Spawning Suspicion

Spawning Suspicion

A Seafood Caper Mystery

MAGGIE TOUSSAINT

Spawning Suspicion
A Seafood Caper Mystery
Book 2

Print ISBN 9780999705421
COPYRIGHT: 2020 Margaret Toussaint

Contact information: maggietoussaint@darientel.net
Cover Art by Margaret Toussaint

Muddle House Publishing
1146 Tolomato Drive SE
Darien, GA 31305

Published in the United States of America

Dedication

This book is dedicated to my husband.

Acknowledgments

Thanks go to my critique partner Polly Iyer who read this story as it grew and provided valuable input. Polly's help with this cover selection was greatly appreciated. Thank you to my editor Beth "Jaden" Terrell for sharpening the story to a fine point. Thanks also to the folks at Henery Press for sharing the logo they created for book one of this series, Seas the Day. Any errors in this story are my own.

Chapter One

Dang. No extension cords. Which meant no hot crab stew, which meant an unhappy Ladies Auxiliary.

"Any luck, River?" my fiancé asked over my shoulder.

I turned from my catering van to face him. "I have no idea where they are, but I can't dwell on that mystery right now. Perhaps the ladies will loan me what I need."

"Or I could run home and get yours."

Pete's solution sounded better. Having an extra set of hands at catering events, especially hands of the man I loved, gave me options. I searched his face, my gaze snagging on his concerned eyes. "Would you?"

"Sure."

"I keep electric supplies in the appliance cabinet."

He tossed the van keys in the air and caught them with a flourish. "Be right back."

Problem solved. I darted inside and arranged the dessert trays in a colorful, three-tiered display. My mouth watered at the decadent aromas of chocolate cake slices, lemon tartlets, macadamia nut cookies, and cherry crunch squares. After running out of desserts at last year's event, I doubled the desserts in this year's quote, much to the delight of the Ladies Auxiliary event chair.

One more glance at the cold section of the buffet table confirmed that the veggie, tuna, and turkey wrap platters were stacked atop chilled mats and encircled by sliced veggies and mounds of fresh fruit. Only the crab stew station remained to be set up, and for that I needed those electrical connections.

Meanwhile, I connected the warming pots in the prep kitchen to keep the stew hot. Soon, I'd checked everything else off my list. I glanced at my watch again and hoped Pete made it back in time.

"Here I am," Pete said, sauntering in like there weren't eight and a half minutes before the doors opened. "No cords at home, so I stopped at Island Hardware."

I clutched the sack he offered to my heart. "Thanks. You are my hero." I wheeled my big pots on the transport cart to the empty station. As soon as the power lights on the pots glowed orange I breathed easier.

We made it.

"I am completely at your service, River," Pete said, giving me that toe-curling smile and a knowing eye waggle.

Mercy.

Better get this back on a professional footing quickly. "I appreciate your help so much. First time I've ever forgotten anything. You saved the day."

"First time for everything, and you did what any good manager would do, River. You delegated the task to an associate while you readied everything else. This feast looks and smells wonderful."

I gave his shoulder a squeeze. "Thanks for the confidence boost."

"You're doing great."

~*~

Right on schedule, the doors opened and forty ladies descended like a flock of migratory birds, all a-flutter and chirping in their pastel plumage. I asked Pete to serve the crab stew to keep the portions uniform. Meanwhile, I refilled wrap platters, veggies, fruits, and desserts as needed and replenished the drink station when it ran low.

Dressed in the Holloway Catering uniform of black slacks and a crisp white shirt, Pete gave off a James Bond aura as he served, schlepped, and chatted with the ladies at crab stew central. The smiling women ate it up.

Laurena Garcia doffed her plastic top hat to me. "Congratulations on another wonderful meal. My ladies say this job is yours for as long as you'll have us."

"Thanks. I appreciate your business."

She pressed a check in my hand. "My pleasure. Great idea to double the desserts. Not that we need the calories, but we all want to taste everything. And it's so good, especially the crab stew. What's your recipe?"

"Family secret," I said, pocketing the money.

An hour later not a crumb remained, and the ladies were enjoying each other's company. Pete and I packed the van as they began their awards program and headed home.

"It's a rush to pull off a production like that," Pete said, his gem green eyes glowing with approval. "I'm impressed by your talent. You make catering look easy."

"It's all in the prep. I learned that lesson long ago. But this job had a hitch, remember I forgot the power strip and extension cords."

"A small oversight you easily corrected."

"Still, clients expect flawless service with no hiccups. So do I."

"It's okay, hon. You're human. You have the universe's permission to be yourself."

My mobile phone buzzed. I'd placed it on the console when we climbed into the van. Georgia law prevented drivers from using cell phones while driving so I used a button on the steering wheel to answer the call. "Holloway Catering. This is River Holloway. How may I help you?"

My brother's voice blasted through the car. "River, thank goodness you picked up. I'm in jail. The cops think I did something terrible, because of Viv."

Jail? Oh, no. This couldn't be happening. Doug's career had traction and his girlfriend adored him. I'd known Viv Declan since we were in grade school together. "Slow down," I said. "I don't understand. Did they arrest you or Viv?"

"Both of us. This can't be happening. I've got jobs scheduled. I can't rot in jail. Get me out of here."

My thoughts spun in all directions as I navigated one of Shell Island's many traffic circles. "Do you have a lawyer?"

"I asked for a public defender, but he hasn't arrived."

"Should I call Mark Horton again?" We'd used that lawyer when Doug acted out after Mama died.

"No. I can't afford him."

"But if they have you under false pretenses, he'll set them straight. Might be worth it to have a pro at the helm."

From the passenger seat, Pete held up a note. I read it. *Ask him what the charge is.*

I nodded at Pete and stared ahead at the busy two-lane road. "What happened?

"Viv and I were there."

I didn't have to feign confusion. "Where?"

"Curtis Marlin's house."

Curtis died in his grandmother's house a few days ago. A former high school basketball star turned playboy, Curtis hardly worked but he'd always played hard. People orbited him, as if they could be cool through association. His bad boy charm never worked on me. Who had time to be a teenage rebel when you had to go to school and be responsible for the household's cooking and cleaning?

"He died of natural causes," I said.

"No." Doug's breath hitched. "Now it's murder."

Icy sensations feathered the nape of my neck. Oh, no. "Since when do you and Curtis hang out?"

"I knew him by name only. We saw him at the marina recently, and he invited us to come out sometime."

My fingers tightened on the steering wheel. "You visited his house the night he died."

"Yeah. They say we killed him."

Chapter Two

The bright sunlight paled and traffic sounds faded. Not good, so not good. My little brother had a knack for wrong-place-wrong-time, but murder? This was awful. Worse, I promised Mom I'd look after Doug.

Pete must've seen the dread in my expression. He leaned over and whispered, "Doug is responsible for his actions."

Easy for him to say. Doug and I were the last of our line. I'd looked out for him for years, but Pete had a point. At twenty-eight and four years younger than me, Doug needed to take ownership of his life.

However, old habits surfaced. "How can I help?"

"Can you call your deputy friend and smooth things over?"

I winced, knowing neither of us would like my reply. "Deputy Gil Franklin is on vacation. I can't bug him until he returns."

"You're my lifeline, Sis. I can't do this alone. I'm not strong like you."

My gut tightened. Doug always made excuses for the messes he created. His tendency to blame others had worn thin over the years. "You are strong, Doug. You finished school, started a business, and worked hard. That's the definition of strong."

"So? Cops say I killed Curtis. That I'm jealous of him. They're wrong, and I need you to prove it."

The sun still shone brightly, but the glow faded beneath the weight of responsibility my brother was applying to me. "How did he die?"

"Poison. But I didn't do it."

"If I look into things, I may find an answer you don't like," I cautioned.

"You're good at finding things. Figure out who killed Curtis so we can go free."

"Not so easy. Like you, I barely knew Curtis. My impression is he drifted through life on the party train."

"I had the same feeling about him."

I slowed to allow the person who turned in front of me to clear the road. "What kind of poison, Doug?"

"They didn't say. Their accusation stunned me. I dummied up and said lawyer. Please, make it go away."

How I wished I could reach through the phone and hug my brother, but a hug wouldn't fix this. "This is very serious. Murder investigations take on a life of their own, and there's often collateral damage. My involvement could hurt you."

"Please, I need your help. I didn't do this and neither did Viv. That's all the time I'm allowed. Gotta go."

The line went dead. Swear words billowed in my head, and I bottled them up inside as I rotely kept driving. *Not now,* I kept thinking. Not when Doug had a chance at a future. He'd found someone who shared his zest for life. He had a handyman career he loved. *Not fair.*

"Talk to me, River," Pete said, his hand resting on my shoulder.

His touch soothed some of the tightness in my belly. "Doug has this effect on me. I get so upset I can't speak. Now he's tangled up in a homicide, and he expects me to save him. I want to stomp around and kick something. Why can't the universe cut him a break? Why does he land in a jam every time?"

"Get it all out, hon."

Tears welled in my eyes, and I blinked furiously to clear the moisture. "Riding to Doug's rescue is exhausting, and that's years of experience talking." I grabbed a deep breath and realized I no longer felt like a powder keg. "He's lucky to have me."

"That he is."

"He says he didn't murder Curtis Marlin, and I believe him. The cops are wrong."

Pete made a circular motion with his other hand. "Keep talking."

The stiff wave of anger I'd felt had rolled off my shoulders. "Doug could go to prison for life. It's one thing to help a friend in trouble, but I can't be objective about my brother. What if I can't do it? What if solving that other case was a fluke?"

"What if it wasn't?" Pete asked. "Doug believes you can help him. So do I."

"Okay. Okay. I get it. Don't let fear win. Focus on my track record of finding things. But homicide is big league, nothing like finding lost keys, glasses, or dogs."

"You have a knack for investigating, hon. The same skill set that allows you to roll out a delicious catered feast on time lends itself to sorting out a mystery."

"I'm gonna do it, but it took me a few minutes to wrap my head around the magnitude first. Thanks for accelerating the process."

"You're welcome."

Slowing for the turn into my driveway, I decided to make calls on Doug's behalf as soon as possible. I drove around to the commercial kitchen behind my house. The vinyl-clad outbuilding met the legal requirements for commercial food prep, and it housed my catering business. Quickly, I placed the ramp across the gap between the van and the stoop.

Then I dialed Fran at the Sheriff's Office. Fran said Doug's arraignment was tomorrow because the judge had a family emergency. Nothing we could do until then.

A retort rose in my throat that I had a family emergency too, but ruffling feathers would be counterproductive. "When does Deputy Gil Franklin return?" I asked.

"He's on leave through tomorrow," Fran said. "See you later."

Helplessness welled inside me, choking me. Doug would spend the night in jail. And Viv. Who would she call for help? It wasn't like her brother Darry was available to help her. He lit out for Alaska months ago.

Maybe Viv phoned her sister-in-law, Anita Declan, who'd stayed behind with their two young children. If so, combining forces might help our loved ones. I dialed her number.

The call rolled to voice mail, so I left a message. "Anita, this is River Holloway. Deputies arrested my brother and your sister-in-law today for the murder of Curtis Marlin. Let's pool resources to make this go away. Please call me."

Pete stopped unloading the van and stood beside me. "What'd you find out?"

"Doug is stuck in jail tonight," I said. "I hate that, and I wish I could get him out now."

He cradled my hand in his. "He can handle a night behind bars. We'll get him out tomorrow."

"My brother is like a friendly puppy in the mine field of life. He rarely associates consequences with actions."

"Everyone makes mistakes. Cut yourself some slack. You're his sister, and of course you look out for him. He'll be fine."

His wry tone caught my ear. "You know something?"

"I know Doug." When I protested, he raised a cautionary palm. "Hear me out. You've always been Doug's safety net. You fixed his previous mistakes. Even if his name is cleared, people will remember Doug Holloway was accused of murder. This stigma could haunt him for the rest of his life."

"He's innocent," I said loyally. "I know it."

"We'll help him, River. That's a promise, but until we know the evidence against him, we don't know what we're up against."

I nodded my understanding, unloaded the van, and stowed everything in its place, with Pete's help. We strolled to the main house together, and it felt good to have his company in this trying time.

Major, a feral cat who'd moved into our yard, watched our approach from a deck bench. The black cat appeared during another case and helped me solve it. Today he regarded us with an intense feline glare.

I started toward him, hoping I'd finally earned his trust, but Major skittered into the woods.

"He doesn't like me," I said to Pete who'd witnessed the rebuff.

"The cat likes you. You're his meal ticket. He does that stare down thing to remind you to feed him twice a day."

Pete's explanation of the cat's behavior made sense, but it didn't touch my rising tide of despair. I hated feeling hopeless, hated that I couldn't immediately ride to Doug's rescue, hated knowing there was a chance I might fail. Reality tasted bitter in my mouth.

Despite the sunny afternoon, I rubbed the chill from my arms. "It would be nice to hug a pet to hug right now," I said. "My brother's in jail on a murder charge."

Pete drew me into his arms. "Will I do instead?"

"Yes."

He kissed me and fingered the necklace inside my white blouse. "I wish you'd wear my ring on your finger."

The flashy diamond suited Pete through and through, but the stone's large size hampered repeated hand washing, hauling equipment, and cooking. I worried I'd lose it or break it so I wore the ring on a chain around my neck.

"Everyone knows we're engaged," I said.

His eyebrows rose. "About that. Decided on a wedding date yet?"

"I can't focus on our marriage with Doug in jail."

"The only way for Doug to be truly free is to find the killer."

"That's my plan," I said, glad he saw it my way. "I'll figure this out, and then Doug will be cleared."

"We'll figure it out." Pete caught my chin and gave me a penetrating stare much like the cat. "And get married."

"You are my heart and soul," I protested, needing to focus on one big deal at a time. "But a marriage certificate is a piece of paper."

Pete kissed me until my toes curled. "It's a legal document that insures your financial security if anything happens to me. You may not need that assurance, but I do."

I caressed his lips. "You're relentless."

A grin filled his face. "I go after what I want, make no mistake about that. And you, River Holloway, are at the top of my list."

On that we agreed. I couldn't imagine my life without him. "All right. Deal."

Chapter Three

Thursday morning dawned with a rare morning thunderstorm that matched my dark mood. I should start prepping for the Melanie Walker wedding reception on Sunday, but I couldn't leave my brother in jail. I had to do both.

After breakfast, Pete drove us to the Law Enforcement Center over on the mainland. I didn't know the man at the lobby window, but he told me Doug's arraignment time at magistrate court. I returned to Pete's truck. "Doug goes before the judge at eleven."

"We're headed to the courthouse?"

I clicked my seatbelt in place. "Not yet. I need to see the bail bondsman on Worchester Street first."

Pete quirked an eyebrow. "I'm pretty good at math and your most valuable asset is your property. You'd risk your place for Doug?"

"Far as I'm concerned, the house belongs to both of us. Mom willed me the property, but it's Doug's home too."

"Interesting your mother didn't share her main asset with both heirs."

"Please, no Doug-bashing. I'm putting the house up for his bail. He's my brother."

"If he skips, you'll lose the house and your commercial kitchen."

I couldn't breathe for a long moment, not until I crushed that garlic clove of doubt. "He wouldn't do that to me."

"I hope you're right."

~*~

Arrestees and lawyers cycled through magistrate court. The stories of people who'd beaten loved ones, stolen from neighbors, and more depressed my spirits. Finally Doug's turn arrived. Guards led Doug inside, his face pale and sickly in the jailhouse jumpsuit.

He searched the courtroom as he entered, his expression brightening at the sight of me. I gave a little wave, nervous about what the judge would decide. Doug's court-appointed attorney, Celia Applegate, looked younger than he did, though they must be close in age.

The prosecution argued for no bail in this accessory to murder case given the defendant's prior criminal record. Ms. Applegate argued Doug made amends for his earlier mistake and now he operated a small business. In addition, Doug's strong ties to the community proved he wasn't a flight risk. Doug pled not guilty. Bail was set at six hundred thousand dollars.

The amount staggered me. Pete's assertions hit home. Doug could go to prison. From experience, I knew the drill of getting the bail paperwork through the system, and of showing up at five that afternoon for prisoner release. I also knew to bring Doug a change of clothes.

To his credit, after meeting with the bail bondsman Pete didn't say I told you so. He drove us to the island, and we both dove into work. I prepared sauces for the wedding party, and he urged his legal team to wrangle his investment's return from the failed North Merrick business he walked away from.

A year ago, Pete had traveled to California to make his mark on the world. The merger of his interests with Dalbert North's should've been the be-all end-all deal of deals for Pete. He'd plugged the financial leaks in the sinking company and his future looked bright. But then the people behind the leaks, drug cartel associates, struck back. Pete used an employee sting to get those bad actors out of the company.

All seemed fine for a few weeks, then the cartel hit harder, this time using physical force to get rid of Pete and his allies in the company. When an employee got shot and Pete got stabbed, he left and came home to me. Every day he healed more in mind, body, and spirit.

I had faith that if Pete wanted to own the entire island by year's end, he'd accomplish it. Pete Merrick could move mountains and had in the past.

Now that Pete was off my worry list, my brother moved to the top. With Mom in poor health throughout Doug's teens, I'd become a substitute parent. Doug had made his share of bad decisions as he'd matured, but I never expected him to be charged with accessory to murder.

My gosh. Curtis Marlin. Somehow his iconic teenaged James Dean image clung to him as an adult. And now, his death threatened to rip my family apart. The sheriff's rush to judgement irked me. If our county wanted justice to be served, Sheriff Vargas would lose the upcoming election. Meanwhile, he'd fingered Viv and Doug as killers in the Curtis Marlin case. I had to clear my brother's name. Viv's too.

Five rolled around and we waited in the jail lobby for Doug to emerge. My nerves pinged and angst pinched my belly. Pete gripped my cold hand, and it felt good to have him sitting beside me.

To my surprise, Anita Declan bustled in with her infant and toddler. She marched straight to the front desk window. "My sister-in-law is innocent," Anita gritted in a deep voice, surprising for a woman in a pressed pink blouse, deftly applied make up, and big hair. "Release Viv Declan immediately."

"Can't do that, ma'am," the sergeant said. "She's accused of murder, and her bail is set at a million dollars. If you post her bail, she can get out."

"You can't possibly have any evidence to back that outrageous amount for bail," Anita countered, fury in her tone. "Let her go."

"Her fingerprints are on the murder weapon, so her bail is set accordingly."

"Do I look like I have a million dollars? We barely have the clothes on our backs. I can't help myself let alone Viv. She's innocent, and this is her first brush with the law. You should release her on her own recognizance."

"Not on a murder charge, ma'am."

"This is ridiculous," Anita said, jittering in place and stabbing her finger on the counter. "I want to see Viv right now. I'm her family."

"I'll check on her status. Have a seat."

Anita turned around, saw me, and blushed. "Viv never had a problem like this until she dated your brother."

"Calm down, Anita," I said, not appreciating her remark but understanding her frustration. "Doug didn't do this and neither did Viv. We have to sort this out."

"I can't calm down. This is a nightmare. First Darry abandoned me, and now my sister-in-law's in jail. I can't sleep, I can't eat, and the kids are driving me crazy."

Her heartfelt words created an instant well of empathy. "I'll hold Zoey, if you like," I said, standing beside her.

Anita blinked. "I'm sorry, River. I've been barely surviving for months now, and I'm at wit's end. I'm not used to people offering to help."

"You're not alone," I said, reaching for the sleeping baby. "People will help if you let them."

Anita released her toddler's hand, handed her daughter to me, and sank into a plastic chair. Little Harry darted to the other end of the room and repeatedly ran his toy truck over the glass front of the snack machine.

"I'm used to self-sufficiency," Anita began, "but I can't remember the last time I slept through the night. I'm a hot mess. No wonder Darry left. Why would he come home to this?"

I sat beside her, cuddling the sleeping baby close, inhaling her clean scent. "It'll work out. Pete is headed over to the vending machine to get me a soda. He'll get you one too."

"I am?" Pete asked, searching my face and then rising. "I will."

He returned with cans of soda, candy bars, and a package of animal crackers. "All right if your son has these?"

13

"What?" Anita looked up and smiled for the first time. "Sure. Harry loves treats."

Pete opened the crackers for the youngster and the child climbed in his lap to eat them. The sugary drink settled my nerves, and Viv looked calmer too.

A little while later, Doug plodded through the jail doors into the lobby, his expression grim. As one, Pete, Anita, and I rose. Doug hurried over to hug me. "Can't we get Viv out too? I'll stay if Viv has to stay."

"I'm sorry. I used the house for your bail. That's everything I have."

"This isn't right," Doug insisted. "Viv shouldn't be rotting in jail for a crime she didn't commit." He glared at Anita. "Can't you do something?"

"I came," Anita said, raising her empty hands. "That's the best I can do. I'm about to be evicted from my rental. I don't know where my husband is, and I have no assets. They laughed at me in the bail office when I tried to use my car for collateral. That old beater isn't worth two grand, and I'm lucky I got it running to drive over to the mainland today."

"I didn't know," Doug said, his face pinched. "You should've said something earlier. Viv and I would've helped you."

"I need a decent job and a babysitter," Anita said sharply. "Can you do that for me?"

Doug flinched at her tone but stood his ground. "If you can paint, I could use a hand tomorrow to keep me on schedule. You can work with me on that job if you like."

"What about the kids?" Anita asked.

"Sorry, no kids allowed," Doug said.

"Mother's Morning Out runs on Fridays at the Methodist Church," I piped in as little Zoey stirred in my arms. "That'll give you a few hours of coverage, and it's a free service. Pete and I can keep the kids in the afternoon."

Anita's jaw dropped. "You'd do that for me?"

"Yes. And together we'll figure out how to clear Doug and Viv from these false charges."

The sergeant returned. "Mrs. Declan, your sister-in-law is in questioning. She isn't available for visitation today. Come back tomorrow."

Anita nodded, a teary glint in her eye. "Thank you for checking."

We helped Anita get the kids settled in her car. "I'll come to Viv's place first thing in the morning after I drop the kids at the church," Anita said. "I appreciate this opportunity."

As she drove off, I said to Doug, "You did a good thing in helping her."

His cheeks flamed red. "Why didn't she tell us about her dire straits? Viv and I would've helped her weeks ago."

"Some people are uncomfortable asking for help, much less accepting it." At least Anita reached for the lifeline we offered. It would allow her a way to start getting back on her feet.

If only it were so easy to clear Doug and Viv.

Chapter Four

Doug called at daybreak Friday morning. "I'm screwed. My tools got stolen outta my truck while I sat in jail."

I blinked away sleep, willing the fog in my brain to clear. "What time is it?"

"Six," he said. "I can't work without those tools. What am I going to do?"

"I thought you were painting today. Surely you can buy a paintbrush and a roller."

"The idea is to make money, not to spend it."

I winced at the sharp edge of his voice. "Call your insurance agent. Find out how much you can expect to cover the loss."

"Uh," Doug said, drawing out the word. "I didn't insure my new tools."

I bolted upright in bed. "Doug! We talked about that. You agreed you needed that protection."

"I needed the money for something else," Doug said.

"What could be more important than your future? We bought those tools with the last of Mom's estate after we paid for your trade school."

"You can't give me your credit card number?"

"No. The only thing I can offer you are the tools in the carport. There should be a paintbrush and a roller set out there, though God knows how old they are."

"I need new stuff. It doesn't present a good appearance to show up with rusty old junk."

"You should've locked everything up tight and insured it. Then you wouldn't be in a jam. What'd you spend that insurance money on, anyway?"

"Viv. I spent it on Viv," he said. "I wanted her to like me."

"Oh, for goodness sake. She already liked you. I can't believe you blew two thousand dollars and have nothing to show for it. And while I have you on the phone the power strip and extension cords from my business are missing. I couldn't find them for a catering job, and I know I put them back after I use them for work. Did you take them?"

The silence on the phone rang with guilt. "Doug, I had an event on Wednesday, and I needed those cords. Your thoughtlessness impacted my ability to do my job."

"Sorry," he said. "I needed them."

"You're welcome to anything in the house, but those aren't household items. I purchased them for my business. You can't forage in the commercial kitchen whenever you want. My livelihood depends upon having those items available for jobs. Plus, you had no right to go in there without my permission."

"I apologized."

"That doesn't cut it," I said into the phone. "Take responsibility for your actions."

"You're awful touchy this morning. It's Pete, isn't it? I knew he'd turn you against me."

"Leave Pete out of this. This is about you being a man and owning up to your mistakes."

I hung up on him, blood thrumming in my ears. Pete's earlier words rang in my ears. In big sister mode, I'd enabled my brother for years. Time for Doug to solve his own problems.

"You all right?" Pete asked beside me.

"Fine," I said automatically. "My brother upset me. Sorry for disturbing you."

"I noticed you held your ground."

My chin rose. "I did."

"He didn't expect that."

"No. He blamed you, but I set him straight."

"I heard that too. Good for you."

"It had to be done, but it feels wrong."

"Give it time," he said, reaching for me. "You looked great with that baby in your arms yesterday. What do you say about making our own?"

I nestled into his embrace. "I'd say yes."

~*~

Friday morning flew by with wedding reception prep, including checking that the chicken was thawing on schedule and making potato au gratin for a hundred and twenty people. I got all six pans to the bake-me stage and stashed them in my walk-in refrigerator.

After lunch, Pete and I drove to the Methodist Church to pick up Anita's kids. A young woman showed us how to install the car seats in Pete's truck. Little Harry chortled with glee at being up so high, while Zoey fell asleep after being buckled in.

At home, we put the baby on a soft pallet on the floor and Harry played with his toy trucks until he dropped. Pete and I closed our eyes on the sectional sofa for nearly ten minutes before the baby stirred.

My eyes flared wide with alarm. I dislodged myself from Pete who clung sleepily to me. "Come 'ere," he said. "Not ready to go again."

"I need to get Zoey before she wakes her brother. He hasn't had a long enough nap."

I collected Zoey, fixed her a bottle, and handed her to Pete because Harry wandered in the living room. Cookies and milk refueled him, and they did wonders for me. With pleasant weather outside, we texted Anita for permission to take the kids to the park. The time passed quickly. Soon four o'clock arrived, and Anita met us by the swings.

"Thanks," she said, hugging little Zoey to her chest while Harry continued to romp in the park with Pete. "This is a godsend. The money I made for six hours of painting will give us a cushion for a few days. I swallowed my pride and applied for food stamps so we should be okay foodwise. I need steady employment to pay the rent."

"It isn't much, but I need an extra set of hands on Sunday catering the Melanie Walker wedding. You can't bring the kids, and Pete will also be helping me. My catering staff is expected to wear a white long-sleeved blouse, black pants, and black shoes. Can you manage that?"

"Yes. Thanks. I'll ask my sister in Savannah to come down and watch the kids."

"Be at my place by Sunday noon. We're loading the van then and heading over to Creekside Lodge. The meal is served at three thirty, and we should be finished serving by five."

Dollar signs flared in her eyes. "Five hours of pay. Great. I appreciate this so much. Thanks again for watching the kids today. This is the first hope I've felt in a long time."

We transferred the car seats to her vehicle and waved goodbye. I glanced at Pete. "You thinking what I'm thinking?"

"Only if you're thinking ice cream."

"Got it in one."

~*~

Doug arrived at dinner time, power cords in hand and red-faced. "I'm sorry I took these. It won't happen again."

"Thanks. I'm glad they weren't stolen with the rest of your stuff."

"I decorated Viv's bedroom with Christmas lights for a special treat one evening, and we liked it so much we left it up. I'd forgotten I used your cords. I bought my own today so it won't happen again."

"Great.

He hung his head. "I wish I could get Viv out of jail. It felt weird sleeping at her place without her. And then all today I kept thinking of her locked in that tiny cell. That isn't right."

I waved to the kitchen table set for two. "Won't you join us for dinner?"

"Sure. It smells like lasagna."

I added another place setting and poured Doug a glass of tea. "It's Pete's favorite."

"Mine too." Doug sank into his chair. "How'd it go with the kids today?"

"They had a lot of energy, but we survived."

"You were a natural with the kids, River," Pete said, sitting across from Doug. "You'll be a great mom."

"One day. Pete got right into the swing of being a dad too." I rolled my aching shoulders. "Being a full-time parent must develop your stamina. Or maybe parents consume more caffeine and sugar, I don't know, but I'm extra tired tonight."

"Y'all will be good parents. I'd like to have a family someday too, but first we have to get Viv out of jail."

I transferred squares of lasagna to each plate and added tossed salad. "Tell us more about the night Curtis died."

"The evening started with dinner at the marina. We danced a bit, but we didn't feel like hitting a bar or going home. That's when Viv remembered the standing invitation to visit Curtis's place and he owed her some money. She texted him and he invited us to come over to hang out with him and his high school basketball team buddies."

"Who are they?" I asked, carrying plates to the table.

"They have nicknames. So, DeAndre "Heavy D" Haywood, Tyrone "Ty" Carvell, and Egbert "Eggs" Butler were with Curtis when we arrived at his place. The crazy loud music made it hard to talk and be heard. Viv turned it down to talk to Curtis, and he called her a degrading name because she hangs out with guys. I wanted to fight Curtis, and Viv wanted to hit him too, but clearly he'd had too much to drink. I demanded he apologize. He did, but his words slurred. He complained of a headache, and he acted uncoordinated. As in, he reached for his gin and tonic and missed the glass. I've never seen anyone so loaded."

I ate in silence for a few moments to digest what he'd said. "Those symptoms may have been related to the poisoning. Anyone else drinking the same thing as Curtis?"

Doug grimaced. "No. Heavy D, Ty, and Eggs brought over a case of beer and iced it down in the sink. Viv and I shared a beer."

"Did the cops tell you the name of the poison?"

"Not directly, but they asked questions about working on my truck, especially if I'd topped off the antifreeze lately. Who adds antifreeze in coastal Georgia in late April? Chances of it freezing around here before late November are zero."

"Antifreeze. That is odd. What does that have to do with anything?"

"Antifreeze is a poison. I looked it up when I got home. It must have been in his drink."

"Did you touch the gin or tonic bottle?"

"Nope. I touched the doorknob and one beer bottle. They printed both of those and that's how they knew Viv and I were there."

Didn't sound like grounds for arrest. "But Viv touched something else?"

"I didn't think so at first, but then I remembered Curtis asked her to fix him another drink before we left. The cops said the only prints on the gin bottle belonged to Curtis and Viv. Plus, they found a jug of antifreeze in her trunk. Somebody framed Viv. She wouldn't hurt Curtis. They're friends. Were, I mean. They were friends."

"Sounds like bad policing to me, not unusual for Sheriff Vargas. Those basketball guys could've wiped their prints from that bottle. Now we have three suspects and a means of death." I caught Pete's eye. "The case against you and Viv feels thin to me. Do they have anything else?"

Doug looked like he'd swallowed a frog. "A few weeks ago, Viv went to the bar alone. Curtis approached and talked to her for a bit. They had another round of drinks, and he left without paying. Viv got stuck with his tab and when she saw the amount, she yelled, 'I'm gonna kill you, Curtis Marlin.' Only, she didn't mean kill him in the literal sense, and she paid for his drinks."

"That is a considerable amount of evidence against Viv. The death threat, possession of antifreeze, and the forensic evidence on the gin bottle all point to Viv as the killer."

Doug shook his head. "She didn't do it."

"I believe you. Why did you rate an accessory to murder charge?"

"Because I accompanied Viv that night and because of my romantic relationship with her. They tried to make me say I'd bought the antifreeze for Viv but I didn't. They said I got rid of

Maggie Toussaint

Curtis because he was my competition for Viv. Over and over
again I told them these things weren't true, but they hammered
away in hopes of a different answer. They say poisoning is a
premeditated crime and that I had to know Viv's plans, that I
knew she brought the poison to his house that night. They say I
aided and abetted Viv in the commission of Curtis's murder.
We're both innocent. It had to be one of those basketball jocks.
Will you investigate them?"

"I'll ask around. Given the evidence against Viv and given the
fact you two are each other's alibi that night, the cops won't
easily dismiss the charges. This case could go to trial."

He gave a little moan. "You've got to make it go away. This is
a nightmare."

"This is a big deal, Doug. You two won't be cleared unless the
cops have stronger evidence against someone else. I'll see about
those basketball guys. Meanwhile, avoid our suspect pool and
skip the funeral. Cops watch people at murder victim's funerals."

"I don't even know when the funeral is," Doug said, eating his
last bite of lasagna and looking longingly over at the pan.

"Next week, I imagine. Meanwhile, I've got a wedding to cater
and a murder to solve."

Chapter Five

Pete slapped the Saturday morning paper beside me on the kitchen counter. "Unbelievable."

In bold typeface, the headline read "Love Triangle Gone Wrong." Beneath the lurid headline, a smaller font size announced, "a gripping tale of broken hearts, revenge, and grisly homicide."

"This can't be true," I said, as I finished plating our mushroom and swiss cheese omelets. "Doug and Viv are a couple now. Viv doesn't love Curtis. I should call the paper and give this reporter a piece of my mind."

"It'll blow over," Pete said. "I've seen this before. Responding in kind will only fan the flames. There's a strong possibility you'd be misquoted in a follow-up piece."

"The cops shouldn't let this kind of stuff go to print."

"You're protective of your brother, but this country values freedom of speech. The reporter is trying to sell newspapers."

"I know you're right, but I want to be mad a little longer. This is my brother's reputation we're talking about."

My cell phone rang. When I picked it up over by the sink, I saw Major sitting outside on his favorite bench, waiting stoically for his breakfast. I made a mental note to feed the cat next. Glancing at the phone, I didn't recognize the number but I took the call anyway because this doubled as my business line. To my surprise a recorded message stated the visiting hours at the jail today and announced that inmate Viv Declan had requested to see me.

I ended the call and sat at the table again. "How weird. I just got a robo call from jail. Viv wants to see me. I wonder if she saw the newspaper article."

"Doubt they have paper delivery in jail," he said between bites. "How can I help you today?"

"I can handle today's wedding reception prep, but I'll make time to see Viv first. When I get home, I'll start the first batch of chicken and slow-cook the green beans. Beans always taste better the second day. Tonight it'll be salad prep and getting the bread ready for the oven. Tomorrow I'll be up at three cooking."

He stilled and cocked an eyebrow. "You won't need me that early, will you?"

"Sleep in. That way you can help with Sunday clean up and make sure I don't fall asleep driving home. What are your plans today?"

"My funds from the North Merrick divesture will clear soon. I've been studying local businesses and creating a business plan. I should rent office space soon so you get the dining room table back."

"You're welcome to keep using the table. It's usually stacked with mail and catalogs anyway. I'm delighted you're thinking ahead though, and even more delighted you plan to invest in Shell Island."

"You've put down roots here, and I'll do the same. Do your thing. I've got the dishes."

"Thanks." I carried Major's meal outside and sat down to finish my morning coffee on the lounger. The cat downed his food quickly, but he didn't scamper away. He lay down near his bowl, purring loudly. I wanted to reach over and pet him, but he didn't like to be touched. The only time I'd ever held him he'd been unconscious.

Time to get moving.

It didn't take long to pull on jeans and a blouse, tie my hair back, brush my teeth, and apply lip gloss. Then I kissed Pete goodbye and headed outside. To my surprise, Major perched on the hood of Mom's old Buick. He yowled when I approached the van and then paced in circles atop the car. It seemed he wanted me to take the Buick.

Oh well, it didn't matter to me which vehicle I drove, and Mom's old car needed to be run. I shifted direction and Major jumped down from the hood. He supervised as I unlocked the door, and then he darted inside and leapt onto the backseat.

"You're a strange cat," I said, "but thanks for the company. One day I hope you'll allow me to be your friend."

I rolled down the windows so we had fresh sea breeze all the way over the causeway. A few miles later, I parked at the jail and left the windows down. "You can't come inside," I told the cat, "and if anyone sees me talking to you, I won't get inside either."

Getting processed into the Visitor Center took a few minutes. I followed the directions at the appointed time and Viv's face showed up on the monitor. "How are you?" I asked.

"I'm a mess," Viv said with a shake of her head. "You have to get me out of here. I can't afford a good lawyer."

She looked pale, and I could barely see her light-colored eyelashes. I hadn't seen Viv without makeup since elementary school. She normally appeared ready to take on the world but today she looked tired, vulnerable, and angry.

"Doug already asked me to figure out what happened," I said. "I don't have many leads, but today's paper claims Curtis died from a love triangle gone bad."

"That's ridiculous. Last year, Curtis and I were friends with benefits for a while. He moved on and so did I. Curtis always had something going on, some deal in the works, and I enjoyed his antics until we broke up."

"What kind of deals?" I asked.

"He was vague about it," Viv said. "Mostly he bragged about a line on a sure thing and this time he'd hit it big."

"That is vague. Do you know his business associates?"

"No. We fell in the category of good-time friends. I shared my life with him but he kept his life private. The only reason Doug and I went there the other night was for a change of pace and to collect the bar tab Curtis owed me. He invited both of us. He didn't care that Doug and I are a couple."

"Who wanted him dead?"

"Hard to say. Mr. Party Hearty lived large, so he got fired a lot. For the record, it's exhausting to party every day."

It didn't appeal to me. "So, Curtis excelled at being a party animal, unemployment, and secret business dealings. Sounds dangerous."

"Seriously, when I dated him, we had fun, until I burnt out. Couldn't work hungover, and I needed my mill job to pay my bills."

"You could've moved in with Curtis," I pointed out.

"I wanted my space and he didn't offer his. We mostly hung out at his place in those days. He hated my two-bedroom apartment. The neighbors complained about noise, and Curtis embraced being rowdy.

"Someone so high energy would be exhausting after a while."

"No kidding. Look, I didn't do this. That alleged death threat I uttered in the bar haunts me. Plus, Curtis asked me to pour that drink. I don't own any antifreeze, and I don't know how that antifreeze got in my trunk. Heck, I didn't know antifreeze would kill you. Why would I kill Curtis anyway? He was who he was."

"What about his three basketball pals? Any of them do their own auto maintenance?"

"Don't know, but Ty, Eggs, and Heavy D used people, same as Curtis. They only came around to drink and reminisce about the good old days. None of them is worth a lick. I don't know where they work, and I know for a fact that Heavy D lives with his aunt."

"What's the deal with the nicknames?"

"A guy thing from the team days," Viv said.

I checked the timer on the call monitor. Only a few more minutes. "Were the guys still there that night when you and Doug left?"

"Yes. The four of them were laughing and drinking when Doug and I left." Viv sighed. "I learned a valuable lesson that night. It didn't feel the same this time."

"How so?"

"Being there felt hollow and fake. Doug is so much more than all of those guys combined. He took up for me when Curtis called me a ho. That's why we left, so Doug wouldn't fight Curtis. No more party train for me. I'm more like you than I knew."

"I don't understand."

"You've always wanted to settle down and have a family. I liked variety and freedom, until Doug. I can see myself with him today, tomorrow, and ten years from now. He makes me better. Now, everything is bonkers, and I'm in jail."

"Doug cares for you, and I will ask questions. Anything else I can do for you? Would you prefer to hire a lawyer instead of the court-appointed one?"

"I can't afford a better lawyer. This is embarrassing to admit but I have no savings. Tell Doug I miss him."

"I will. Hang in there, Viv. I'm asking questions, and I'll focus more come Monday. Tomorrow is the Melanie Walker wedding."

"Oh. I forgot about that. Good for you on not getting fired from that job."

I chuckled. "I came close over the last few weeks."

"You'll be fine."

"Your sister-in-law is helping me. Anita tried to bully the front desk guy into letting you go, but he held fast. I hope she holds her militant attitude in check for Melanie's wedding."

"That should be interesting."

The video call timer counted down the last minute in seconds. I leaned close to the monitor to make every second count. "Why?"

"Anita is furious Darry left her. I'm surprised she has any smiles left in her."

"She's in dire financial straits, Viv, and days from being homeless."

Viv's eyes rounded. "I had no idea."

Going to Alaska for work made no sense considering we lived in Georgia. "Why did your brother go to Alaska?"

"Same pipe dream as Curtis—to strike it rich overnight. He expected the experience would change his life. Darry lit out for Alaska without saying goodbye, as if it were another teenage adventure. I'm angry and disappointed he left Anita and the kids. And me. He left me. Even after I stopped being mad I wanted nothing to do with him."

"And he never came home. Seems relevant."

"He's a man-child. Don't waste your time on him. Say, how's Anita paying her bills?"

"Not sure. She helped Doug paint yesterday and is helping with the wedding tomorrow, but she needs a full-time job. She applied for food stamps. Living in her car is a strong possibility."

"If she's evicted, she can stay at my place. But if I can't work, I won't have a place either. What a mess."

Chapter Six

After starting the green beans, I prepared and cooked half the spice-rubbed chicken needed for the job, otherwise I'd be up all night baking. Then, in late afternoon I took a break from cooking to move some heavy equipment to the venue at Creekside Lodge.

My morning visit with Viv kept cycling through my thoughts. She needed my help. I couldn't wait until Monday to start investigating. I needed to start today.

I locked the commercial kitchen and hustled over to the house. On the way, I saw Major perched atop Mom's old Buick. Did he sense a pending drive? Heath regulations barred animals in the van but the car worked because of the separation via the trunk between cat and catering supplies. I smiled. Road trip for the cat.

Pete sat in the dining room, happily crunching numbers, or so I thought. "Going somewhere?" he asked, rising to greet me.

"Over to Curtis's house for a look-see and then out to Creekside for an equipment delivery."

"I'll come with you."

I smiled. "I hoped you'd tag along. Major wants a car ride so we're taking the Buick."

"Gotcha. I'll drive."

I tossed him the keys. "All right."

Minutes later with the cat in the Buick's backseat and the cavernous trunk loaded with gear, we motored toward Curtis's house. During my childhood, it had been Gertrude Talley's place.

She'd outlived her husband and daughter, making Curtis her only heir. With his death, who owned the Talley-Marlin cottage in the woods?

"What's the address?" Pete asked, interrupting my musings.

"Stay on the main drag until I tell you to turn. Curtis's grandmother, Ms. Gertrude, made candles and soaps and sold them at county fairs. Mom loved those soaps, so we rode out here often in my childhood. I caught my first frog in her yard."

"Guess it didn't turn into a prince," Pete said, maneuvering through the last traffic circle.

"Don't know what I'd a-done with a prince. Life suited me just fine."

He reached over and patted my shoulder. "That's the way it should be, love."

We rode in comfortable silence, then Pete said, "I love having a home office. It's nice having you pop in and taking breaks like this. Life is more engaging since I returned home."

"Hopefully, safer too."

His lips tightened before he spoke. "My injuries are healed. Trust me, I'll do deep research before committing to another business."

"I thought you craved adventure in business deals."

"Our adventures suit me fine," Pete said.

"You don't mind then, that I like to help people?"

"I want you to be happy."

Not the answer I wanted. However, he made a good sleuthing partner, and he didn't discourage my hobby.

While waiting for the light to change, he said, "Speaking of home offices, our ideal house would have space for my home office and your commercial kitchen. Agreed?"

A sudden uneasy feeling zapped my gut. "Yes."

"Some island properties might fit that bill. Now that North Merrick is cashing out my remaining shares, I'll have funds for us to upsize. Would you be interested in looking at properties next week?"

The air in the car felt too thick to breathe. My fingers curled tight at the thought of leaving my home. "It doesn't hurt to look but fair warning: I can't contribute much financially. Frankly, a big mortgage scares me."

"We're a team," Pete said as he accelerated. "I'll cover the down payment and the monthly payments. Don't worry about that, love." I must've protested because he continued smoothly, "Our place should suits all our needs, including our growing family."

Another internal punch to the gut, the topic I'd avoided for weeks. Best to air my fears. "About the family thing. What if...we can't? What if something's wrong with me?"

"First, you're fine. Second, conception happens in its own time. You've been wound tight keeping your business afloat, and I spent a year in hell. I took a lot of punches in that California assault, including a few cheap shots to the groin."

I winced. "Ouch."

"Guys don't talk about dirty punches, but you shouldn't blame yourself for our slowness to conceive." He cleared his throat. "I'm breaking the guy code for you."

"Thanks, I think. What are you saying?"

"We're starting a life together. I'm fine with however that looks. I want kids, but I want you more." He wiped his brow. "Now I see why you pull over when personal conversations get intense. I want to hold you tight to reassure you everything's okay, but there's too much traffic to pull over safely."

My tension eased into a smile. "I'm good. You mean the world to me. Our turn is coming up after the Cheerful Rooster convenience store."

"Turn right at the store?"

"Nope, it's a left after the store."

"Right."

"Left." I burst out laughing at the unexpected byplay. "You're funny."

"Glad to hear you laugh. Between Doug's trouble and the wedding reception prep, you've been swamped." He turned onto the narrow lane, small cottages bordering the road for a few blocks before forest prevailed.

My expression sobered. "Doug is innocent. The cops are certain Viv is guilty and Doug helped her. If I do nothing, they're sitting ducks."

"We'll sort it out. Here's what we know: Curtis is dead. Poisoned."

"Yes, and someone put enough antifreeze in the gin bottle to kill him. Not Doug or Viv."

The road surface became hard packed shell for the last half mile until it dead-ended at the old house. Yellow crime scene tape ringed the house. No other vehicles were present.

"See any cameras?" I asked.

Pete gazed at the eaves of the one-story cottage and at trees with a clear line of sight to the door. "If they're here, they're well hidden."

"I'm glad our recon mission is private." I opened the door, stood, and stretched. Major the cat leapt out and trotted around the house.

"No junk in the yard," Pete said, stopping beside me.

The sun shone brightly, insects buzzed. Except for that tape, this place seemed caught in a time warp. "What?"

"Most island guys have disassembled motors, shooting practice targets, boats, motorcycles, or ATVs. There's nothing here, except for those old rockers."

I followed his gaze to the porch. "Ms. Gertrude's chairs need to be re-caned. I wonder if the heir to the property would sell us those chairs."

"If Curtis had no heirs and no will, his estate could be tied up in probate court for years." He gestured to the dusty window. "Let's see what we can find out about Curtis Marlin."

I stood on tiptoe to peer inside. "Looks like a tornado touched down in there." We circled the house, seeing nothing that would clear Doug and Viv. Major joined us as we completed the loop. "This place is isolated. Maybe scavengers picked the yard clean."

"Perhaps," Pete said. "What about the dreamcatchers? They look new."

Four dreamcatchers ringed the wrap-around porch, two hanging on the front and one on each side. The circular rings bounding the webbing were covered in dark suede and painted with a Native American scene. Dark feathers hung from the rims.

"Those weren't here when Mom and I visited his grandmother. Maybe they're souvenirs from a trip out West or that trip Curtis took to Alaska. Maybe Viv knows where they came from."

"Was he superstitious?"

Major landed on the car hood with a jarring noise, startling me. "I don't know."

"Some folks see dreamcatchers as decorative, others as protectors."

A chill streaked down my spine. "You think Curtis used the dreamcatchers as wards to guard his place?"

"They're supposed to trap bad dreams and keep you safe through the night."

I looked at the dreamcatchers gently twisting in the breeze. "Given he's dead, he needed stronger protection."

Chapter Seven

On the way home, we unloaded equipment at Creekside Lodge and assembled my buffet station in the pool house. I locked the totes of prepared green beans and Tex-Mex white corn in the walk-in refrigerator, stashed my industrial pots in the cabinets, and checked the full icemaker. Everything was ready for tomorrow.

Outside, a white jumbo canopy covered a dozen round tables and chairs. A smattering of seats lined the creek bank where Major patrolled. A mild breeze wafted our way.

"This place is gorgeous." I said, glancing around. "We should consider having our service here."

"I'd like that," Pete said. "Any other places strike your fancy?"

"The pier is special to us, so that's a possibility. And St. Luke's appeals to me, if that's not too formal for you."

"I'm also fine with those places."

"What about a simple ceremony with Father Ben? I don't want a big production or the expense of a large wedding."

"We can afford a large to-do if that's your dream."

I chewed on my lip a bit. "My dream wedding involves the two of us."

Pete grinned. "I'll be there. No worries on that front and the sooner the better."

"I won't change my mind about marrying you. Is there another reason causing you to want the wedding so quickly?"

He didn't answer for a bit. "Life comes at us hard and fast. Circumstances change rapidly. I wasted an entire year coming to my senses. I love you with all my heart, and it spooked me this morning when you weren't enthusiastic about marrying me."

I kissed him. "I want to marry you, but the details of getting married are holding me back."

The tightness in Pete's face eased. "Whew. I thought you had cold feet, but logistics are the issue. I'll work on those."

"We should do them together, Pete."

"Except you're super busy right now and I'm at loose ends between calls to my California lawyer and filing more motions against the failed North Merrick venture."

"I hope your motions are successful, but we'll make it work either way."

"We will," Pete said. "Though it will be easier to rebound with my investment stake. Getting back to the wedding, Father Ben is fine as the officiant. Since we both agree on that detail and if it's okay with you, I'll approach him about date availability."

A weight lifted from my shoulders. "Wonderful."

~*~

After a quiet dinner at home, I returned to my commercial kitchen to review my lists for tomorrow. Stacks of stainless steel deep dish trays on my counters were ready for the remainder of the rubbed chicken as I baked it tomorrow.

Feeling confident about my progress, I chopped salad veggies in my food processor. Soon I had mounds of cucumbers, carrots, celery, radishes, red onion, tomatoes bagged separately, along with grated cheese. I made a gallon each of ranch dressing and citrus vinaigrette and set aside the washed lettuce to tear tomorrow.

Before I started on the yeast rolls, my phone buzzed. I'd missed several frantic text messages from the bride-to-be. She expected me to add three foods to the menu: hot wings, pizza bites, and boiled shrimp.

Heat steamed up my collar. No caterer would add three extra dishes for this size crowd at this late date. I called her.

Melanie answered on the first ring. "We have to change the menu," she yelped. "Malcom wants finger foods. He hates chicken."

They should have thought of that months ago. "I'm sorry to disappoint you, but it's too late to change the menu. We have a contract, and the food you ordered is what's coming tomorrow."

"How hard is it to throw extras on a plate?" Melanie asked.

My entire kitchen brimmed with food and serving trays for her big day. I composed myself so my voice didn't squeak. "Catering a large function is more than throwing a few items on a plate. Why is Malcom upset about the menu now? Didn't he participate when you made the food selections with the original caterer?"

"Never said a word. Too busy with his phone the whole time."

"He had his chance for input. He's a businessman. If he wanted finger foods, he should've spoken up long ago."

Melanie sniffed. "At the rehearsal dinner tonight, he said everyone hates rubber chicken dinners."

My spine stiffened like a steel rod at the insult. "My spiced chicken will melt in his mouth. Trust me, people will rave about your wedding for years. Is it possible you took his remark out of context?"

"I don't know." Melanie cried. "His mother thinks Shell Island smells like a sewer, she said my bridesmaids are trashy, and she hates me. His dad nearly stiffed the wait staff at Fergy's Red Derby. He argued that the excellent service for the rehearsal dinner fell below par. He embarrassed me."

"The two of you don't spend much time around his parents?"

"No. Mal says they don't understand him."

She sounded calmer now. I'd hit on the right approach. "He loves you. He's getting the woman of his dreams. He'll be happy and he'll love my chicken. It's okay, Melanie."

"I am the woman of his dreams. He's lucky to get me."

"There you go. You'll be a beautiful bride. Don't worry about the food. It will be delicious."

"Thank you, River. I feel better after talking to you."

"See you tomorrow."

After I ended the call, I pulled the yeast roll dough from the warm oven and began fitting dough balls on trays. The yeasty aroma brought a sense of peace and contentment.

Pete entered and perched on an island stool. "How much longer until you're done?"

"I only need to finish these rolls. Did something come up?"

"Everything's fine with me. It looks like you've used up every square inch of space in here. And this kitchen smells great. I'm lucky to be part of your life."

"You're sweet and the feeling is mutual." I caught his eye. "Melanie just called to add three dishes to the menu based on a comment her fiancé made tonight."

His gaze intensified. "You held fast to your contract, right?"

"I did."

"Good."

Doug knocked on the door and sauntered in, propping a hip against the counter. "You need my help tomorrow for the big shindig? Or am I off the server list until my name is cleared?"

"You're on my list. Not having you would show I don't believe in you. If someone makes a fuss, we'll revisit that decision. My apologies for not confirming with you earlier. I'm not myself these last few days. I definitely need three helpers. So, yes, I need you, Pete, and Anita Declan as my assistants tomorrow. Are you okay with that?"

"Anita's a good worker." He paused abruptly. "I also need to thank you. Your idea of connecting with the bridge ladies as a substitute player worked brilliantly. I've had a steady stream of repair work and referrals from them since I opened my handyman business. These ladies believe I'm innocent. I'm their friend's son who can do no wrong, and I'm grateful to get my handyman business off to such a running start. If work continues at this fast pace, I'll hire a full-time assistant."

I beamed with pride. "I'm proud of what you've accomplished."

Pete pushed by with a kiss. "I'll head back to the house so y'all can have brother-sister time."

Doug took the stool Pete vacated. "What's the plan for tomorrow?"

"I've already set up the buffet station as a food warmer in the pool house. I'll need you and Anita to go out early and get that going. Check that the tables are set for 120 and then stack the salad and dinner plates on the pool house counter."

"Sure. What time should we arrive?"

"Noon."

Doug nodded then drummed his fingers on the counter. "Does it strike you that Pete's mostly sitting around these days?"

My brother was in protective mode again. He didn't know Pete the way I did, so he was quick to judge the man I loved. "That job in California nearly broke him physically, mentally, and financially. In addition to physical therapy, he's using leverage to get his financial investment back. He's also working on a business plan for taking over the entire Village shopping area."

"Wow. I had no idea. Since I've moved in with Viv, I've missed so much over here. But just like you check up on me, I need to ask this. You're sure about marrying him?"

I braced my arms on the counter, feeling the weight of the day all of a sudden. "I'm absolutely certain. I've been in love with him all my adult life. Mom and Pete schemed for months on his proposal strategy, so she approved of him. He's the one for me, and before you ask, it doesn't matter if he's rich or poor."

My hand went to the engagement ring I wore around my neck. In true Pete style the ring featured an over-the-top diamond. Beautiful, but not conducive to making bread rolls or most other food preparation functions. "We're planning a small wedding this spring. Would you do me the honor of giving me away?"

"Of course."

"Great. I'll ask Viv to be my maid of honor too, but we have to get her out of jail first."

"She'll be honored to be your attendant. She's told me about all the stuff the two of you used to do as kids. Those Nancy Drew days are some of the best times of her life."

Never in my wildest dreams would I have thought Doug and Viv would end up a couple, but they were a good fit. The fact that she had a few years on Doug didn't matter to either of them.

"All right then," I said. "Nice to have more wedding details settled. As soon as we nail down the day and location, I'll share them. And so you don't hear it from someone else, Pete and I are house shopping. We need a larger place that will also give him a formal home office."

Doug blinked rapidly. "You're selling this place?"

"Not if I can afford to keep it. Besides, even though Mom willed the house to me, this is your home too. Don't you want it to remain in the family?"

"Hadn't thought about it. I'm getting started with my business and paying half the rent for Viv's apartment suits my budget."

"I understand. I'll keep you posted about our housing plans."

"Great. I'll serve at the Walker-Conway wedding tomorrow, and on Monday you'll figure out how to spring Viv from jail."

"Deal."

Chapter Eight

Sunday morning dawned to the mouthwatering aroma of roasted chickens, dozens of them. With Melanie's wedding at two thirty, I had to be out of here by noon.

At seven thirty Pete brought me a fried egg sandwich. "Thanks," I said, wolfing it down. He wore a dress shirt and pants, not his usual Sunday at-home attire. "Headed out?"

"Thought I'd hit early church this morning, if you can spare me. I'll be back in time to load the van and help with all things wedding today."

"Wish I could join you. Say hi to Father Ben for me and tell him I'm working today."

"Will do." He whistled as he hurried away.

The oven timer rang, and I rotated a new batch of chickens into both ovens. I checked my timeline again. Right on schedule. I loaded the baked rolls in the van, along with every serving spoon I owned.

I stepped into the yard to send a text to Anita Declan to go directly to Creekside Lodge at noon instead of meeting me here at home.

Something tickled my leg. I glanced down, intending to brush the insect away. Major paced back and forth in front of me and dragged his tail across my legs. Holy Cow. In the six weeks I'd been feeding this stray black cat, he'd never let me touch him.

"Hey, kitty," I said in my softest voice. "What's this? Didn't you like your breakfast?"

The cat continued his narrow patrol. Hmm. Something bothered him. I glanced around, fearing the glint of a gun barrel or a posse of bad guys storming out of the woods. But the sun shone brightly, the songbirds chirped joyously. Only the cat acted out of character.

Major rubbed against my ankles and shoes, and I reached a hand down to pet him. He didn't freak, and in fact, arched his head under my touch, purring.

I wanted to share this exciting news, but my friends and family were unavailable or in jail. Jail. Poor Viv. She'd been jailed since Wednesday, four long days and nights of confinement.

She'd given me three suspect names yesterday morning, but I hadn't followed up yet on Heavy D, Ty, and Eggs because of preparing for today's job. Guilt eddied in my gut, along with an unwelcome wave of regret. Curtis Marlin's drinking buddies were my best chance of getting Viv out of jail.

I checked my phone timer. I had a few minutes now to search online records for Heavy D's address or phone number. The browser search returned four Haywood addresses on Shell Island. No answer at the Carl Haywood residence and no voice mail either. Allen Haywood's number had been disconnected. Jamaria Haywood didn't answer and her voice mail was full. Only one choice left, Raquel Haywood. I tried the number. Busy and no voice mail option.

I waited and tried again. Busy. I'd try that number later, and the other ones that were in service. Though, since Heavy D lived with his aunt, I leaned toward the two female listings. *Hang in there, Viv. I'll get this snooping done soon.* I pocketed the phone.

The cat sat statue still near me, as if his gaze imparted the secrets of the universe. Deciding I had nothing to lose, I reached for the cat, intending to place him on my lap. He arched and hissed, batting my arm with a paw. I got the message as he scampered away.

Touch not the cat, unless he initiated the touch.

After washing up inside, I toasted the almond toppers for the green beans and checked that the butter twirls held their shape at room temperature.

My phone rang. Melanie Walker. "You're coming aren't you?" she shrieked in my ear. "I had a nightmare that everybody came, but we had no food."

Oh, boy. Wedding jitters on steroids. This would be a long day. I sank onto a stool. "Holloway Catering staff will arrive at noon. With the service at two thirty, we don't anticipate serving dinner until three thirty. Rest assured, your guests will have a delicious meal."

"Mama said to mention we have six extra people. Some distant cousins didn't RSVP, and they crashed the rehearsal dinner last night."

"I have a little flexibility in terms of providing more food, though you will owe me the same per person plate charge for the newcomers. I expect that extra 150 in the final check today. Also, you can't squeeze six more people onto those ten-tops. You need another table and six more chairs. Did you notify the facility?"

"Yeah, but it didn't work out. They said we contracted for 120 people and that's what we're getting. You call and make them listen."

Alarm bells clanged in my head. "They may not have additional tables or place settings at Creekside. If they didn't accommodate your request, your mother should call them."

"I wish. Mom said I had to do this because it's character building. Why should these latecomers get a seat or a meal? I don't even like those cousins. They're obnoxious and drama queens when things don't go their way."

I strove to be helpful. "Did you tell the facility you'd pay their change fee?"

"No. Should I have mentioned it?"

I jotted place settings on my to-do list. "Yes. You're asking the facility to rapidly accommodate more guests. They expect compensation for their time and inconvenience same as I'm expecting additional compensation."

"I can't deal with this today. Can't you make that call?"

"Not if you want a memorable meal for 126 guests."

"I'm busy too. Being the bride is hard work." Melanie hung up on me.

Pete wandered in at ten thirty with a bakery bag of carrot cake muffins and a supersized iced tea. I gulped both down greedily. "I love this personal attention."

"All part of the package," he replied, polishing off two muffins to my single one. "Father Ben agreed to marry us this spring, especially if we steer clear of weekends. There's a catch."

"Oh?"

"A couple's counseling requirement. We need to start right away."

I studied his face. "You're serious?"

He nodded. "We penciled in Wednesday at four. Does that work for you?"

"Uh, sure, I think. Let me check my phone calendar." I scrolled through dates. "That works."

"Great. Only a few more details and we're ready to go."

I set aside my phone. "We'll get there, but not today. This is Melanie Walker's big day."

"Agreed. Let's get to work."

~*~

We loaded the van. As a precaution, Pete and I also packed my grandmother's china, silver flatware, serving pieces, and a tablecloth for the trip. I hoped we didn't need the extra place settings but I didn't want to be caught short, a lesson I'd learned the hard way. We drove the van into the pool house area and unloaded.

Doug and Pete ferried the food to the pool house while Anita and I placed roasted chicken, beans, and corn in the buffet warmers and warming ovens and refrigerated the salad fixings. We poured salad dressings into bowls with ladles, thirteen of each type of dressing. We also plated butter swirls for each table.

Anita pushed the loaded serving cart out to the tables. She returned in a few minutes. "There are only twelve tables with ten place settings each out there."

My heart sunk. Guests were beginning to arrive. The bridal party was dressing inside the mansion. Melanie couldn't break free and deal with this now, though she should've resolved it earlier today. I could call her mother, but the mother of the bride had responsibilities too.

Between the mansion and the pool house, a giant tent covered the dining area. Automatically, I counted the preset tables. Anita was right. Only twelve tables were prepared for guests, which meant there was no place for the additional six guests. And since Melanie hadn't used a seating chart, the latecomers might sit anywhere, bumping guests who'd RSVPed.

Many of the island's movers and shakers were here. Though I had nothing to do with the seating arrangements, chances were that I'd be blame for any mix-up. I'd have to deal with this now.

Having worked events here before, I knew where they stored the tables and chairs between events. I delegated the task of adding another table for six to Pete and Doug. Anita and I made up the table with my tablecloth and dishes from home. The table didn't have a matching floral centerpiece but that couldn't be helped.

Crisis averted.

We had a few moment's respite before the dinner so Anita and I walked to the creekbank. The rising tide gleamed under sunny skies. Melanie had gotten lucky with the weather and the absence of bugs.

"It feels wrong to enjoy this scenery when Viv is in jail," I said after we'd let the sun warm our faces and turned to stroll back to the pool house. "I want to help her but I don't have any real leads."

"I already gave it my all," Anita said, padding beside me. "Between the kids and scratching out a living, I won't be much help."

"Taking care of those children is your priority and that's what you should be doing," I said. "Changing the subject, did you know Curtis?"

Anita's step faltered and then she caught up with me. "Not very well. Most people knew his reputation. Guys that live large like Curtis are frauds."

Her comment sounded heartfelt, and I paused beside the pool, savoring the roasted chicken aroma in the air. "How so?"

She shook her head and sighed. "Don't take anything I say as gospel. I haven't slept through the night since before Zoey was born. My perceptions about men are probably skewed because of Darry taking off with no word."

"I'm sorry that you've had such a terrible time of it, and I feel bad that I didn't know to help you before now."

"That's okay," Anita said. "I kept hoping Darry would return and everything would be all right. I've given up that dream. I've got to make a new plan."

"I'll help any way I can," I said, "but getting back to what you started to say about Curtis. Would you elaborate? It might help me better understand Curtis."

At first I didn't think she'd answer. Palm fronds rustled and snatches of conversation drifted over to us. I was about to suggest we return to the pool house when she spoke.

"We've all known people like Curtis," Anita said. "They're fake, pretending to be something they're not, and for some reason, people accept the tales they spin. If you live a lie, you can't let down your guard. Hence, fakers have few friends."

"That is insightful, and it explains why I keep coming up with his three basketball teammates and Viv as his only friends."

"That sounds right." Anita sighed. "I wish—"

"River!" Geneva Walker shouted.

I turned to see Geneva hurrying my way from the adjacent mansion, the hem of her blue robe snapping around her calves. Her red face put me on notice. Something wasn't right.

"Have you seen Malcom?" Geneva asked standing close and speaking in a stage whisper. "He's missing."

I shook my head, trying to project a calm professionalism and not thinking too far down the road of a missing groom. "I haven't seen him, sorry."

Geneva cried out. "I've worked too hard to pull this wedding off. He can't disappear. Where is he?"

I blinked a few times, not knowing how to help her. "I don't know."

Eyes rounded, Geneva stared at me. "Everyone knows you're good at finding things. Right now I need your locational skills. Please make some calls, River."

Her request put me in a bind. I didn't have time for a "finding" job but the reception dinner couldn't go forward without the wedding. I had to look for the groom and continue the meal preparation. Pete and Doug joined us poolside. "Where's he staying?" I asked. "Did he book a room at the hotel?"

"I comped them a suite for tonight. Malcom asked to check in a night early and I extended the reservation. My people swear he's not in his room. His blue Beemer is gone." Geneva fixed me with a hard stare. "Melanie's crying her eyes out because she's been jilted. His parents are on the way from Savannah and they haven't heard from him. Please find him."

Chapter Nine

Thoughts churned in my head, and one commanded my attention. No groom meant no wedding and no reception. I wanted all of these well-heeled guests to have the opportunity to enjoy the food I'd prepared, as that's how I garnered new clients. If this derailed, the chaos would distract me from investigating the Curtis Marlin murder properly.

I needed the weeding to happen, and I needed to get my brother's charges dropped, and since my time was limited, these two events were linked in my thoughts. Somehow, I had to make it work.

I nodded, clenching my hands together. "I'll look into it."

"Thanks." Geneva turned to go and then whirled back around. "That chicken smells divine. If this goes sideways, I want the food. I'll freeze it and dine on it for the next year."

I chewed my lip so as not to smile. Perhaps this pending disaster could be salvaged. "Yes, ma'am."

Geneva hurried to the big house. I gathered my small staff close. "We need this marriage to happen, and the groom is missing. Each of you call a restaurant or bar and ask if they've seen Malcom Conway. Make a list as you go. I'm calling the cops."

I searched my contact list for Deputy Gil Franklin. This was his day off but I hoped he picked up.

"Yes?" Franklin answered on the first ring.

"Sorry to bug you," I began, "and I wouldn't ask if I had other options."

"It's okay, River. I'm at home. How can I help?"

I stared across the pool with unseeing eyes. "We have a missing person at the wedding I'm catering. Can you find out if there were any wrecks last night or this morning involving Malcom Conway? He drives a blue Beemer with a Chatham County plate."

"I'll check with dispatch," Franklin said. "What's this about?"

"No groom for the two-thirty ceremony," I said, looking at the empty tables under the tent, the poster boards of seating charts. "I'm catering the Melanie Walker and Malcom Conway wedding at Creekside. According to Geneva Walker, Malcom has a room at Ocean Crest Plaza Hotel but neither he nor his car are there now."

"What's he look like?"

"White male is all I know." I paused for a moment. "Thank you for helping on your day off. Malcom hasn't been seen since last night's rehearsal dinner at Fergy's Red Derby."

"Understood. I'll look into the matter."

"Thanks. I appreciate this."

I ended my call, and seeing everyone else busy on their phones, I stared at the vast salt marsh, then I texted Melanie to ask who Malcom's friends were. She replied in thirty seconds. *His friends are my friends.*

I sent another text in reply. *Where would he go to escape the wedding pressure?*

Top Cat Lounge, then to the beaches and sleep in his car, Melanie texted back. *He did that when we quarreled once.*

I gazed at my helpers and relayed Melanie's message. "I can spare Doug or Pete to fetch the groom."

"I'll go," Doug said.

"Check the public beach lots for a blue Beemer but be back no later than two thirty. Call me when you find him."

Doug left and my phone rang, Deputy Franklin. "Got something?" I asked.

"No wrecks or grooms in the hospital. He got a speeding ticket last night. No law enforcement issues since then. The patrol deputy is on the lookout for a blue Beemer."

May as well broach Viv's murder charge. "Appreciated. Um, I have another matter to discuss with you."

"Vivian Declan?" he asked.

My hopes plummeted at his sharp tone. "Yes."

"She'll keep until I'm on duty."

The call ended, and I shared the news with the others.

Anita beamed. "I should be sad for Melanie, but this drama is the most excitement I've had in years. Catering is a hoot. I wish I did this every day."

"Fair warning," I said. "It isn't usually like this, but we're going to keep on schedule with our meal service. I have to believe Doug will find him."

As we worked, bridesmaids swarmed out of the house, each one fluffed in orange-sherbet colored gowns that they hitched up, revealing tanned ankles and bare feet. Melanie flounced out and her white gown had the same fluffy skirt and a sequin-covered bodice. She also gathered handfuls of her gown, revealing bare ankles and feet.

A photographer snapped photos of Melanie and her flock of orange peeps. Geneva strolled over as we filled wire baskets with rolls. "Any word?" she asked.

"Nothing yet."

The color drained from Geneva's face. "His parents are gloating, like they expected this. I hate them. I might not let Malcom marry Melanie."

Time to calm the waters again. "I'm sure there's a reason for his absence."

"Why is he doing this to me?" Geneva asked, her voice thinning. "To Melanie?"

I squeezed her hand gently. "It'll work out. The Geneva Walker I know would continue preparing for her daughter's wedding ceremony. That's what I'm doing."

Geneva drew in a long breath and squared her shoulders. "Malcom is the man Melanie wants, and I support her choice. I'll be the perfect mother of the bride, and no one will be the wiser."

My phone buzzed with a call. "Hold up." I listened then shared the news. "Doug found him at Seashore Park. Is his tux here or at the hotel?"

"Thank goodness." Geneva grinned and pumped her fist. "Malcom's tux is here."

49

"Yes, ma'am." I relayed the message and she hurried away.

"We're coming," Doug said on the phone. "A case of too much to drink. When I woke him, he had no idea what day it is. Guy's got a killer headache."

"See you soon."

Pete hugged me after I ended the call. "You saved the wedding," he said.

"Let's hope it's smooth sailing the rest of the way."

~*~

All too soon the guests gathered for the reception. No one remarked on Doug being a server, and he did an excellent job as usual. Pete and Anita slid into the routine as if they'd served food for years. Right after the cake slicing, the bride darted over and hugged me. "You're the best," Melanie said. "The food wowed everyone, as you promised. Malcom ate every bite of his chicken and half of mine. Mom said you got Malcom here. You're my new best friend."

"Thanks," I said, uncertain of the honor. "I'm happy for you."

"My mom thinks the world of you and so do I. Thank you so much." She dashed away.

"Wow," I mouthed under my breath as I separated out my dishes.

Pete rubbed my back. "Well done."

"Thanks. I couldn't do it without everyone's help." I turned to see my staff watching me. "You were all awesome."

"I followed Doug's lead," Pete said. "Thank goodness you sliced the cake. Pretty sure I'd have mangled that."

I wrote checks to Anita and Doug, sending them on their way at five. Not long after, Geneva walked over with a generous check for me.

"This is too much," I protested, trying to hand it back.

Geneva retreated. "It's what I would've paid that Savannah caterer and you went the extra mile. Bonus points for finding the groom."

"Thank you."

"I'll recommend Holloway Catering to my friends, though most of them were here tonight and loved your food. Maybe you'll share the chicken recipe with me?"

"Maybe."

Pete drove us home under a fiery sunset sky. I started to relax. "You've now seen Holloway Catering in action at two different-sized events. What do you think of my world?" I asked.

He navigated the first traffic circle with ease. "Pieces are always moving, like a three dimensional chess game. I enjoyed being part of the high-energy production."

"This event had unique challenges, but I'm glad it's done." I pointed to my chest. "I'm officially taking off my catering apron for a few days. Need to focus on my next big project."

"Which is?"

"Finding Curtis Marlin's killer."

Chapter Ten

Over coffee on the back deck the next morning, I marveled anew at the large bonus I'd received. If I booked one wedding this size every month, that's all I'd need to stay afloat. Except large weddings with big tips didn't come along every month.

On the plus side, I handed out over a dozen business cards to wedding guests who'd requested them. If past experience held true, I'd get bookings from about a third of those people, so definitely a big win.

My black cat finished his breakfast and drowsed in a nearby pool of sunshine, his purring an audible rumble. I liked having a kitty, but I wished mine were cuddly.

The door opened and a freshly showered Pete joined me. "Still fondling that check, I see."

"Guilty as charged." I stuffed it in a pocket, watching Major dart down the steps. "I'd love to mount it on the wall but I'd rather cash it."

"I know the feeling." Pete laughed. "What's our game plan on this fine Monday?"

"Heading to the bank once my commercial kitchen is shipshape, then I'm going after those basketball teammates on our suspect list. I hope to catch up with Deputy Franklin today too."

"He'll help? I'm surprised. Viv and Doug's arrests imply the cops closed the case."

"They're wrong. We have to give them an alternate suspect, but we need to know what they have."

"That reminds me ... yesterday at the reception, someone mentioned Curtis."

"Who?"

"A brunette bridesmaid. She said Curtis had an STD."

I drained the last bit of my coffee. "The rumor may not be relevant."

"A high-strung person might get even if they caught something from him."

True. "I'll ask the deputy if Curtis showed signs of communicable diseases at autopsy. I can't get past the actual poisoning. Why do that? According to what I discovered today, antifreeze is a painful way to die."

"Everything is online these days," Pete said.

"That's creepy."

"Perhaps. At least bullets weren't flying."

He had experienced a brush with bullets and knives out in California last month. "You're okay, right? I mean, uh, we haven't reinjured anything with our, uh, adventures?"

Pete leaned over and kissed me. "Even if we had, I wouldn't change a thing."

"Good to know."

~*~

Exiting the bank, I saw Heavy D enter the café near the pier. I hurried inside Pete's truck and said, "How about an early lunch in the café today?"

"Good news?" Pete asked.

From his expectant gaze, he hoped I was pregnant. I wish that were true but nothing to report on that front. "More like investigating. A suspect entered the cafe, and we can grab a hot lunch while we observe him."

"Two birds with one stone. Gotcha."

Pete ushered me into the café, and we headed for a table past where Heavy D sat. As we approached, I said, "DeAndre?"

He looked up. "Yes?"

Feeling reckless, I dropped into the seat across him. "You don't know me, but you met my brother Doug. He visited Curtis's house that night. My name is River."

He leveled a finger at me. "You're the caterer. The cookie lady."

"That's me. I'm sorry for your loss."

"Me and Curtis go way back," Heavy D said.

I shot Pete a questioning glance and nodded toward our table and he kept going. "Curtis died from poison." I said. "I can't believe it."

"Me neither. The cops been up in my grill about it too. We didn't see nothing that night. Curtis acted drunk but he always drank too much. We didn't know he'd been poisoned. I don't get it. Who would do my boy Curtis that way?"

"It's a mystery I want to understand, and I hope you'll help. Who were his other friends?"

"Curtis would walk into a bar and twenty people would surround him, but none of those barflies were friends. He never invited them to his place."

"At least one person didn't like him. And I heard an unflattering rumor going around."

"About him winning a million dollars at slots in Reno? That's bogus. If he had big bucks, he'd flash it everywhere."

"Hadn't heard that one. I heard about an STD."

Heavy D snorted. "No way. All of us had a pact from the beginning. No unprotected sex. Some chick musta said that out of spite. Most girls were too needy for Curtis, except for Viv. She fit into the group like a guy. She seemed happy the other night. Then she lit out of there."

The restaurant clatter faded away. "After Curtis called her a ho."

"Yeah. Not cool, and he apologized, but she left anyway. He spouted crap like that, but he never meant it."

"The cops think she poisoned him to get even."

"Not hardly. Curtis called her worse over the years, and she didn't get testy. Somebody else did this. Some sneaky son of a gun."

"You got any ideas?"

"I'm not ratting out my teammates."

So he suspected a teammate. Interesting. "Someone knew what Curtis drank and doctored his gin. Somebody sneaky."

"Yeah. Weren't no call to kill Curtis. He was all right."

"Thanks for helping me try to free Viv." I slid a business card his way "If you remember anything, call me."

He palmed the card. "Sure thing."

I slid out and joined Pete. We ordered BLTs and the vegetable soup.

Heavy D finished his meal and stopped by our table. "I been studying on this, and you didn't hear it from me. Curtis and Ty recently had their vehicles serviced at the same garage. Island Tire and Auto."

"Okay."

Heavy D fixed me with a glare. "They have antifreeze in car shops."

My head kicked back. "Oh. Thanks for the tip."

"Not saying the shop or Ty did anything bad, but it's something, you know?"

"Appreciate it."

"One more thing I told the cops. That night, Curtis drank so much his speech slurred. Even though Viv served him that last gin and tonic, Curtis met us at the door with that Beefeater's bottle in hand."

"Anybody else drink it?"

"Me and the boys drank our beer. Viv and Doug split a beer. They barely stayed ten minutes. Curtis fell asleep on the sofa and we split. It freaks me out now. We could've saved him."

"You didn't know. No one blames you."

"Doesn't matter. My heart is heavy." He thumped his chest twice with his palm and shuffled off.

"I hope he'll be all right," I said.

"He's trying to process it," Pete said. "I've been there before. When bizarre things happen, there's no easy explanation. You pick up the pieces and go on."

"I understand, only I'd hoped he'd act guilty. He's genuinely upset his friend is dead."

"I don't know his normal mood, but I agree with you. He seems like a straight shooter. He didn't have to volunteer anything."

"My van needs an oil change so I'll make an appointment at Island Tire and Auto Repair. Perhaps they have containers of antifreeze in the waiting room."

"Today?"

"Tomorrow. I want to compare notes with the deputy today."

"Good luck. At least we'll have two vehicles today. I have a business appointment this afternoon."

"Oh?"

"A realtor's showing me commercial properties and a few homes. Wanna come with?"

"We'll cover more ground separately. You handle the real estate angle. I'll work on the free-Viv plan."

Chapter Eleven

"Ms. Declan's fingerprints are on the tainted gin bottle. We have her dead to rights," Deputy Franklin said, his voice clear and confident.

The communal workstation at the cop shop sat empty except for the two of us. Still, privacy was an illusion. Other deputies could enter at any moment.

"There should have been other prints on that bottle," I said. "Whoever killed Curtis must've wiped it. Viv didn't bring the booze or dose it. I've known Vivian Declan for more than twenty years. No way would she poison anyone. That's not her style, besides, she's dating my brother. If she harbored romantic feelings for Curtis, she wouldn't have taken Doug to Curtis's house."

"Eyewitnesses claim Curtis called her a derogatory name. She killed in retribution."

Overhead a fluorescent light buzzed. If I worked here, I'd fix that. "Sadly, Viv became immune to that man's trash talk. I checked with Heavy D. He said Curtis had the Beefeater's bottle when he, Ty, and Eggs arrived. Viv poured Curtis a drink, at his request. You have the wrong suspect."

"Sure you want to go down that route?" Franklin asked, shifting his weight in the chair.

"What do you mean?"

"If Viv is innocent, then your brother has a strong motive. He killed Curtis to avenge the verbal abuse Viv received."

"No way. Doug can't kill a spider in the house. He scoops them up and frees them outside." I realized my hands were waving in the air. I sat on them. "He wouldn't hurt Curtis because my brother is a live-and-let-live person. Once Curtis acted like a jerk, Doug acted true to his nature and left to avoid conflict."

"The other three guys alibi out. None of them touched his drink at any time. They were questioned individually and their stories match. They spent the night at Sully's place, amidst more heavy partying."

"Their alibi at Sully's is too far downstream to matter. Those three were at the Marlin house before and after Doug and Viv arrived. That trio could've poisoned Curtis in either time window. For that matter, the booze could've been poisoned any time prior to the party."

"True, but poisoning is a deliberate and personal crime. The sheriff is convinced the people at the Marlin house that night are the only suspects. With the sheriff buying the basketball guys moving in lockstep that night, they aren't his prime suspects. Viv is, and Doug is by association."

"Doug and Viv were together too, but you think that makes them guilty. They're innocent. If not the basketball guys or Doug and Viv, someone else dosed the gin."

"Very unlikely. Curtis Marlin had a limited range of close associates. The fingerprints in the house belong to the victim and the five visitors that night. The evidence doesn't support another suspect."

"That should've been a clue. Curtis gave wild parties. His house should've been loaded with fingerprints. I can't believe no other prints were present." I had to open his eyes to my truth. "Even if Curtis compulsively cleaned house, there's another explanation. Criminals wear gloves. Why aren't you looking for someone sneaky?"

Franklin's expression tightened and shuttered. "The simplest answer is usually the right one. The evidence points to these five, three of whom have solid alibis."

"I disagree. How did Curtis afford his party-boy lifestyle? His sketchy work history and his impoverished grandmother wouldn't support a flea."

"We reviewed his finances."

The deputy's smug attitude irked me. "Here's what I know about Curtis: He worked at the Coffee Shack briefly and got axed for coming in late. He waited tables at the Creekside until they switched him to bartender. He got fired for being drunk on the job. Grandma Talley served as his financial lifeline until she died. Far as I know, Curtis didn't work after her death, except for his trip to Alaska. If he gained income illegally, there's a connection to someone sneaky."

"We documented the victim's spotty employment history and the subsequent loan he took out on Mrs. Talley's property. His payments were in arrears, and his bank started foreclosure proceedings. Banks don't poison customers who stop paying. They follow an established process to remove debtors from their customer base. We reviewed Marlin's phone records and identified frequent callers. Nothing indicates other people. The sheriff and the D.A. are satisfied they have a strong case against Vivian Declan. Doug will be tried as her accomplice."

My chest tightened, and I struggled for a breath. The cops had stopped looking for other suspects. Doug and Viv faced a super-sized disaster.

"What about the rumors flying around the island? I heard Curtis won big in Reno and had an STD. Either situation could be a motive for his death."

"We don't deal in rumors, Ms. Holloway. I urge you to accept our findings."

"I can't give up on my brother or Viv. Curtis had an enemy, someone who couldn't stomach his arrogance or his foul mouth."

Did his expression soften? I kept going. "Heavy D said Curtis and Ty recently had their cars serviced at Island Tire and Auto. Car places have antifreeze. What if Curtis got belligerent and upset Ty? His poisoning could be payback."

Franklin shook his head. "You can buy antifreeze anywhere."

"I'll find out who really killed Curtis." I stood up to leave. "I intend to visit Island Tire and question the staff."

His hand rose, palm out. "Hold up." He stared at the far wall momentarily and swore under his breath. "I'll visit the car shop and ask questions, informally."

The investigation remained closed, but he'd question these people who had recent business dealings with Curtis. Still a win in my book.

"Thank you," I said, still planning to scope the place myself.

Chapter Twelve

At home, I soaked three whole flounder in buttermilk for dinner. Pete had a sweet tooth so I made brownies from scratch. I prepped potatoes and sweet potatoes and put them in a timed oven to bake. I had finished making the salad when Pete came home.

He swept into the kitchen like an offshore breeze, his face bright with happiness. "I found the perfect house. You have to see it right now. The realtor is waiting for our return."

"Give me a sec to square the food away." I put our dinner on hold and turned. "Let's see this perfect house."

Pete hurried me outside. "You'll fall in love with the kitchen. It's twice as big as this one and you can do all your cooking in it."

"I'm excited to see it, but commercial kitchens have specific regulations. This kitchen may not fit the bill."

"The kitchen is perfect. I'm not worried about that." He waved off my comment. "You'll love it. Big rooms. Three spare bedrooms. We'd have room for our family to expand and room for Doug if he wants to live with us."

"If I can clear his name."

"You will, hon. You're that good." He gave my hand a squeeze, cranked his truck, and eased down the shaded road. "This house is a fresh start for us, River."

We turned onto the main road and accelerated through the first traffic circle. "There's a formal dining room set off by French doors." Contagious excitement rang in Pete's words. "That'll be my home office. The landscaping is spectacular."

"I can't wait to see it."

A slender, narrow-hipped woman with big hair in a peach skirted suit and heels met us in the driveway. Soon we strolled through a beautiful estate home. The ceilings were lofty, the windows floor-to-ceiling and trimmed with sheers and custom drapes. After viewing the great room from the foyer, Pete insisted we go upstairs and save the kitchen for last.

Four large bedrooms with adjoining bathrooms rounded out the top floor, each room grander than the last. The master bathroom had enough floor space for a flash mob. It would be fun to live in this space, I thought, nodding at each amenity.

Finally, we padded down the sweeping staircase and the kitchen came into view. The light gray walls complemented the stainless steel kitchen appliances. Granite countertops in a charcoal gray gave the room a sleek look. I drew my hand lovingly over the countertop. I'd love to roll out pie crusts on this surface.

"You like it?" Pete asked.

"I do. This designer had a passion for cooking."

"Great. I love the house and you do too. I'll make an offer on the house today."

Conscious of Toni listening to our every word, I leaned close to his ear. "Pete, may we talk in private?"

Questions filled his eyes, but he turned to Toni. "We'd like to discuss this."

Toni's megawatt smile dimmed momentarily. "Of course. I'll wait outside. Take your time."

Pete took my hand once we were alone. "What's going on?"

"You've made a lovely choice. This house is modern and upscale. We could live here easily. But this isn't a commercial kitchen. It isn't a separate entity, and the yard is filled with patios, a pool, and thick hedges, so there's no room for a commercial kitchen. Worse, there's no room to insert my kitchen either, plus, we'd have to ask the homeowner's association permission first. Some people don't want a small business next to them."

He didn't respond for a long minute.

"I didn't consider that," he said.

"It is beautiful, and it has room for a growing family. The walk-in closets and this kitchen are to-die-for. However, this house doesn't work for my home-based business as is."

"I'll ask Toni about the HOA rules." He brightened. "Okay with you if we sacrifice the pool for your commercial kitchen?"

"Sure," I said. "Let's ask her."

Outside, Toni stoically relayed the neighborhood's regulations. My vinyl-siding unattached modular unit didn't meet neighborhood standards. Worse, the neighborhood board reviewed home businesses on a case-by-case basis. She knew that for certain because she had a home office for her real estate business here. Even Pete's home office needed to be approved.

"Sorry." Pete sighed. "This house and neighborhood don't work for us."

"I have upscale listings elsewhere I'd love to show you," Toni said.

Pete glanced at me. I shrugged. He turned to the realtor. "We'll regroup first. Thanks for your time."

Toni left, and we sat in Pete's truck.

"I'm sorry it didn't work out because I know you want that fresh start in a place that's ours," I said. "Maybe at some point I can afford an offsite commercial kitchen and we can live in this neighborhood."

"It's not that," Pete said. "I'm used to finding solutions, but in my haste I nearly made things worse. I wanted you to have a grand house to atone for me nearly wrecking us last year."

"We don't need a palace, or at least I don't. We have a place to stay indefinitely, even if it isn't a good long-term fit. We'll keep looking."

He reached across the console and laced his fingers through mine. "I'll do better next time."

"It's okay. Buying a house as a couple is new to both of us."

"One good thing came out of this," Pete said. "Earlier, I spoke to Toni about safety, and she guaranteed me this neighborhood is safe. I mentioned the recent homicide on the island. Toni brushed it off as a bad location, then she said the cops had the wrong guy. She dated Ty Carvell a few years ago, but not for long because of his terrible temper. She said his place has holes in every wall from his fists."

"I'll mention his temper to Deputy Franklin."

Pete nodded and shifted the gear lever into drive. "How'd your meeting with him go this afternoon?"

"He agreed to ask questions at the garage, but I made an appointment for the van tomorrow to form my own opinion."

"It's nice knowing the deputy is responsive."

"He's humoring me." I frowned. "The sheriff closed the case. We have to prove him wrong."

Chapter Thirteen

Pete surprised me by driving to the pier. "Let's take a walk before we go home."

He didn't have to ask twice. Felt like I'd been cooped up all day. We parked and joined the throng on the pier. People fished, crabbed, or strolled like us, while others waited for the Monday sunset to paint the sky.

We padded to the distant bench we preferred. Sunglasses in place, I eagerly turned my face to the setting sun, basking in the warmth. "This view always satisfies, and it takes away my worries."

"About that, I need to apologize again for rushing into the real estate market," Pete said. "I should've paid more attention to your business needs, but we need more space for our offices and family. I feel adrift in your house. It doesn't seem like mine because everything is yours. I'd prefer we bought furniture together so it feels like our place."

As breakers rolled to shore underneath us and crashed into the Johnson rock-wall barrier, his statement struck me with equal force. How dense I must be for not realizing he felt uncomfortable at my place.

I'd made room for his clothes, but in truth, he camped out in my space. And my home had furnishings from my parents and grandparents. Nothing new or modern. I gulped. Pete deserved more than that.

"My turn to apologize. I didn't consider how things looked from your perspective. Of course, we'll make whatever changes you like to our place, whether it's where we are now or in a different location. Both of us should feel welcome in our home. We'll find what's right for us."

He grinned. "That's the spirit."

"I hadn't given new furniture a thought as I've been scrounging to make ends meet for what seems like forever, and everything in this house is comfortable and familiar. I wish you'd said something before now."

"It's okay. I needed time to heal and decide on a business direction before I even thought about our housing needs. Still working on business direction, but I thought I'd be doing us a favor by identifying a place that met all of our needs. I got a wakeup call today too."

"Okay, it's a couple thing, and we're both used to acting independently. So, we'll do better, right? This is a minor speed bump for an engaged couple."

"Right.

An athletic-looking man wearing black compression tights under gray shorts, a form fitted high tech lightweight shirt, and an Atlanta Hawks ball cap limped our way. The muscles in his buff arms looked like they'd been chiseled from stone. I elbowed Pete lightly in the side. "What are the odds? That's Eggs, one of our suspects."

"He's heading this way," Pete said softly.

Eggs stopped in front of me, sun at his back, his face in shadow. "Heard you're looking for me. What's this about?"

"You're the guy they call Eggs, right?" I asked.

"So what?"

"I'm River Holloway, this is my fiancé, Pete Merrick."

The guys exchanged stern looks and handshakes. "How come you're sniffing around me and my friends?" Eggs asked.

I could do tough guy inscrutable too. "Cops arrested my brother and Viv Declan for Curtis Marlin's murder. They didn't do it. Heavy D said that Curtis's gin bottle was there when y'all arrived that night."

"True."

"Viv and Doug were framed."

"Not by me or my crew. Curtis was our brother." His tough-guy voice cracked as he spoke. "We're broken up because of this."

"I'm looking for an alternate suspect and if it's not you three, it has to be someone else. Who had a grudge against Curtis?"

Eggs laughed so hard he cried. "You're kidding, right? Curtis alternately talked smack or bummed money from everyone in earshot. He did people that way."

"You can't think of anyone who is sneaky and wanted Curtis dead?"

"That little old girl is like that."

"Which girl?"

"Viv. She screwed everything up."

"How so?"

"Curtis liked that chick, but she left him last year. Said she was done."

"Did he have an STD?"

Eggs snorted. "Curtis always tested clean, I promise you. We four had a condom clause. No unprotected sex."

"Why'd Viv leave?"

"The mill. Curtis got on a tear about the mill screwing up the river and the ocean. He called mill workers stone cold killers. Viv told him where he could shove his opinion and scratched off."

"People have complained about the mill for years," I reminded. "Viv moved on months ago. If I believed you, why would she wait so long to kill him?"

"Revenge is best served cold."

"You think she planned this? That she knew how much antifreeze to use?"

"Why else would she drag her new boyfriend out there if not to rub Curtis's face in it? Way I see it, my boy had to insult her to make her leave."

The wind changed direction and hair blew across my face. I thumbed it behind my ear. "It doesn't make sense. Viv's talked to Curtis since they stopped dating. He kept inviting her to his house."

"Probably because he wanted her to pay his bills again." Eggs looked away for a long moment. "And, around Viv he felt like the carefree guy from his glory days, until she walked out."

This story didn't ring true. "Good try. Why'd they really break up?"

He scowled, turned as if to go, and then faced me. "Oldest story in the world."

I strained to hear his softer tone. "Yes?"

"A tiger can't change his stripes."

"I don't understand."

"Viv found Curtis in bed with another woman. Hurricane Viv whirled out, and it's a wonder the windows didn't implode. Curtis apologized, but Viv said he betrayed her on purpose."

My intuition pinged with truth. "I understand their breakup now, but why would Viv wait so long to kill him? She's a direct individual. If she wanted Curtis dead, she would've gone after him immediately."

Eggs shrugged. "Hard to say how a woman thinks."

"Viv didn't kill Curtis," I insisted. Pete stirred beside me, and I placed a cautionary hand on his leg. "She's not vindictive. When things go wrong, she moves on. She doesn't hold a grudge. She wipes the dust off her feet and leaves."

"After the breakup, Curtis watched her work the bar crowd. When she'd leave with a guy, he'd drink himself blind. The night he died he drank plenty before she paraded her latest boy toy in front of him, no offense to your brother, ma'am."

How odd. So much unrequited love. Perhaps another woman took offense? "After Viv and Curtis broke up, did Curtis date anyone who fell in love with him?"

He shook his head. "Not following you."

"Was there a love triangle between Viv, Curtis, and another woman, like the one Viv found in their bed? If someone hated Curtis for using her as a Viv surrogate, killing him and framing Viv makes sense."

Eggs expression blanked, then he shook his head. "Nice try, except he didn't bring chicks to his place more than once after Viv."

"Who did he date?"

"I didn't pay close attention, but one gal got riled up because he didn't want her. She got hitched yesterday. Melody something."

I caught Pete's gaze. "Melanie Walker?"

"Yeah. Thinks everything's about her, but she's more screwed up than Curtis, only her mom's checkbook fixes her problems."

"I didn't know they dated."

"They hooked up occasionally."

I winced. I did not need to know this about Melanie. "Anyone else?"

He slanted his eyes away before he answered. "Not that I recall."

I dug out a business card for him. "If you remember another name, please call. I'd appreciate the help."

"You coming to the funeral tomorrow?"

"I'll be there."

"Steer clear of me and the guys." He turned and limped away.

I waited until he was out of earshot. "That was interesting."

"He's upset. It would be wise to avoid him."

"You think he would use lethal force?"

"I think we don't know enough about him. His emotions are running him, so it would be wise to give him space for now."

"Noted."

Sunset painted the sky in bold oranges and golds. I pushed thoughts of murder investigations away and relished the fiery, bronzed colors of sea and sky. The intense red and orange hues deepened by the minute, changing crimson and tangerine into burgundy and burnt umber.

Pete wrapped his arm around my shoulder, and we watched the dazzling light show. "Beautiful," he murmured.

"It always inspires me."

"You're beautiful, sweetheart. I'm a lucky to be with you."

I stroked the side of his face. "Thanks. And I know that look. You're want me to commit to a wedding date. What dates are you considering?"

"End of April or early May, depending on when we finish the counseling requirement."

April would arrive in a few more days. I gulped. "That's soon, but let's compare calendars with Father Ben at our appointment."

"Great. The next decision is style of dress. Do you prefer jeans, suits and dresses, or tuxes and gowns?"

If she were alive, Mom would have a fit if I got married in jeans, but what did I want? It came to me in the next breath. "I want a simple ceremony but my mind immediately pictured a white gown. I need a few days to decide."

"You got it."

"Did you believe Eggs?"

"I did. The bit about the Walker woman surprised me."

"Sadly, she previously lured away another man from Viv. Knowing Melanie's in-your-face style, poisoning would take too long to suit her, so she's not a suspect candidate. She'd be more likely to shoot a man pointblank in the face."

"Remind me to never cross her."

Chapter Fourteen

The next day, the windowless walls and dim lighting in the cavernous funeral home chapel bothered me. Not a place I'd ordinarily visit because I loved natural sunlight. But I needed fresh leads so I would stay. I strode confidently through the gloom, sitting midway between the front and back.

Heavy D, Eggs, and Ty sat on the second row in a small cluster of other mourners that included the elderly spitfire sisters, Ola Mae Reed and Valerie Slade. I studied their snowy heads and elegant dark attire. Both women looked as if they'd been to the beauty shop and the mall.

As if sensing my gaze, Ola Mae turned and did a little finger wave. I nodded and she seemed pleased. My gaze shifted to the stoneware urn displayed on the raised stage. That must be Curtis Marlin's ashes. If he had no surviving family, what happened to his remains?

The air shifted as someone slid in back of me. I glimpsed the newcomer in my peripheral vision. Deputy Gil Franklin. Oh, joy. With a choice of 200 seats in here, he'd chosen the one directly behind me.

One stooped elderly man occupied the front row, and fewer than ten people attended the ceremony. The worship leader gave the readings and homily, as well as played the piano and sang. Though I'd come to observe attendees, I found myself listening to the man's words.

Despite the generic platitudes about a young life cut short, the leader's words of cherishing friends and family uplifted me. I wished Pete were here, but he was hot on the property trail again with Realtor Toni. Now that he understood our specific needs, he hoped to find the perfect place and check this item off his to-do list.

I rose when the service ended, intending to eavesdrop while paying my respects. I set my sights on the older man talking to the worship leader.

Movement registered nearby. "I need to speak with you," Deputy Franklin said softly.

"After I pay my respects." I shot him a Mona Lisa smile in the thin light.

He scowled. "I'll wait in the lobby."

Ola Mae and her sister Valerie trapped me in my row as the lighting brightened to a burnished twilight. "Good riddance to that copper," Ola Mae said. "He's barking up the wrong suspect tree."

"He wants to talk to me," I said. "About the case. I can't believe the cops arrested Viv Declan and my brother for this murder."

Valerie tsked. "Policing 101. The easiest answer is the one they like. God forbid they dig for the actual killer."

"I heard you put your house up to post bail for your brother," Ola Mae said.

"I did, and I'd do it again. Doug and Viv are innocent. I hate that Viv is stuck in jail."

Ola Mae patted my shoulder. "It'll be all right."

"I hope so, but this victim's secrets are hard to come by." I gestured furtively toward the trio of former basketball stars conversing up front. "His friends closed ranks. Most people are happy about the arrests. Not me."

"You're a good shepherd to our islanders," Valerie said. "We're grateful for your efforts."

Steam warmed my collar. "Thank you. My parents taught me to treat others as I'd like to be treated so that's my goal."

"Most people today have poor home training," Ola Mae observed. "You're a gem."

"You two are looking fine this morning," I said, shifting the focus from me to them.

Ola Mae preened under the compliment. "Our previous funeral attire lasted decades but the outfits wore out. We consider these ensembles investment pieces and hope we'll get another twenty years out of them."

The basketball guys strode past like they were driving to the hoop. Heavy D gave a tip of his black hat as he passed. Eggs ignored me. Ty turned as he walked and growled at me, "Stay away from me and my crew."

"I'm sorry for your loss," I said to his back, taking an instant dislike to the man.

Valerie appeared oblivious of the exchange. She fanned her face as she watched the trio exit the chapel. "My stars. What fine looking fellas. Can we invite them over, Ola Mae?"

"When goats sing. Come on, Valerie, time to leave. We have a full schedule today."

That left me and the stranger, the gentleman couldn't take his gaze off the urn. I padded down the aisle, circling to enter the center of his field of vision so as not to startle him. "I'm River Holloway, a former schoolmate of Curtis, and I'm sorry for your loss."

The man rubbed the tears on his cheek and cleared his throat, a deep rumbling effort that took a few tries before he spoke. "Ross Talley, of Birmingham, Alabama. I'm his great uncle, his grandfather's brother. I barely knew this man, and yet he's the last of my brother's line. His parents never amounted to a hill of red peas before that fatal motorcycle crash fifteen years ago. God love her, my sister-in-law did her best by Curtis, but he turned out sorry like his parents and sent Gertrude to an early grave." His eyes clouded. "I shouldn't be gossiping in a holy place, but it's the truth."

"It's all right, Mr. Talley."

He shook his head and looked at the urn. "I can't haul those ashes on my flight home to Alabama. Duty and preference are incompatible in this instance."

His grief touched my heart. How could I help him? I brainstormed alternate solutions. "Is there a family plot on the island?"

"No. We shipped my brother and sister-in-law's bodies to Birmingham. It cost a fortune, but our entire family is buried in Alabama. When Gertrude died, I drove over in a truck, hoping to carry our family heirloom furniture home but I wasted my time. Not one piece of our family antiques remained. She must've sold the pieces to survive because that's the only way she ever would've parted with them. Since then I've wondered if Curtis pawned her furniture."

"I know nothing about the furniture but you mentioned shipping. Perhaps the funeral home will ship his ashes to Birmingham for you."

"Must be rules and red tape about that."

"It never hurts to ask. And if it is impossible, you could scatter his ashes on the Talley property here."

"Good idea. Thank you."

I reached into my purse. "If you need anything while you're on Shell Island, here's my number."

Talley absently pocketed the card. "When people don't fit in their skin, there's always collateral damage. Such a wasted life." He studied the urn again before gazing up the aisle. "I've had my fill of death for today."

I offered my arm. "Need an escort?"

He brushed away my offer. "I may be ninety, but I ain't dead yet. Pay attention, missy. Stop moving and you die."

Momentum mattered in life. I understood that completely. "Nice to meet you."

He nodded and kept plodding forward.

I gave him the honors and then when he'd gone, strode up the aisle, no wiser for coming. Next stop the lobby, Deputy Franklin, and hopefully some answers.

Chapter Fifteen

Once I cleared the chapel, the red-faced deputy clamped his hand on my arm and led me outdoors. "Is there a problem?" I asked, digging for my sunglasses in the sudden glare.

"You're trying my patience," the deputy said. "You interviewed those teammates already and you grilled Ross Talley just now. The man's ninety-five if he's a day."

"I expressed my condolences. You're wrong about his age. He's ninety."

"What else did he say?"

"He's upset about the hardship Curtis and his parents caused Gertrude Talley. Speaking of Curtis, I heard he dated Melanie Walker."

Franklin's blue eyes narrowed in disapproval. "She's on her honeymoon."

"That's right."

"Forget it. I'm not bothering anyone on their honeymoon on a hearsay basis."

"What about the car place? Learn anything there?"

"According to the shop owner, Curtis and Ty got into a shouting match in the waiting room, with both men threatening to kill each other. Ty punched the soda machine and stormed out. Curtis tried to pay Ty's bill, but his card didn't work. Curtis left without paying either bill, then the shop owner filed a complaint."

"What a mess. Will they file a claim against the estate?"

"Yes. Which brings me to my next point. Talking to persons of interest in a case can be dangerous. As I just stated, Ty Carvell has a volatile temper."

"I wouldn't dream of confronting him, but Heavy D and Eggs strike me as decent people who tell the truth."

"Regardless of your insights, leave investigating to the professionals."

"Fat chance. You cops think Viv and my brother are guilty. I can't afford a private investigator. I'm all they've got."

"Vivian Declan's fingerprints are on that bottle. She served him the poison. She's guilty. End of story."

"Viv's been framed and you guys bought it, hook, line, and sinker. You quit looking for the real culprit, just as the killer intended."

"If new information develops, we will consider it."

I barred my arms across my body. "How decent of you."

He bristled at my sarcastic tone. "I talked to the car shop people because you asked."

"Off the record."

"It'll go on the record. The altercation between Curtis and Ty may be relevant later."

Hope sparked. "You're still investigating?"

"I'm monitoring the parties involved, in addition to my other duties."

"You looking for that promotion to Investigator?"

"That's not a secret."

I could work with that.

~*~

After lunch I drove to the elementary school to tutor fourth graders in fractions, a weekly volunteer activity. The children's boundless energy distracted me from the murder and the possibility of my brother and Viv going to prison. The session passed quickly, then I drove to Island Tire and Auto.

Lenny checked me in. I handed him my key and wandered around the small waiting area. The parts counter next door was visible through the glass partition. On the car shop side, the lobby had no displays of antifreeze or any other car fluids. A triple tiered rack of tires filled one wall and tainted the air.

Four chairs clustered near the door, across from the tires.

Lenny returned to the counter and saw me staring at the dented soda machine. "Does this work?" I asked.

"The dent is superficial. I've got a call in to our body shop dent guy to come and fix it."

"Oh." I fed the coin slot and sipped a cola, casually sauntering back to the counter. "Did the tire rack fall on the machine?"

"Naw. Had a hot-fisted guy in here the other day. I would call him a customer but he didn't pay his bill." He nodded toward his monitor and then turned it for me. "Got his photo on the lock screen so I won't make that mistake again."

I looked hard at the grainy photos. Bingo. "I recognize Curtis Marlin and Ty Carvell." Those six photos were likely banned customers. "You can delete Curtis Marlin as he passed away recently."

Lenny shrugged and swiveled the monitor to face him. "Maybe the owner will remove it, but he kept letting Marlin and his pals slide on payment. Not me."

Deputy Franklin hadn't mentioned unpaid bills. "Did they owe a lot of money?"

"More'n I make in a week."

"Oh." I looked around for the owner's name. Blinked when I recognized it. "Reggie Gray was their basketball coach. I didn't realize this place belonged to Coach Gray."

"Bought it off his uncle some years back. Thought it would be his fallback job but he lost his coaching job right after he bought this place. He shook up this business, hired new mechanics and service techs, and now this place turns a healthy profit. I've worked here five years."

I sipped my drink and glanced around. "So why'd Coach Gray cut the guys slack on their bills?"

Lenny leaned in close. "He says he failed them. Thought his guys would go places. Not one of them landed a college scholarship. According to Reggie, team guys usually get comped their bills in college towns while they're playing. He said he owes them, or he did. The gravy train ran out."

Hmm. "At least now, he has one less deadbeat customer. Guess that explains why he isn't making Ty pay for the soda machine repair."

Lenny looked like he would say something else but the mechanic bustled in with my key. "Van's ready, ma'am," Lenny said, hanging onto the key as he printed paperwork. "We topped off all your fluids. You're good to go."

I handed him my credit card. "What happens to old antifreeze around here?"

"We follow all the disposal rules. Have to, or we'd be shut down."

"Do jugs ever walk away?"

"Not that I'm aware of."

I glanced over and both work bays were empty. Two mechanics stood outside taking a smoke break. A bright yellow bottle of antifreeze sat on the open garage's floor. If someone timed it right, they could grab fluids from an unattended bay.

Lenny handed me back my card, I signed the papers and received my key. I pulled away, checking to see if cameras covered the bays. They did.

My shoulders slumped. Not the findings I hoped for but my van received a needed oil change. Instead of an upset creditor, I'd found a sympathetic mentor. I had to do better by Doug and Viv.

Case facts surfaced in my thoughts. The basketball trio, Viv, and Doug saw Curtis the night he died. Curtis had a prior relationship with Melanie Walker. He sabotaged his relationship with Viv but still cared for her.

Other than having parents who died in a motorcycle accident and being raised by Grandma Talley, I knew little about Curtis's personal life. But I knew a Curtis expert.

I drove to the mainland and within fifteen minutes, I sat in the jail's visitor area with Viv on the other side of the monitor. Dark circles ringed her dull brown eyes. Her usually lustrous and bouncy hair hung limply around her pale face.

"We'll get you out of here, Viv," I said. "Hang in there."

"I'm worried about my job. Doug notified my boss that I'd been detained, but Ernest has hinted for months that I make too much money. I'm certain he'll fire me. I can't pay my rent without my job."

"I'm working on finding answers. Of Heavy D, Ty, and Eggs, Ty is the most volatile, but that very trait suggests he wouldn't kill someone with poison. He'd use his fists."

Viv gave a wan smile. "That's Ty all right."

"We need new leads. Who else has a grudge against Curtis?"

"He owes people money. That remained constant over the years."

"Who?"

She named banks, the car place, and the county tax assessor.

"What about individuals? Something like a personal debt."

Viv shrugged. "He borrowed from me and the basketball guys, and probably every woman he ever dated."

"Melanie Walker?"

"I hate her guts."

Chapter Sixteen

"Déjà vu moment for me, just like senior prom," Viv said, eyes glistening. "I walked in on Melanie and Curtis in our bed."

"How awful." The rawness of her hurt ate at me. I wished I could hug her. "Now I'm sorry I catered Melanie's wedding. You should've told me earlier."

"You needed the business," Viv said. "I understood. Besides, it isn't like she'll stick with this new guy. This is Melanie's third marriage, after all. But a word to the wise. Advise Pete to steer clear of that woman. Something makes men jump in bed with her."

"Pete wouldn't do that."

"That's what I thought too. Curtis claimed she came on to him, and he never turned down sex. He said sleeping with her meant nothing to him, but his betrayal ruined it for me. I never trusted him again."

"Totally get that. Any truth to the rumor they might have, er, hooked up recently?"

"I wouldn't know. I steered clear of Curtis for months. In the last few weeks, we began talking at bars."

"Heavy D said he never got over you."

Viv snorted, a loud obnoxious sound. She clamped her hand over her mouth. "Sorry. That's ridiculous. He didn't speak to me for months, stared right through me. Get this. He hollered at me from their shared bed, both of them buck naked, that she meant nothing to him."

"I'm so sorry you went through that," I said. The five minute warning light blinked, signaling the end of our visit neared. "Anything else about him that might help the investigation?"

"He drank too much," Viv said, "but you already know that. He played cards with some buddies, a regular poker game on Friday night."

I brightened. Gamblers frequently incurred large debts. "Did he gamble?"

"All the time."

"That might explain his money troubles. Where did he play? Who else attended?"

"Don't know. Curtis kept secrets close to his vest."

This seemed relevant. "Would his former teammates know?"

Viv shrugged, then the monitor light flashed. Time to say goodbye. "I'll keep looking. Stay strong, Viv."

"Jail stinks. Please get me out of here!"

I placed my palm by the camera and she did the same. "Working on it," I said as the screen went dark.

~*~

Poor Viv, I thought as I drove home. My nerves were shot just from the procedures to see her on a monitor. I needed a shower, a massage, and a plate of warm cookies. Heck, I'd start with the cookies.

I wound my way over the causeway, and with each tire revolution, my sense of powerlessness eased. Salt air wafted over the tidal creeks and marshes through my open windows. As I motored onto the island, a musky forest aroma with a lilt of flowers mixed with the sea breeze.

My thoughts gelled at the reassuring scent of home.

Viv couldn't breathe in jail. Her free-spirited nature would fade in enforced confinement. She needed island air as much as I did. I shuddered and thanked God for my freedom. I had to find the real killer fast.

The Melanie Walker suspect possibility, while interesting, didn't work. Melanie moved on and married a wealthy man. I thought back to Sunday, when I'd been proud of my staff for

81

saving the day. The happy married couple were still in Aruba on their honeymoon.

Which left me with the poker night lead. On TV, men played poker at friend's houses. If Heavy D or Eggs didn't know where Curtis played poker, I'd hit another blank wall.

At the first stop light, I called Heavy D. After the hello-how-are-yous, I asked about poker night.

"Not my bag," Heavy D said. "Got no money to spare, and I never understood how Curtis played so much. He loved gambling and often bet money he didn't have. I never understood how he kept it going."

"Anything you remember about his regular game would help, as in the weeknight, place, or players."

"A long time ago, he invited me to join a Friday night game, but I don't remember where. I enjoy hanging with my crew, but my money stays in my pocket. Feel me?"

"I feel you. Are Ty and Eggs gamblers?"

"Ty, not so much. Not sure about Eggs."

I had the same sense about Ty and Eggs. Ty would never be able to bluff, not with his hair-trigger personality. Eggs seemed to meet life on his own terms.

"I've been wondering about your nicknames. Where'd those come from?"

"We had two DeAndres on the basketball team. I played center and the other DeAndre subbed at point guard. Because of my size, I became Heavy D. Ty is short for Tyrone, and believe it or not, Eggs is short for Egbert, which he hates. All Egberts in his line are called Eggs, and you can see why."

"Oh. I thought he had a thing for deviled eggs."

"That boy puts eggs away, for sure, but that's not how he caught the name."

"Thanks. I'll look into this poker game connection."

"Sorry I couldn't help more."

"It's okay. Thanks for taking my call."

Curtis had been dead five days, and I had no idea who killed him. At this rate, Viv and Doug would spend the rest of their lives behind bars. I couldn't let that happen. I recapped what I knew. Heavy D, Eggs, and Ty's mutual alibi cleared them, and Viv and

Doug didn't do it. Melanie Walker Conway played life hard and fast. She could've poisoned Curtis, especially if he called her a ho, but she'd been too busy lately to doctor his gin. Not Melanie.

I needed suspects with strong reasons to kill Curtis.

Pete's truck slumbered in the drive when I returned home. I hurried inside to greet him.

He met me at the door. "I want to show you a few places. Just us. We'll look from the curb and if any float your boat, we'll call Toni to show them."

"I'd like that."

"Great. One more thing. Father Ben called this afternoon. He cancelled our session tomorrow. He now needs to attend a regional church meeting in Thomasville because he's an alternate for another priest who can't make it."

"Sorry to hear that. I have sympathy for anyone stuck in long meetings."

"Be that as it may, completing our marriage counseling requirements in the condensed timeframe will be challenging. We'll have longer sessions or multiple sessions per week."

"Father Ben is fair. He'll make it work."

"He'd better. He's penciled in May 10 for our wedding, if that works with your schedule."

I thumbed my phone on and zipped to that day in the calendar app. "It works. We have a wedding date. Viv and I need to go gown shopping as soon as we can spring her from jail."

"Good plan. I'll take Doug to be fitted for tuxes."

Lightning fast, my thoughts shot to the truth that two members of our wedding party were on the hook for a major crime. And just as quick, that stark reality faded. I believed in a future which also included my brother and friend's freedom. I never gave up on Pete last year and I wouldn't give up on Doug and Viv either. Somehow, I'd find a way to save them. I hoped.

Chapter Seventeen

We drove by six properties in upscale neighborhoods. Of those, one had curb appeal. It crested the upper end of Pete's price range because of the acreage attached. However, it sat vacant for years and needed extensive restoration. With the hidden costs of fixer-uppers, we decided to pass. In this climate, once mold and mildew took hold, they were the devil to beat.

Ice cream cones in hand, we sat outside Island Creamery. Sunlight warmed my skin and a light breeze filled the air with ocean freshness. "I wish house shopping was easier," I said. "I'm frustrated too. My place is too small for our current needs but it's what we have."

"It's my fault for raising our expectations so high," Pete said. "Previously, I had no restrictions when house shopping. Probably why my homes meant nothing to me. We need a place that works for both of us, our businesses, your brother, and our future kids."

He would end with our lack of kids. I'd rather not think about my failure to conceive now. "I'm glad we can discuss this. If you are as irritated with me as that realtor is, we're in for a rocky start on finding the right house."

"No irritation on my end. Toni's focused on quick sales. She won't bug me again unless something new to the market meets our needs."

"That's a relief." I finished my cone and sat back to enjoy the afternoon promenade. People with ice cream cones meandered by, hand in hand, kids danced around their parents like orbiting moons. Dogs walked sedately on leashes, sniffing the salt air as if it were the elixir of life.

After a bit, my thoughts circled back to Curtis. "Pete, you know about any poker games on Shell Island?" I asked. "Specifically, a Friday night game?"

"Poker? You thinking to become a card shark?"

"No way. This is about the murder case. Viv said Curtis had a gambling habit. I asked Heavy D, but he didn't know where Curtis played, only that he'd played on Friday nights."

"Poker. Hmm. There used to be a game at the golf course, but I'm unsure of the night."

I sat up straight. "Can you call to ask about the night? And to ask if Curtis played there?"

"I'll make a few calls."

The sun kissed the treetops on the western horizon as I settled back into the bench, Pete's arm snug around my shoulder. My phone rang. I glanced at the display and took the call. "Doug, is everything okay?"

"River, you won't believe this," Doug cried, his voice jubilant. "We're still pinching ourselves."

"We who?" I asked.

"Viv's in the truck with me. Someone paid her bail."

I covered the phone microphone with my hand and whispered to Pete, "Did you post Viv's bail?"

He shook his head.

I spoke into the phone. "Who paid it?"

"The bail bondsman wouldn't say," Doug said. "The donor demanded anonymity. Isn't this great! We're headed to Viv's place now."

"How about a celebration dinner at the house?" I offered. "I'll treat you two to something amazing."

"Uh, thanks but no thanks. Tonight's for us. Maybe tomorrow?"

Ah. "Of course. Call me tomorrow and tell me what time works for y'all."

"We'll have a strategy session. Viv can't go back to jail. Me either. We'd rather hide out in a third world country than rot in a prison cell."

"Wait a minute." My words came out in slow-mo. I couldn't believe Doug would be so callous. "If you skip bail, I lose our home and you become a fugitive. Forever."

"Oh, yeah. Forgot that part."

He sounded flip, and my stomach started to freefall. Didn't he understand the consequences here? Time to reinforce my message. "I'm homeless if you jump ship."

"Bummer for you."

"Doug!"

"Kidding. Catch you later."

The call ended. I turned to Pete. "An anonymous donor paid Viv's bail. Doug spoke about leaving town so they didn't go to prison."

"I'll talk to him."

"He knows better, but it's no joking matter. That property's been in our family for three generations."

"I'll handle it," Pete repeated, a little sharper.

Knowing Doug, that conversation wouldn't go well. "The only fresh angle we have is the poker lead. Otherwise, we're back to the three basketball teammates. Now that I've talked to Heavy D and Eggs and learned about Ty's punch-first personality, it's hard to think of them as poisoners. They seem normal."

"That's what people say about serial killers."

I pounded a fist into my palm. "I don't want Doug living on the lam or us sleeping in my van. Let's go home. Cooking clears my thoughts."

When we got home though, the front door yawned wide and my insides churned like an outboard propeller. "Did we forget to lock the door?" I asked Pete.

He came around to my side of the van. "Don't think so. Wait here while I check it out."

I scurried after him. "Not so fast. I feel safer with you."

"Okay." Pete studied the door jam and the lock. "It doesn't appear to be forced open." He hollered inside. "Anybody here?"

A faint cry sounded from the interior. I listened closely. "It's Major. He's in the house somewhere."

I followed Pete toward the kitchen, heading in the direction of the faint mewing. We flicked on lights as we went. Major's cries became more demanding as we neared the back of the house. I called him. "Here, kitty, kitty."

Major meowed loudly. The sound came from the laundry room. Odd, we never closed that door unless we had company. Pete opened the door and Major streaked out like he had a crab claw clamped to his tail.

Pete and I exchanged a puzzled glance. "How'd the cat open the front door and get trapped in the laundry room?" I asked.

"Don't know," Pete said. "Let's search the house for signs of an intruder."

We stuck close together as we padded from room to room, checking hiding places and window locks. "I don't see anything out of place or missing." I said. "Nothing's been pawed through or upended."

"Must be a fluke," Pete said. "Somehow the cat pushed the front door open and then got sassy with the laundry room door and paid for his mischief by getting stuck inside."

"Seems farfetched, but its more credible than aliens or bad guys, so let's go with it."

"Bad guys," Pete repeated slowly. "Should we call Deputy Franklin?"

"What would we tell him? Nothing was disturbed. Looks like the front door blew open and the cat explored the house."

"We need a sturdier lock for that door. I don't like the idea that we aren't secure in here. Who else has keys to this house?"

"Me, you, and Doug."

"Not bad, but I'd like to change all the locks. That okay with you?"

"Works for me." I sounded confident, but inside I circled back to the intruder theory. Someone who picked locks like a pro wouldn't leave any evidence behind.

Was someone after us?

After me?

Chapter Eighteen

I spread the last spatula of chocolate icing on the cake. Doug loved my Death by Chocolate cake. Tonight's homecoming dinner would feature everyone's favorites, including crab cakes, Brunswick stew, broccoli, and spicy coleslaw. I tidied the kitchen, and the day yawned before me. Without busy hands, my thoughts veered to the question I most needed to answer: Who killed Curtis Marlin?

Pete's words about keeping an open mind echoed in my head. I only knew what Heavy D, Ty, and Eggs told me about each other. Talking to other squad members might yield another perspective. I dug my sophomore yearbook out of the hall closet and studied the basketball team. The guys and two others had been the regular starters. Of those two, Russell died in a freak boating accident, and nobody had heard from Chauncey in years. However, the photo reminded me I had an insider option for team history. Better yet, this person owed me a favor.

I drove to Island Lumber and found Haven Potts. "River Holloway, what can I do you for?" he asked amid stacks of two by fours.

"Hey. I was hoping to run into you here," I said. "Is your little terrier staying close to home these days?"

"We'll never forget you found Ginger for us. The replacement lock on the gate works great. The kids can't open it, and Ginger stays safe in her backyard when she's outdoors."

I dug in my purse for the yearbook and opened it to the team photo page I'd marked. "Very good. Look, I hope you have a minute to spare. I need your help. I'm researching the high school basketball team back in the day."

Haven glanced at the page and back at me. "This is about Curtis and his crew?"

"Yes. I talked with Heavy D and Eggs, and they denied having a grudge against Curtis. But I need to be thorough." I leaned in close. "Do any of those three men have a motive for killing Curtis?"

"Let's do this in my office where it's more private." Haven escorted me to a tidy masculine office with lots of clean surfaces. We both took a seat and he continued. "Everyone near Curtis for more than sixty seconds had reason to kill him. The guy bummed money from everyone and had zero social skills. Once, one team wannabe, a short kid that chased the loose balls at warm up, caught his wrath. Curtis made a cruel remark about the size of the kid's, um, genitalia, and the kid ran from the gym never to return."

That was mean. The more I learned about Curtis, the less I thought of him. "That's a long time to hold a grudge, if he waited until now to act."

Haven steepled his fingers on his desk and chuckled. "That guy hurt Curtis worse than you know. He grew up to be president of the bank. Reese Woodman."

The name sparked a memory. "Reese took the school tennis team to states, right?"

"Yep. He got even with Curtis by turning him down for a loan. He told me about it three months ago. And Reese may have returned the genitalia slur while Curtis sat in his office begging for money, but you didn't hear it from me." He gave me a sly look. "Grown men aren't petty or anything."

"Gotcha." My rising hopes to cast Reese in the killer role plummeted. Slowly, my gaze drifted back to the team photo. "What about the others? Did they have motives to kill Curtis?"

"Those three guys must've been immune to Curtis's rotgut mouth. I never understood why they idolized Curtis."

"BMOC," I said.

"Could be Big Man On Campus syndrome, but nobody on my senior class team ever got the star treatment like Curtis. And then for him to be so cutting and hateful to anyone who didn't suit him. I won't bore you with the names he called me."

"You had reason to kill him?"

"Who didn't?"

"Did you? Kill him?"

"No way," Haven said emphatically. "I got a wife and two little kids I want to see grow up. Handing Curtis his just desserts would land me in prison. Not worth it. However, I always figured karma would catch him and, by George, it did."

Kids. Did Curtis insult someone's children? I leaned closer. "Do Heavy D, Ty, or Eggs have kids?"

"I started late so my kids are still in preschool. I've never seen the guys at preschool functions, so I'm leaning toward no. Unless they're deadbeat dads. Anything is possible."

Chasing down kids could be a rabbit hole. I needed to focus on the murder. "You got any dirt on the guys?"

Haven scowled. "In high school we thought those three walked on water and yet somehow they all fell into the deep because of Curtis."

His remark ignited a spark of hope. "What do you mean?"

"Curtis manipulated them. He made it so the guys could only be friends with him, you know?"

"Please explain."

"Eggs had a bright future, until he got arrested for shoplifting a pair of high-end sunglasses that Curtis admired while they shopped. The security sensor alarmed when Eggs left. Eggs got community service and a criminal record because of those glasses being in his backpack. Curtis did that to him."

"That's terrible." It took me a few seconds to close my mouth. "What happened to Ty?"

"Curtis wrecked Ty's social life. Bonnie the cheerleader had a crush on Ty. When he ignored her, she ran straight to Curtis. Soon, a rumor about Ty being gay spread like a crown fire. No girl gave him the time of day after that, including the girl he liked, and gay guys kept asking him out. Ty never got over it."

"That's where his temper comes from?"

"That's where his rage comes from. The guy came with a quick fuse."

I rocked back in my seat, no longer sure we attended the same school. "Good grief. I had no idea all this high school drama happened. I lived in the bubble of Drivers Ed and Life Skills classes."

"You were a great cook even back then. Lucky you to find your passion so soon."

"I guess. Thank goodness Curtis never noticed me. What'd he do to Heavy D?"

"Brace yourself." Haven drew in a loud breath. "Curtis told a college recruiter Heavy D had a coke problem."

I recoiled at the news. "No."

Haven went on as if I hadn't spoken. "Curtis lied about the cocaine issue. Without recruitment and a scholarship, Heavy D couldn't afford college. Oddly, the scout took an interest in Curtis after that, and Curtis told everyone he'd get an offer from that college. He didn't, and neither did D. I didn't know about this next part until recently. Heavy D encountered the scout earlier this year, and the scout remarked how good D looked, considering. Then Heavy D heard the lie Curtis told. Ty and Eggs had to forcefully restrain D from pounding Curtis."

How sad. Curtis had been outright mean, manipulative, and lied without conscience. I couldn't help thinking he deserved what he got.

"What made Curtis so hateful?"

"No idea."

"Why did the guys remain friends with a bully like Curtis?"

"Maybe they couldn't break the Curtis habit," Haven said. "You know, the price they paid for popularity."

That rationale didn't work for me. I tried a different approach. "If Curtis manipulated that athletic talent scout to pass on Heavy D, why didn't the scout sign Curtis?"

"Apparently the Curtis charm wasn't universal. Like you, I'm glad Curtis ignored me, and I now live the life of my dreams."

I stared around his tidy office. "Lumber figured in your dreams?"

91

"My dad and I built projects all the time. He said the world needed doctors and lawyers, but it also needed carpenters and pipefitters too."

I attended college at Mom's insistence and even earned a two-year degree, but cooking held my interest from start to finish. "Your dad was a smart man."

"I didn't appreciate how smart until he died." Haven cocked his head to listen as an announcement blared over the loudspeaker in his office. "Shoot. There's a problem at register two. Gotta run."

"Thanks, Haven. I've taken up enough of your time. Take care."

As I drove home, I considered what I'd learned about the dead man. Curtis had a history of manipulating and harming others. He'd targeted Heavy D, Ty, and Eggs. His influence continued beyond high school, and he'd limited future prospects of his besties out of spite. He'd lived on borrowed time for years. How depressing.

Enough about Curtis Marlin.

Tonight we celebrated Viv's release from jail. I spent the afternoon making dinner, starting with crab cakes. After I shaped and chilled the cakes, I made a batch of angel hair coleslaw with a splash of hot sauce to give it kick. A little bit of shredded carrot, a smaller amount of shredded onion, a dab of horseradish, the right amounts of sweet and sour, and voila, coleslaw.

Next, I steamed fresh broccoli and pan fried the crab. A pot of thawed Brunswick stew simmered on a back burner. Pete strolled in as I finished. "Smells great," he said.

I sniffed the air and shook my head. "You may be the only person in North America that loves the aroma of broccoli."

"It's the cake and crab cake scents I'm loving. I don't smell any broccoli."

I lightly tapped his hand. "No fair sneaking bites. We need enough for our guests. This is a celebration dinner for four, in case you forgot Doug and Viv are joining us."

"I forgot nothing. Sure you don't need something tested?"

Tires crunched on the driveway outside. I playfully batted his hand away. "Be a thoughtful host and escort Doug and Viv inside."

While I set the kitchen table, I noticed the cat staring at me as if willing his dinner to appear. Major's thick, shiny coat gave him a healthy appearance, and he no longer looked emaciated. Anyone catching sight of him would see a pampered house cat. Except Major hated being closed up. He wanted to be free.

Same as Viv.

And my brother.

I'd find a way to keep them free or die trying.

Chapter Nineteen

"I can't stop taking deep breaths," Viv said between gulps of dinner. "Fresh air smells wonderful. Jail isn't the place for independent thinkers. The guards tell you when to stop and go, and the jail cliques dictate the rest. Jail food tastes like cardboard, and everyone watches you pee. It's humbling. Don't get me started on the shower situation."

I glanced down at the empty serving dish of Brunswick stew I'd thawed at Viv's request. This batch of the spicy pulled pork and veggie slow-cooked entrée tasted yummy and stuck to your ribs. Both guys and Viv ate seconds of stew and cornbread.

"We're glad you're out," I said. "I'd hoped to identify the real killer right away but so far no luck. Who's your mystery benefactor?"

"I have no idea," Viv said, her eyes bright, "but I'm so grateful. If I knew, I'd cut their lawn and clean their house for a year. It is delightful to talk without women screaming, fighting, or pulling hair."

"Yeah, you're free!" I crowed and everyone chimed in. Once the noise level dropped, I continued, "Seriously, I was shocked at how Curtis treated people. How did you stand his manipulative behavior, Viv?"

Viv chugged her glass of iced tea before she answered. "By the time I dated Curtis, I realized everyone had baggage. He certainly did, but he could be charming and persuasive. When he focused on me, I basked in that spotlight. Seduction appealed to him, but

I tired of his negative qualities fast. That's ancient history. Did you learn anything to help us?"

I refilled her tea and set the pitcher on the table. "A reliable source revealed Curtis's dirty deeds in school. Apparently layers of high school existed that I never noticed. It's like I went to a different school."

"I hear you," Viv said. "In Curtis's senior year, the basketball team ruled the school. I focused on helping my parents keep a roof over our heads and food in our bellies, same as you." She scowled at me. "You didn't answer my question. What did you discover?"

"I have no proof, only rumors." I ran my fingers around the rim of my glass as I gathered my nerve. "Remember hearing about Ty being gay?"

Viv paused while buttering another slice of cornbread. Her expression clouded then cleared. "Sure."

"He's not. My source said Bonnie the cheerleader wanted Ty, but he turned her down. Right after that the false rumors about his sexual orientation started."

"Huh." Viv's head ticked to the side in a considering manner. "What's with his gay friends?"

"Also Curtis's doing."

"Why didn't Ty ask another girl out?"

"You'd have to ask him."

Viv shuddered. "No, thanks. What about Eggs?" Her face looked stricken. "Oh, no. The sunglasses incident."

"Yes. Allegedly, Curtis planted the glasses on Eggs in the store. Eggs insisted he didn't take them. Within the week, Curtis wore those glasses every day."

"To taunt Eggs?"

"Perhaps, but from what I surmised, self-gratification motivated Curtis. It isn't clear if he bought or stole them."

"Good gravy. What'd he do to Heavy D and how did he survive?"

I filled her in on what Haven told me about Curtis sabotaging Heavy D's talent scout.

Viv sat sniper-still during the telling. "He must've been furious. D put himself through college to earn his parks and recreation degree. It took him twice as long to graduate."

"I remember. Imagine if he'd had a free ride to college, or if Eggs had no juvie record, or if Ty had dated girls in high school. Their lives would've been so different."

"All three men had reason to kill Curtis. His actions hurt them in life-changing ways." Viv went silent for a moment. "My brother hung out with Curtis. I'll bet Curtis hurt Darry."

I made an open palm gesture, wondering how she'd missed the obvious. "Your brother's in Alaska."

Viv blinked. "So?"

"Can't be in two places at once. He couldn't have killed Curtis."

"But still, in light of this news about Curtis's total skunkiness I should call Darry. Maybe enough time has passed that he'll answer my call. We parted on bad terms." She made a face. "He was an idiot to leave Anita and the kids behind, but he said he had to go alone."

I got a funny feeling. "Surely he planned to send for them."

"That's what I thought too, but they're still here. I haven't heard from him since November."

"How odd."

Viv scowled. "Darry has too many responsibilities to act like this is a prolonged senior trip to Costa Rica. He's gotta do right by his family. I'll try him now."

Doug, Pete, and I waited as she made the call. In the ensuing silence, we heard the out-of-service recorded message. Then the line went dead.

"No phone? I can't reach my brother," Viv said, her face turning pale. "He could be dead, and I wouldn't know."

Oh, my. Not once did I consider her fun-loving brother might be missing. I tried putting a positive spin on this news. "You would've heard if he died. Cops would've notified his family."

"Not if he got mugged or lost his identification." Her chin quivered. "Darry!"

Chapter Twenty

Thirty minutes later, Deputy Gil Franklin ate a slice of Death by Chocolate cake a la mode at my kitchen table with us while he took down Viv's missing person report on her brother. "How long since you heard from him?" he asked.

"Not since he left." As she paced the room, Viv explained the fight they'd had. "That would be in mid-November. I never knew why Darry thought job opportunities in Alaska abounded in November. I told him it wasn't like spring break in Florida with fun and sun, but he said he had to go. That it would fix everything. We argued bitterly over him leaving his family behind."

Pete and I sat at the table with Doug, who crossed his arms and scowled at Franklin.

"You didn't consider his welfare until now?" Franklin asked.

"Declans are stubborn. He needed to apologize to me, and he didn't. When he didn't call at Christmas, I put him out of my mind. I should've reached out to him then, but pride held me back. I recently found out he made no financial provisions for his family. That floored me."

"Why didn't his wife report him missing?" the deputy asked.

"She must be upset," Viv said, pausing by the hall doorway. "Anita is close to being evicted. She worked for Doug and River this week, so she has grocery money, but that's it. I'll do what I can to help his wife and kids, but thanks to this bogus murder charge, my support is limited." She blushed. "I got fired today. Now I need a new job and no one's hiring accused murderers."

"Viv! You should have mentioned it earlier," I said, going over and hugging her. "Neither you nor Doug said a word about that."

Viv's arms hung lank until I released her. "Knew it would happen. My boss dropped hints for months that I cost too much money. A new hire out of school will accept minimum wage for the same work. Case in point, he hired an eighteen-year-old the day I got arrested."

"That's low," I said. "You need a better job."

"I'm good at mechanical systems. The mill is the only game in town when it comes to big industrial sites."

"Maybe, but the hospital and the schools have large mechanical systems. If we put our minds to it, we could think of other places you could try. In any event, we'll figure it out," I said, rubbing her stiff back. "Soon as we learn who killed Curtis."

The deputy cleared his throat. "Getting back to the reason I'm here, why make this report now?"

Viv took a deep breath and glanced my way before facing the deputy. "At dinner, River shared new information she'd learned about Curtis. That prompted me to call my brother. His number is disconnected. He hasn't called since he left, and far as I know, he didn't call or write Anita either. I should've noticed he'd dropped off the face of the earth sooner, but my anger toward him barely cooled. I'm still upset, but now I'm worried too."

"His driver's license is on file, so I have his description. Are his fingerprints on file?"

"Not that I know of." Viv grimaced. "I hope he's alive and well."

"I'll notify the Alaska State Troopers. How did he travel to Alaska?"

Viv's eyes widened. "I assumed he flew, but who knows? Anita has their car so he didn't drive. Ask her."

The deputy gestured at an empty chair. "Why isn't she making this report?"

"Her kids are in bed," I said, returning to sit by Pete. "We called, and she said to go ahead without her. She can't afford a sitter, and she didn't want us over there talking and waking the kids."

Franklin rubbed his chin and stared into the twilight for a long moment. "You sure your brother went to Alaska?"

"At this point, I'm not sure of anything," Viv said, sinking into a chair by Doug. "Two weeks ago I had no cares. I had a job and a new guy in my life. Now everything's soured. How quickly things change. But to answer your question, yes. He went to Alaska. He never lied to me."

"You still have me." Doug reached for her hand. "You're not alone."

"Thanks, Doug, and thank you, River," Viv said. "I couldn't face this by myself."

"Does your brother have any tattoos, scars, birthmarks, piercings, or previous broken bones?" the deputy asked.

Viv's jaw dropped. "You think he's in a morgue?"

Franklin studied her for a long moment. "I need multiple ways to physically identify Darry Declan. Tattoos?"

"One set of hot pink lips on his butt, the result of a week-long drunken adventure in Daytona. Two hearts tattooed on his chest. One says Harry and the other Zoey. Those are his kids."

"Not the wife's name?"

Viv shook her head.

"Anything else remarkable about his physical features?"

"No."

"Thanks. I'll interview Mrs. Declan next and upload the report." He turned to me. "What's this new information you discovered?"

"Curtis manipulated everyone, even his friends." I repeated what I told Viv. "He abused his friends to satisfy his personal agenda, regardless of the fallout. Heavy D, Ty, and Eggs have strong reasons to hate Curtis. Tonight, when Viv realized how vicious Curtis had been toward his friends, her concern for her brother mushroomed because of Curtis persuading his brother to go to Alaska. When she couldn't reach Darry, she reported him missing."

The wall clock ticked in the ensuing silence. "Doesn't follow for me. Why would the basketball guys wait years to go after Curtis for high school mischief?"

I took my time answering. "I like DeAndre the best of the three, but he just learned about Curtis's malicious interference in his basketball career two months ago. Didn't the three of them alibi each other?"

"They drove to a house party together," Franklin said, pushing his empty plate to the side. "Witnesses placed them there all night."

"One of them could've laced that gin bottle ahead of time." Viv gripped one hand over the other so hard her knuckles bulged. "My prints were obvious and the most likely reason is the killer wiped the bottle clean. I mean, shouldn't there have been prints from the liquor store?"

Franklin grunted. "Good point."

"I didn't kill Curtis. You can take that to the bank," Viv said. "I confess to being a terrible sister these last few months because of my anger at my brother. Jail helped me realize that family and friends are important. I don't want to drift through life. I'm making my life count. I want to be like River."

Heat warmed my face. "Thanks for the compliment, but don't sell yourself short. You're already amazing. We have to flush out the killer." I glared at the deputy. "Have enough to reopen the case?"

"I've got a new missing persons case, and I'll mention the background information to the sheriff if you name your source. I need to interview him first."

I drew in a breath through clenched teeth. "He spoke in confidence."

"No name, no additional investigation."

"Tell him," Viv urged.

"Please hand me your notebook," I said and then scribbled a name on the page, closing the top cover to protect the name.

Franklin glanced inside at the name and nodded. "Thanks for the chocolate cake. Remind me to order one for my birthday."

His help came at a bitter cost. Haven Potts wouldn't appreciate being dragged into a murder investigation, but if I didn't reveal his name, Franklin wouldn't investigate. "Sure."

After the deputy left, I picked up the new key on the counter. "One more thing, Doug. The other day we found our front door open. There was no sign of an intruder, only the cat trapped in the laundry room. Since we don't know what happened, we changed the locks and have a new key for you."

Doug swapped his old key for the new one. "Thanks."

Soon Pete and I were alone and doing the dishes. "Seems like we're at dead low water. Darry's unaccounted for, I betrayed a friend's confidence, and Viv and Doug have a murder charge hanging over them."

"Franklin's a straight shooter." Pete dried and shelved my pots and pans. "He's got the connections to search for Darry in Alaska. As for the investigation, don't sell yourself short. You uncovered a new lead for the police. You'll figure out who killed Curtis soon, of that I have no doubt."

"Thanks for believing in me." I thought about it for a moment. "I should warn Haven." But my call rolled to voice mail and I left a message.

"It'll work out." He tossed the wet dish towel in the laundry room hamper. "Changing gears for a moment. Think Doug would double as my best man?"

Pete had been adopted and both his adoptive parents died when he turned eighteen. He'd lit out to make his mark on the world, always returning to Shell Island and me, his high school sweetheart.

I beamed at him. "He'd be honored."

"We also need witnesses. Doug and Viv are logical choices."

"Great, so we're all set."

"Almost. What about a wedding registry?"

"I'd rather shop for things we like as we need them. As for silver and china, we're good. I have sets from my grandmother, mother, and an aunt."

"I've seen your china cabinet." He grinned. "But I thought you might want your own patterns."

"No need. I treasure the sets I already own." I stopped, unsure of where to go in this tangled mess of establishing our traditions. "Sorry, my sentimental streak is a mile wide. If you want us to have our own dishes and silverware, I'll make room in the cabinet."

"Three sets of fancy plates are plenty. I suggested the registry because I didn't want to cheap out or ignore tradition in my rush to the altar."

"We're good. And don't worry about cheaping out. Once we start outfitting a space for us, you'll sing a different tune."

Chapter Twenty-One

Major the cat sniffed my coffee cup on Thursday morning, his tail twitching from side to side. He'd jumped on the side table once I settled to listen to the birds welcome the day. Not wanting to spook him, I sat quietly.

After showering, Pete planned to go straight to Island Creamery this morning, forgoing breakfast so I didn't need to cook a hot meal. I enjoyed the quiet time with my thoughts. The mainland bridal boutique would be a good place to shop for a wedding gown. If I struck out there, Jacksonville, FL, or Savannah, GA, would have what Viv and I needed.

Without warning, the cat pounced in my lap. My breath hitched as Major circled then curled in my lap like he did this every day. Contented purring filled the air. Tentatively, I stroked his head, and he leaned into the touch.

He'd come so far from the rangy, frightened, but determined feral cat who followed me home. I'd often wondered what he thought about when he stared off at nothing. Did he long for his old life? A lifelong feral cat wouldn't jump in my lap after a few weeks of regular groceries. He must've been someone's pet before.

Should I get a red collar for him? Nope. He wasn't the accessories type. At his next vet visit, I'd ask if he could be chipped. That would allow me peace of mind.

The back door opened but Pete didn't join me on the deck.

"Look who's the cat whisperer," he said from the doorway. "You've charmed him."

"I'm not sure what this is about, but I'm enjoying his company."

"Great. I'm headed out, but first, I checked your schedule and reserved May 10 through the 15 for our wedding and honeymoon. Is that okay with you?"

Honeymoon. Oops. I'd forgotten that part. "Sure."

"I'll check in at noon today. I'll also text you about our next appointment time with Father Ben."

"Today's Thursday, so I'm at tutoring this morning," I reminded him.

I must have moved wrong because the cat darted into the woods at full speed. "So much for cuddle time," I said. "On the plus side, nearly two minutes lapsed before he bolted."

"You're earning his trust, little by little." Pete stepped onto the deck and lifted me easily.

"Your arm. Put me down," I exclaimed. The knife wound he sustained during a very physical corporate takeover in California lingered in my thoughts. I'd nearly lost him.

"My arm healed, and physical therapy made it strong again." He gave me a proper kiss and said goodbye.

I wandered into the kitchen, made peanut butter toast for breakfast, and then remembered the stack of letters to be mailed. I glanced at my phone's digital calendar, seeing that Pete had already blocked out the days he'd mentioned with "wedding and honeymoon."

Scrolling up, I saw a note about contributing a dessert to the church potluck this Sunday. I could make a couple of icebox cakes now and they'd keep just fine. After a quick check of my cookbook, I had an ingredient list and an errand list.

When I stopped at the post office to mail those letters, Ola Mae Reed and her sister Valorie Slade chatted with Lizzie Collins from the bridge group by the outgoing mail slot. Ola Mae waved me over.

"Have you heard the news," she said, once again in her everyday garb of a pale blue pantsuit. "Somebody's breaking into houses and stealing food."

"Food? Not TVs or computers?" I asked. "What kind of burglar steals food?"

"A hungry one," Valerie said. She wore a light coral ensemble similar to her sister's. "Folks who never locked their doors before are locking them now. They don't want anyone touching their food."

"Huh." The pine-fresh scent of the freshly mopped floor filled my lungs. "If someone needs food, why don't they go to the churches? We have food pantries at two island locations."

"It's a mystery," Ola Mae said, "which is why we're glad to see you. You can figure this out."

"I'm busy with the Curtis Marlin homicide."

"No reason why you can't investigate both cases," Ola Mae said. "Stealing food is clearly a test. This thief will take us all to the cleaners. Mark my words."

Her comment tickled me. "You believe food theft is a gateway crime?"

Ola Mae shook a bony finger at me. "A bad element is testing the waters. Last month that crooked deputy nearly turned this place into a mob hangout. Those mobsters aren't done with us yet. They want to see if we're paying attention."

That sounded dire. And awful. I surrendered. "Are the food thefts in the paper? Is there a list of victims?"

"He hit nearly every other house in Windward Oaks."

Windward Oaks. A mid-island, blue collar neighborhood. When I attended junior high, many band kids lived there. I remembered because my bus route included the neighborhood.

"What's the sheriff doing?" I asked.

"Stepping up patrols." Lizzie Collins snorted. "That burglar's burrowed in there like a lazy worm in ripe corn. Extra patrols will likely force him to East View or over to Village Estates and then where will we be?"

Nobody wanted burglars in their backyard. "Who got robbed?"

"Marita Arnold just blew through here. She got hit," Valerie said. "Can't miss her place. Corner house with the gnomes in the yard."

I loved these ladies to death but if I didn't leave soon, they'd think of ten more tasks for me to do today. I edged toward the door and daylight. "Thanks. I'll make inquiries, but the food thief isn't my top priority."

Ola Mae and Valerie gave smiles worthy of Mona Lisa. "We know."

Lizzie Collins strolled outside with me. "Say, I'm having my neighbors over to celebrate their anniversary on Saturday, can you cater that dinner for me?"

Business. Yay. I checked my calendar. "I have availability on Saturday evening. What did you have in mind?"

She told me, I agreed, and five minutes later, I had a deposit in hand. Not bad for a trip to the post office. I considered the stops on my errand list again. Probably not enough time to grocery shop, put the food away at home, and get to tutoring. Made more sense to do things in reverse order, starting with a visit to Marita Arnold.

I drove to Marita's modest two-bedroom home and knocked on her door. I noted her single car garage overflowed with a bit of everything while her older model car sat in the driveway. The door creaked open. I extended a hand. "Mrs. Arnold, I'm River Holloway. Mutual friends suggested I stop by and talk to you about your burglary."

"Land sakes, child," Marita said, her voice thready and labored. "Come inside and have coffee with me."

I followed the heavyset woman into a cozy and cluttered living room done in pastel tones. "I'm due at the elementary school for tutoring soon, so I can't stay for coffee, though thank you for the offer. Tell me about your theft."

She took a hit off an inhaler in her hand. "I didn't see him and don't know how much he stole. He took stuff because there's room on the pantry shelf now."

"May I see?"

"Sure."

Stacked dishes filled the sink, dirty pots rested on the stovetop. Marita waved toward the mess. "I felt poorly last night and didn't do the dishes yet. Asthma is not my friend."

Sympathy welled. This time of year asthmatics got socked with a double whammy of steamy weather and tree pollen, so much so that this woman couldn't even manage easy household chores. "I'll catch those. It won't take me five minutes."

"Appreciate the offer, but it will motivate me to keep moving today." She opened a door to a deep pantry, and I gazed inside.

"You have a ton of food in here," I said.

"Isn't it great? If the world ended today, I wouldn't starve."

If the world ended, she'd be dead. I didn't take her for a conspiracy buff but looks could be deceiving. "You're a prepper?"

"Not sure what that is, but I'm ready in case something happens. Anyway, see that spot?"

She pointed to the only bare place in the entire pantry. Looked like maybe three sixteen-ounce cans could've fit there. I saw cans of vegetables, soups, chicken, and tuna. Boxes of pasta and cereals populated two other loaded shelves. Bottled water cases filled the floor area to the first shelf. Rolls of paper towels crowned the top of the closet.

I stepped back so she could close the pantry door. "Nothing else missing?"

"Not in here." She shut the door hard, turned my way, and gestured to the right. "A package of powdered donuts on the counter disappeared. I didn't eat them, and I live alone."

"When did this happen?"

"Over the weekend. After hearing the burglar news at the post office, I realized I got hit too."

"Do you lock your doors?"

"Usually, but last Saturday, I didn't close the garage door. I never lock the interior door to the garage."

"You should lock it until this burglar is caught."

"That's what the post office ladies said." She reached over and twisted the lock. "There. Locked."

I jerked a thumb in the direction I'd entered. "What about the front door?"

"Locked all the time."

"Did you file a police report?"

"Nah. Too much trouble for a few cans of soup and a pack of stale donuts."

"Call the sheriff's office and ask for Deputy Franklin. He'll want to know what happened."

"If you think it's important."

"It is." I glanced at my watch. "I should be going. Keep your doors locked. You don't want to surprise a burglar in here."

Her watery eyes rounded. "Hadn't thought of that. Will do."

~*~

The rest of the morning and early afternoon passed in a blur of activity. I returned to my commercial kitchen by mid-afternoon and had begun working on those icebox cakes when Deputy Franklin knocked. I opened the door.

"You're a hard woman to track down," he said.

"I had a busy day." I motioned him in, belatedly realizing flour covered my striped apron. I folded the top part over the soiled area. "What can I do for you?"

"Stop giving out my name to little old ladies, for starters," he said, stepping inside and closing the door.

I edged over to the sink and washed my hands. "Marita Arnold had a burglary. It's relevant to the theft pattern in her neighborhood."

"We've already stepped up patrols over there. No reported thefts since the weekend. The thief moved on."

"Maybe the thief stole enough to last for a few days."

"There is that."

"Did you talk to Haven Potts?"

Franklin nodded. "He confirmed the information. The sheriff and D.A. will decide if the lead is worth pursuing."

I rocked back on my heels as his words socked me in the gut. "You're kidding."

"Afraid not. Due to the time lag between when these incidents happened and now, the sheriff believes these incidents are unrelated."

"Even though DeAndre Haywood recently learned how he'd been screwed by Curtis in high school?"

"Nobody, including me, thinks DeAndre Haywood would hurt a flea."

I expected a fair hearing of my new information. Anger fueled my words. "But they think Viv and Doug are stone cold killers?"

He ticked off points on his long fingers. "Viv had a past romantic relationship with the victim that ended badly, she flaunted her new boyfriend under his nose, and then she served him tainted booze. She publicly threatened to kill him. Her trunk revealed a jug of antifreeze. She had motive and opportunity. That case is winnable."

I saw red for a long moment. "I strongly disagree. Worse, our island residents continue to suffer from the sheriff's hasty decisions. You should run for sheriff next time around."

"Not planning on jumping into politics. But the real reason I dropped by is my ex-wife wants to have a Sweet Sixteen party for our daughter. What would it cost for you to cater it?"

"Didn't see that coming," I said, reaching for my phone and accessing the digital calendar. "Let's check the date and then we'll talk price based on your selections."

"You'd do it even though you're mad at me?"

"I run a for-profit business. No reason to turn down a paying customer."

"All right. Her birthday is in the middle of a week. We prefer the following Saturday."

He gave me the date, and it fell in the range of days marked wedding. I couldn't accommodate his request. "I'm sorry. I'm not available then. That week I'm booked solid through May 15."

His expression tightened. "Let me check with the ex and see if another date works."

"There are other caterers on the island if the date is non-negotiable. I can recommend someone if you like."

"I don't know the other caterers. You're detail-oriented, and you cook like a dream. We'll make it work."

I tucked my phone in a pocket. "Thanks for the compliment. Sorry I can't accommodate your first choice of dates."

He shrugged. "Life is a negotiation, especially when dealing with exes."

"Despite what the sheriff decides, will you talk with DeAndre?"

"I might. Good day."

I watched him stride away. Major eyed him from the deck, scampering under a crape myrtle when the cop hurried by.

Pete sauntered over a few minutes later. "Everything okay with the deputy?"

"I guess."

"When I sent him back here a few minutes ago, he seemed wound tight. Did he ask for more chocolate cake?"

I blinked. "I forgot to offer him anything to eat or drink. He surprised me with a catering job possibility, so my thoughts jumbled."

"Got a feeling he wanted it that way. Any chance of Doug and Viv getting cleared?"

"Not good at all. The sheriff and D.A. believe the case against Viv is a slam dunk. We have to find the killer, but the more I learn about Curtis, the more I'm glad he's gone."

"Understandable. What leads do you have?"

"I've got two ideas, but the best one is the most hazardous."

"And that is?"

"Visit the widowed sisters. When I saw them this morning, I had the sense they knew more than they were telling."

"Didn't they poison their husbands?"

I nodded. "Allegedly, so they're poisoning experts."

"Don't eat anything over there."

"I won't. Say, what about our skipped marriage counseling appointment?"

"Father Ben said we'd double up next week."

I groaned. "What could we possibly talk about for two hours?"

Pete chewed his lip. "Could be anything."

Chapter Twenty-Two

Ola Mae and her sister Valerie beamed when they saw my icebox cake at ten thirty Friday morning. They invited me into the parlor where the marble-topped furniture and fringed lamps pushed the heck out of antique status. While Ola Mae ushered me to a seat, Valerie bustled off to the kitchen.

"Everything looks bright in here," I said, my fingers trailing over the pristine, whipped butter-colored walls before I settled in a lady-sized, rose-patterned chair. "Looks like you painted."

Ola Mae's pale eyes twinkled. "There's this new handy-dandy painter in town. I believe you know him. He's from Doug's Pro Home Repair."

A smile welled in my heart. "He does nice work."

"We're pleased. It's been twenty years since these walls saw paint. We were overdue." She gestured to her furniture. "He's so careful with our pieces, and he drapes everything. Been a long time since we had that kind of service."

"I'm glad it's working out. I stopped by to follow up on a few items."

Valerie walked in with a tray containing three glasses of iced tea and three slices of my cake. I set my tea and cake on the end table beside me and waited for her to get settled.

"Catch me up," Valerie said. "Did I miss anything?"

Ola Mae harrumphed. "I mentioned how happy we are with our painter. You didn't miss anything." She turned to me. "Please continue, River."

"Thank you. I spoke to Marita Arnold. I even suggested she get in touch with a deputy. Did y'all hear about any more burglaries?"

The sisters exchanged glances before Ola Mae answered. "Not us. You?"

I gestured with open palms. "Nothing. Deputy Franklin said the burglaries occurred on Saturday and Sunday. Seeing as how it's Friday and no more activity, he thinks the thief is gone."

Valerie made a clucking noise. "Our local cops have a lousy track record."

"Guessing here, but it feels like there's something you're not saying," I said.

"Wel-l-l-l. I noticed a stranger in Windward Oaks," Valerie said. "On Tuesday, when I visited a friend over there."

"What did this stranger look like?"

"He wore those patterned hunting clothes. I can't call the name to mind."

"Camos," I said. "You saw a man?"

"Yep. Men walk different than women. He looked grubby too."

"Anything else? Race, body build, hair color?"

"White, skinny, and average height. He wore a dirty green ballcap over scraggly hair. Possibly brown or black hair. Not sure."

"Shoulder length?"

"Lands sakes, River. You ask too many questions."

"It's important. Anything you can remember might help."

"I'd say collar length then. Honestly, as I sped past him he bent to tie his shoe. I didn't see his face." Valerie paused as if searching her memories. "Oh. One more thing. He carried a dark bag on his back, the kind the kids wear to school."

"A backpack?"

"That's it."

"That's more information than we had before. Thank you for that." I took a moment to savor a bite of icebox cake. It tasted just right. "Did y'all hear Viv Declan made bail?"

Ola Mae nodded. "Saw her in the post office. She'll be all right, soon as you figure out who nixed Curtis Marlin."

"An anonymous donor paid Viv's bail. It is unusual."

"Nice to know there are Good Samaritans in the world," Ola Mae said, reaching for her cake too. "This world is harsh to those on the short end of justice."

"Yes," Valerie said, "I am pleased to see Vivian around town. It's a pity someone framed her."

"I'm glad she's free. Any ideas about who paid it?"

Ola Mae shook her head. "I haven't heard anything. Have you, Sis?"

Valerie had forked up a bite of her cake and paused midway to her mouth. "Haven't heard a word."

"Seems strange, but society is unaccustomed to unselfish acts like that. Her arrest cost her a job so now she's looking for work."

"She's young," Ola Mae said. "She'll find a better job, but we're counting on you, River, to catch the killer. By the way, this is the best icebox cake I've eaten in twenty years. I don't understand why you aren't booked morning, noon, and night."

I glowed from her praise but shrugged off the booking remark. "Anybody can cook and most think of catering for formal occasions only. In addition, long time islanders are often on fixed incomes and can't afford me."

Valerie made a dismissive wave with her hand. "You could create homecooked lunches for thirty or forty people and sell them for fifteen dollars, easy. You could start once a week or so, on a subscription basis and charge an extra two dollars for delivery."

I stilled at the idea. Maybe it would work for me, maybe not. "That's a market I've never considered."

"Aren't you the least busy during the weekdays?"

"I have a few midweek functions, but islanders use caterers mostly on the weekend."

"Try it on Wednesdays," Valerie said. "You have two customers right here. Create an app so people could order and pay through their cell phones."

My eyebrows shot up. "You use apps?"

"Oh, yeah. We track the weather, the traffic, the stock market, and the latest news."

"Thanks. I'll consider the idea." I drew in a deep breath. "Say, you two have been here for years. What do you know about Curtis Marlin's family?"

"He is the last of his line, far as we knew," Valerie said. "Until the funeral, we didn't know he had other relatives. I forget that guy's name from Alabama."

"Ross Talley," I added quickly. "He's Grandma Talley's brother-in-law from Birmingham. I spoke with him after the funeral and he didn't want Curtis's ashes."

"What?" Ola Mae said. "That's ridiculous. We thought he took them home for burial."

I winced. "I hope so. Even Curtis deserves a proper burial. Getting back to the Marlins, Curtis's parents died in a motorcycle crash and his grandmother raised him. How did his father act back in the day?"

"He flirted with Ola Mae." Valerie said. "She liked the attention until she found out he had a wife."

I caught the flush of red creeping up Ola Mae's neck. "He had a roving eye?"

"That's right, and a serious gambling problem," Ola Mae added. "They rode that motorbike because he couldn't afford a car. Our acquaintance is why I remember the crash so clearly. A strong summer squall swept through and they hydroplaned. One moment Gilbert and Sunny Marlin lived and breathed, the next they slammed headfirst into a semi on the causeway. That road stayed closed all day while the cops cleaned up the mess."

"Hush up, Ola Mae," Valerie said. "River doesn't need gruesome images in her sunshine thoughts."

"Sounds terrible."

"Even so, Mrs. Talley rose to the occasion. Did you know Curtis never helped in her garden? She grew most of their food, canned it, and ate frugally all year long. Her husband's tiny pension didn't stretch far, so she had a time of it."

"I had no idea."

"I'll tell you a secret," Ola Mae butted in. "When she got down to her last dollar, she came by with a piece of marble-topped furniture. We bought everything she sold. Every table in this room used to be hers, most of the chairs too."

I glanced at the dated furnishings with new eyes, and my breath hitched in my throat. The poor woman. She'd sold family heirlooms to provide for her grandson. I remembered his great uncle had mentioned the furniture.

I cleared my throat softly. "Ross Talley noticed the missing furniture during his visit. If you decide to sell it, he will likely buy it back."

"We'll keep that in mind," Valerie said smoothly, rising to gather the empty plates on the tray. She smiled at my full glass of tea. "Not thirsty today, dear?"

"I'm good." I would never be thirsty in this house. I stood, taking her clear hint the visit had concluded. "Thank you both for your time. Perhaps the food thief information will help me find the real killer. Say, are y'all familiar with poker games on the island?"

Ola Mae grinned. "Danny's Place has a game tonight, but you didn't hear it from me."

"Can anybody go?"

"Yep. It's open to all, but be forewarned. Serious card sharks play there. It isn't a game for rookies like you who couldn't bluff to save her life."

This poker game would be a great place to gather more information about Curtis. "I'm asking for a friend."

Chapter Twenty-Three

Pete jumped at the chance to play poker at Danny's Place that evening, just as I'd hoped. As soon as he left, I put my secondary plan into effect. Pete may be a better poker player, but I wanted to read the guys myself. And my spicy snacks were the perfect entrée into the game room.

To pull this off, I had started preparations earlier today by creating a bourbon-laced glaze for a twenty-piece chicken drumette pack. I quickly whipped those into the oven and went to work toasting pecans with butter and brown sugar. While those baked, I spruced up with a shower and a flattering top over jeans.

My mouth watered as I walked back into the kitchen. I packed up my goodies, creating a vent hole in the cardboard chicken container. Major insisted we take the Buick, so me and the cat drove to Danny's Place. I parked near Pete's truck and headed inside. This bar was situated in a failing strip mall about as far as you could get from the water on an island.

Pickup trucks numbered as the primary vehicle in the crowded lot. The door opened and a couple stumbled out, wrapped in each other's arms. They didn't see me but they noticed the wing flavorings.

"Something smells divine," the woman said, "and I want it."

I cleared my throat and tried to brush past them. "Special delivery, excuse me."

The man sniffed and stopped. "I'll give you fifty bucks for whatever's in that bag."

"Sorry. This order's prepaid."

As I brushed by, the woman muttered, "Should've offered her more. I bet her food is good."

Encouraged, I made my way to the bar counter and motioned to the bartender, "Delivery for the poker game."

"Who are you?" the female barkeep asked.

"River Holloway."

Her eyes narrowed. "They've never had a food delivery before."

"My boyfriend's never played with them before. Thought a few snacks would help break the ice with the guys."

"Can you cook?"

"I'm a caterer by trade."

She sniffed the air. "I'll help you, but it'll cost you one serving of everything in that bag."

"Deal. Best if I don't serve you out here."

The bartender put down the rag she'd used to polish the counter. "Right. I'll show you the way. Name's Carmelo, by the way."

"Nice to meet you."

"I've heard of you. Did that highfaluting wedding for Melanie Thomas, I believe."

"That was me."

She came around the counter and motioned me to follow her toward the restrooms. "Well, I be danged. River, if your cooking is as good as your reputation, I hope your guy fits right in to poker night."

No response seemed necessary. Carmelo knocked on an Employees Only door and waited. A man I didn't recognize came to the door. "What?"

Carmelo gestured my way. "Got a lady here who wants to feed you schmucks."

I peered into the dark room. Four men sat around a table, and Pete, who had his back to me. "I thought you guys might enjoy a few snacks while you played," I said. "I have caramelized nuts and bourbon-glazed chicken wings."

Pete turned. "River? What are you doing here?"

The redness of his face caught me off-guard, but his genuine surprise enhanced my plan. "I cooked a snack for your new friends. I hope that's okay."

A guy with a booming voice said, "She got you on a short leash, Merrick?"

"River, we're good here," Pete said.

I kept swinging the open chicken container gently in the doorway. "My apologies. I didn't mean to cause a disruption. Sorry to have bothered y'all."

"Hold up," Boomer said in an accented voice. "Something smells delicious. Leave the food. I'd love me some chicken right about now."

"Me too," the baseball capped guy next to him said, also sounding like Spanish was his first language. "Might as well bring it in."

Carmelo bustled us inside and over to an empty table. Not a hint of décor in this room and the lighting came from a single bulb fixture directly over the table.

"I'll make everyone a plate and get out of here," I said. "I didn't know this was a guy's-only game."

"We've had gals play before," Boomer said, "but it works better when it's just guys. Nobody has to watch their language or fight over who's taking the gal home."

"This gal's mine," Pete said. "Making that clear before you eat her food."

"She a good cook?" Ball Cap asked.

"The best."

While they chatted and played cards, I served Carmelo a plate. Her eyes rolled in bliss as she bit into the chicken drumette. "Mercy. I need this recipe, girlfriend. You can come to Danny's Place anytime you like."

She scooted away and I created five plates with a tiny handful of nuts and one drumette each. Since Boomer and Ball Cap seemed to be the group's spokespersons, I served them first. Neither of them went for the food. The older guy with a full shock of white hair on Pete's right tried his chicken first. He immediately threw in his cards and ate everything but the bones on his plate.

By then I'd served everyone and retreated into the shadows of the room to observe. The game wound down and the older guy turned to me. "Is there more chicken?"

"Sure." I started forward with the tongs and served him another piece from my tray. By then the others started on their food. Pete shot me a questioning look, and I smiled at him. He seemed to relax.

Boomer tossed his cards in the pot and said, "Bring that grub over here."

Soon all pretense of cards were gone. Boomer turned out to be Gino Romano and Ball Cap's real name was Willie. The older guy was Dylan and the person who hadn't spoken, a man with startling blue eyes was Nate.

I kept doling out the drumettes one at a time, and then I'd make a pass by each plate adding a scoop of toasted pecans.

"Merrick, you're a lucky guy," Gino said, licking his fingers. "This gal cooks like a dream."

"River's business is food. She's Holloway Catering."

"Damn fine vittles," Nate said. "Sure hope you stick with us, Merrick. Hope your personal chef tags along every time you come. Lucky for you we have a spot open. One of our regulars checked out for good."

"Who's that?" Pete asked, pushing his bone-filled plate to the side and gathering the cards to shuffle them.

"Guy named Curtis Marlin. You heard of him?"

"I read the papers," Pete said. "Was he a good poker player?"

I stepped into the shadows and tried to melt into the wall.

"He died owing all of us money, but he could sure spin a tale," Gino said. "That guy kept us in stitches. You any good at jokes?"

"Not my thing. I'm a business turnaround guy. Serious is my M.O."

"Good thing you got this woman's food to recommend you," Willie said. "You keep us in grub like this and you're welcome here anytime."

"I want the nut recipe," Dylan said. "Haven't had anything this good since my Mom made these for the holidays."

Pete waved me forward, and I lit up inside because my fly-on-the-wall plan was working. "I can tell you how to make them right now, but it would be better if you called or emailed me for the recipe later," I said. "Would you like one of my cards?"

"I would like one," Dylan said. "How much does it cost to hire you?"

I placed a card beside him. "If you have an event you'd like catered, I'll be glad to sit down with you for a quote. I stay pretty busy." I glanced around the table. "Anyone else want a card?"

"I'll take one," Gino said. "What kind of events do you cover?"

"Weddings, funerals, parties, dinner parties, the Chamber of Commerce awards dinner, corporate functions, holiday parties, reunions, club luncheons, that sort of thing."

"You got my vote," Willie said. "Gimme a business card. You never know when I'll hold an event."

Dylan burst out laughing. "Hell would freeze over first. Don't waste a card on him."

"I want a card," Willie said. "We could have her cater the barbecue on the fourth of July."

"Now that's a fine idea," Dylan said. "Best you've had in three years."

"Popular dates fill up fast," I said. "Be sure to confer with me about availability ahead of time. There's a significant deposit to reserve a date."

"You expensive?"

"My pricing is competitive."

"What does that mean?"

"A caterer costs more than doing it yourself, but my customers say it's worth the added expense. If you're serious about booking a date, call me during business hours." I shot each of them a smile in turn. "I didn't mean to disrupt your game, so I'll gather my stuff and scoot."

"Our door is always open to you, Ms. Holloway," Gino said.

"It's River."

"All right, River. Join us anytime. You're welcome here."

~*~

Late that evening, as I wrapped another pound cake for the freezer, Pete bounded into my commercial kitchen. The weight of the day rolled away and I flashed him a welcoming smile. "How'd it go?"

"Guess who won big tonight?" he said, twirling me around the room.

I swatted playfully at his arms. "Let me set this pound cake down."

He released me and flashed a wad of cash. "I walked out with two hundred dollars over my stake. Each player won a few games, but I won the largest pots."

"Did they take it easy so you'd come back?"

"Who cares? Tonight I'm a winner. I needed this and didn't know it. The failure of North Merrick shook my faith in my intuition. Tonight, I read the guys and my observations were on point. Man, I'm on top of the world."

He whirled us around the room again, ending with a dramatic dip and a toe-curling kiss.

His excitement lit me up too. "Maybe you should play cards regularly."

"With a new wife and a new business on my horizon, I'm too busy to be a regular, but I might drop by now and then. What fun to relax and be myself. Thanks for bringing over that icebreaker food. After the initial surprise wore off, I saw why you did it. The guys opened up once their bellies were full."

"I'm happy this evening recharged you. With the dust settling from your previous business, you can move ahead in every way."

"With you," he said, nuzzling my nose.

"With life," I gently corrected, extricating myself to freeze the pound cake and finish sanitizing the counters. "But play time is important too. Only look at what a few hours of poker did for your mood."

"I feel amazing." He stretched and sighed. "The challenge of learning their tells revved my engines. I dialed in all the creativity, ingenuity, and finesse that North Merrick quenched. I feel like a new man. I'm glad you asked me to go."

"Me too."

He drifted close to me. "We're good together, babe. And I loved the secret agent aspect of the night. It's a rush."

"Did you learn anything about Curtis from the poker guys?"

"Gino griped about Curtis dying. He owed the guys thousands of dollars, and he owed Gino more. They plan to leverage the estate to get repaid. I kept my mouth shut, and they kept talking."

"Wonderful. How'd his debt get so high? Didn't they make him settle up before he played again?"

"Not that kind of a game," Pete said. "If Curtis won, they took a slice of his winnings to go against his debt. Otherwise, they let his debt ride."

"I don't understand that friendly-but-keeping-score mindset at all."

"The guys liked Curtis. The stories he told must've been golden, or they would've kicked him to the curb."

"Gotcha. Guys have different rules for friends."

He grinned. "Something like that."

I did some mental math. Big debt. Dead guy. Seems like there should be an "equal" sign between those factors. "Did a poker guy kill Curtis because of the debt?"

"A dead man pays no one. Curtis told crazy stories about his life. If he had a flat tire on the road, for instance, some punks would mug him. That sort of thing."

Huh. Curtis Marlin's alleged depths surprised me. "So he behaved when it suited him. He shared tales of misfortunes to entertain the poker guys. He charmed the basketball guys too, or they wouldn't seek him out."

"Sounds about right."

I couldn't get around the debt Curtis owed. "He owed the poker guys big money, but he owed Gino the most."

"Yeah. Close to five grand."

"What's Gino's last name again?" I asked.

"Romano, like the Italian cheese. Gino Romano. Trips off the tongue, doesn't it?"

I eyed him speculatively. "How much did you drink tonight?"

"Coupla beers. Some guys did shots between beers. Maybe that's how I beat them. I didn't cloud my mind with booze."

"Beer has alcohol in it."

"You're right," Pete said with a calculating smile, "but I can nurse a beer for hours."

I laughed at the intensity in his eyes. "Glad you didn't lose your man card at the poker game."

"The man card works fine, hon." He reached for me. "Let's go next door to our place and give it a spin."

~*~

On Saturday, I caught up with Deputy Franklin at Seashore Park. He stood in the shade talking to three teenaged girls in skimpy bikinis. When he saw my van, he left the teens and strode over to my window.

"Good morning," he said. "You staying out of trouble?"

I shifted the gear stick into park and faced him. "Mostly. I learned something new last night. Curtis Marlin had a gambling problem and owed at least four local men over a thousand dollars."

"Gambling problem?" Franklin scratched the back of his neck. "First I've heard of it. Tell me more."

"I don't know much more, but those men had a financial motive to kill Curtis. Viv and Doug did not."

"Who's your source for the information?"

"Pete played in a poker game last night and Curtis's name came up."

"I'll bet it did. How'd he know to play with these men?"

"Research. Pete wants to clear Doug and Viv as much as I do."

Franklin glanced away, his bright blue eyes narrowing as if he spotted a ship on the horizon. "Names. I need names."

"Willie, Dylan, Nate, and Gino. I don't know last names except for Gino. He's Gino Romano."

Those laser sharp eyes cut back to my face. "Danny's Place?"

I nodded. "You know them?"

"Those are heavy hitters. Rumor around town says Romano's connected to the mob, but we have no proof."

Bees buzzed at the nearby trash can. An overripe odor had me wrinkling my nose. "Pete said Curtis owed Gino five thousand dollars."

"Would Pete wear a wire and go back in there?"

I shrugged. "You'd have to ask him."

"The sheriff will be interested in this wrinkle. I can't guarantee he'll consider dropping the charge against Viv or Doug, but this may be useful in the overall scheme of things."

"He shouldn't have shut down the investigation so quickly, even if he is running for re-election. Did you catch up with Heavy D?"

"DeAndre Haywood refused to speak to me. Said he'd already cooperated. He implied harassment, racial bias, and a lawsuit."

"Can he do that?"

A convertible of teenaged boys rolled by, radio blaring. Franklin gave them the eye and they kept going. He turned back to me. "In today's world, anyone can sue anyone else."

"Even so, I'm surprised at his change in attitude."

"It happens. Suspects get legal advice and use buzz words to push us back. I don't want to be the deputy that bankrupts the system. Unless we have direct evidence against Heavy D, I can't touch him."

"What about Ty and Eggs?"

"You can bet they're all spouting the same rhetoric. Of course, if one of those three is a bad actor, they'll be true to their nature soon enough, and we'll have grounds to haul them in for questioning."

"Is that likely?"

"You never know," he said. "This job continues to surprise me."

With my Curtis angle going nowhere, I shifted to another island crime. "What about the food burglar? Have a line on him?"

"I don't, and there's no indication the food thefts connect to the Marlin case. They're two different crimes."

"I heard a physical description of the burglar."

"You have been busy. Let's hear it." He flipped to a new page in his notebook.

I gave him Valerie Slade's description of the man in camo.

He finished jotting things down and pocketed the small notebook. "Similar ID to other sightings of this man. I'll contact her for an official report. Thanks for the tip."

"You're welcome."

"What else is on your sleuthing menu today?"

"A quiet afternoon and evening at home with my fiancé."

"Good. Say, I spoke with my ex about the Sweet Sixteen party. We'd like to book the following Saturday."

"Let me check." I scrolled though my phone calendar. "I have something the Friday night prior but it isn't a large event. How many are you expecting for your daughter's party?"

"That's the ex's department."

"With back-to-back events, I'll either need a simplified menu or a limit of twenty people. Should I meet with your ex for the menu selection?"

"Let me tell her there's a cap, then we'll plan the food. Please hold that date for us."

I added it to my phone calendar. "I'll hold it two days. By then, I expect a 40 percent deposit. If someone else requests that date in the interim, I'll give you a day to pay a deposit. Otherwise, the reservation goes away."

"Shouldn't be a problem. I'll be in touch once I've spoken to the ex."

He strode away to his cruiser, surefooted in the sandy parking lot. For the first time, things looked brighter for Doug and Viv. The poker guys and basketball teammates had motive to kill Curtis.

I took a minute to decide if I wanted to squeeze in a beach walk, and as I hesitated I had the distinct feeling I should leave. I glanced at my arms expecting to see goosebumps, but my skin looked normal. The uneasy sensation must be a nervous response, but why? I scanned the half-empty parking lot for signs of danger. People came and went. Nobody paid any attention to my van or me, but the prickly sensation continued, as if someone watched me.

I drove away and the edginess subsided.

Nerves.

Must be.

Chapter Twenty-Four

I was five minutes from home when Dylan Barresi called and instructed me to meet him at the pier to discuss a catering job. "Are you one of the poker guys?" I asked, not remembering anyone in my client list named Barresi who spoke with an accent.

"Sometimes. I'll be at the pier in ten minutes. If you want the job, be there."

He hung up. I changed course at a traffic circle and headed straight to the pier. Luckily, I kept sample menus in my business tote, plus I had access to my prices in the tablet I carried in my purse. I parked the van and stood next to it.

I texted Pete my location and errand. He called right away. "Are you nuts? At least one of those guys is mob related. Those Latino accents are real."

"Apparently Dylan Barresi likes my cooking and wants to hire me."

"Be careful."

"Always."

I ended the call and scanned the crowd of people strolling with kids and dogs, but I didn't see the older gentleman from last night. I hoped he showed up soon, as I had a catering job for four this evening and a limited amount of free time today. A younger man beside a black limo across the way waved at me. I pointed to my chest. He nodded.

Hugging the large tote with menus and planners to my chest, I hoofed it to the limo. "Yes?"

"Mr. Barresi is ready for your meeting now."

Another Latino accent. "I don't see him."

The man opened the car door and waved me in.

I edged closer to the limo, not sure how I felt about taking a meeting in the parking lot. "Mr. Barresi?"

"It's Dylan. We met last night. Please join me."

His voice sounded raspier than last night but I recognized him. "I don't understand."

"I don't take meetings in public places."

Horns honked from the limo blocking the traffic loop. "I'd feel more comfortable if you joined me in the park. We can sit on a bench and no one will bother us."

"If you want my business, missy, you'll step into my mobile office."

The driver glared at me. I'd never been in a limo before and curiosity overrode my innate caution. "Okay. I can accommodate your request."

"Good for you."

The driver's phone rang as I sat across from Dylan. The sumptuous leather upholstery and pristine carpet smelled brand new. "Nice office," I said.

His gaze shifted over my head to the driver as we slowly rolled forward. "It works for me. We are often on the road and I prefer privacy."

Moments later, I heard an electric whir behind me and turned to see a partition had opened.

"Is there an issue, Vince?" Dylan asked.

"The package is missing."

"Find it."

"Yessir."

The partition closed and we once again had privacy. The car turned and accelerated on King's Way. "Where are we going?" I asked.

"Nowhere and everywhere. Don't like most folks to get too close to me. For you, I make the exception."

Time to get down to business. "What size event are you planning, Dylan?"

"Right to the heart of the matter. I like your style, River."

127

"How can Holloway Catering help you, sir?"

"I plan to host six people at my place this coming Friday at five p.m. I want snack food like you brought for the poker guys. Lots of tailgate-style snacks."

"Sure." I checked my phone calendar. "The date works for me. How many kids and adults?"

"Six men. No kids. Big appetites."

I wrote down six big eaters. "And your budget?"

"What'll it cost me?" he countered.

"Depends on your menu choices." I pulled out a binder with tailgate food choices and made suggestions. He studied the food photos and me. "What do you recommend?"

"Everything I make tastes good, so your menu is about the foods you want to serve." Feeling like a TV gameshow hostess, I pointed to several glossy photos of complementary tailgate foods. "Any food allergies I should know about?"

His brows rose. "You planning to off one of us?"

"I apologize for alarming you. I want to ensure all the dishes will work for your guests. Nuts, shellfish, and wheat are a few of the more common food allergies."

"I especially want nuts and shellfish. The rest is up to you. Also I want a big batch of those spiced pecans just for me."

Not a lot of help, but I'd started a project with less direction before. "I'll need to work up some figures to give you my price. Should I call you later with that number?"

He barred his arms across his chest and glared at me. "No time like the present."

Great. No pressure at all. But I wanted the job, so I pulled out a contract and itemized each dish and created a column of prices to total. He surprised me by adding it correctly in his head while I used a calculator. We settled on a price for wings, spiced pecans, broccoli salad, ham and cheese sliders, cornbread muffins, chilled and peeled boiled shrimp with cocktail sauce, melon balls, and strawberry cheesecake. I signed the contract sheet and so did he.

I took a photo of the itemized list I'd detailed and handed him the original. "I'll need a 40 percent deposit within two days to hold the date and the rest will be due the day of the event."

He nodded. "You'll have the money."

"Where do I bring the food? I usually arrive onsite about two hours ahead of time to set up."

"Vince will come get the food from your place of business at three. No set up is necessary for my event."

I flashed my the-client-is-always-right smile. "Okay then. We're all done here."

Dylan mashed a button and the partition opened again. "She needs money for the deposit." He quoted the amount, and the partition closed.

"I dreamed of your pecans last night," Dylan said.

"I'm happy to share my recipe with you. They're easy to make."

"Thought about it. Rather get them directly from you." He chuckled. "You can't get rid of me that easy."

I kept my wince of displeasure to myself. Dylan Barresi's tone implied cheer, but his eyes radiated a threat. He definitely won the prize for most eccentric client.

The limo slowed, and I saw the pier out my window and breathed easier. "As soon as I have your check, we're good to go."

Dylan nodded. I tried the door. Locked. "Uh, how do I get out of here?"

"Vince will open the door when it's time."

My hand reflexively pulled on the door handle again. It took me a moment to calm my breathing. "I don't appreciate being held captive in your car."

He matched my icy tone with a glacial stare. "If you were a captive, you'd know it."

"You're joking."

Dylan Barresi flashed a terrifying basilisk smile. I quaked at the thought of being this man's captive. "You know, on second thought, I'm not the right caterer for you. I decline the job."

"Do that and you'll end up in court or worse. We have a signed contract."

"The fine print says I can refuse a job if the client is unreasonable. Personal threats qualify as unreasonable."

An uneasy silence filled the limo. "You can't quit. I already promised the guys," he said. "Why does this type of misunderstanding always happen with women?"

"We don't like threats. You want my catering service?"

"I certainly do."

"Then I expect a little common courtesy."

He looked away first and swore softly. "In my line of work weakness will get you killed."

Somehow I'd gone from being frightened of this man to feeling energized around him. I didn't know what that meant about me, but I wouldn't let him bully me. "I'm not your employee, and it doesn't appear we can reach a mutual agreement. I don't want this job."

"What'll it take? More money?"

"This isn't about money. Treat me with respect. Treat all women with respect."

He drew into himself for a long moment. During that mini-eternity, I wondered if I'd pushed him too far, if I'd made an enemy of a potentially ruthless man.

"I apologize," Dylan said. "I thought operating from a position of strength would give me an edge in our negotiations."

My back teeth gritted together. "I do not negotiate on price. My prices are fair, and I resent you thinking I protested to extort money from you."

"Again, my mistake. I'm used to dealing with a different caliber of person. Will you take the job?"

"Why should I? You're an incorrigible bully."

"My money's as good as anyone's. We have a deal." When I said nothing he added, "I'm sure you don't like all your clients. I promise you can deal directly with Vince."

"Is he your protégé?"

"Is that a trick question?" Again, I held my silence, and he filled it with words. "Vince will treat you like spun glass or he's out a job, even if he is my nephew."

Fortunately Vince opened the door at that moment and handed me a thick brown envelope. "What's this?" I asked, searching both men's faces.

Dylan Barresi attempted another smile. "Your deposit, Ms. Holloway. Vince will come by for the food two hours before the event on Friday. A pleasure doing business with you."

I stumbled out in the sunshine and watched as Vince drove the big vehicle out of sight. Pete trotted over and guided me out of the roadway. "Where were you?"

"Everywhere and nowhere. You were right. Dylan Barresi plays by different rules."

"He kidnapped you. I'm calling the cops."

"Don't. He has a few communication issues. We worked it out and signed a catering contract." I waved the thick envelope. "I accepted his deposit."

"I don't like it. You won't work that job alone. I'll be there every step of the way."

"No need. I won't deal with Barresi again. Vince will pick up the food from my kitchen."

"You are more than likely catering for the mob."

I shrugged. "Mobsters have to eat too."

"River!"

"He won't threaten me again, not if he wants those spiced pecans."

Chapter Twenty-Five

Ola Mae Reed phoned at lunchtime. I caught the call as I took a quick cooking break on my deck with a large tumbler of iced tea. The lasagna I'd cooked for lunch would be ready any minute now. It had been a busy day so far and the catered meal for two couples tonight would keep me busy through the evening.

"River, did you hear the news?" Ola Mae asked. "The cops arrested Ty Carvell this morning."

The world stilled as if marsh fog blanketed my yard. Could this be Doug and Viv's salvation? I dared to hope so. "For murdering Curtis?"

"For fighting. He beat the tarnation out of a guy at the wine bar. Nearly killed the man. People say he's a bad seed. This could be the break you need to clear Viv and Doug's names."

"If only, but the sheriff doesn't link different crime types, according to Deputy Franklin."

A small white sedan rolled up my drive. Viv leapt out and barreled my way. Judging by the wrinkles in her clothing and her mussed hair, I guessed she'd come straight from a nap.

"This sheriff is a joke," Ola Mae said. "We could do better. Your deputy is a straight shooter. He should be sheriff."

"True," I responded. "Sorry to cut this short. Someone's here. I have to go. Thanks for the news."

Major took one look at Viv and darted into the woods.

Viv flopped down on my lounger, narrowly missing my feet. "You heard?" she asked.

"If you're talking about Ty's arrest, yes."

"If they've got him, I'm in the clear."

"He's arrested for something else. Sheriff Vargas treats each case as a stand-alone. Ty's incarceration for fighting may not help you."

"That's not fair. He's a person of interest in the Curtis Marlin homicide. Him getting arrested for aggravated assault and battery should direct attention his way."

"I agree in principle, but the sheriff doesn't. We can't rely on them to find the killer. If we prove Ty poisoned Curtis, at least they'll know where to find him."

"Well," Viv huffed and stopped. "I don't like that one bit. What a buzz kill. I hoped to end this nightmare and get my job back."

"Not over, but you will be cleared if I have anything to say about it, and from what you said before you needed another job anyway."

Viv's fingers threaded through her tangled hair, and she cried out in anguish. "I hate this. Except for Doug, my life is a shambles."

"It will get better. Things are breaking loose. We're closing in on the truth."

"Easy for you to say. You're engaged to a great guy, your business is growing, and you own your home."

I shook my head. "You forget the *year* I had with Pete gone and hardly any word from him. And my business doesn't fully support me. I still pick up odd jobs to make ends meet. As for my home, I didn't pay off the mortgage. My parents and grandparents did."

"People respect you, Miss Sunshine with cookies. They want to help you."

"I'll tell you a secret. The reason I hand out cookies is to remind people of my business. It's good advertising."

"I get it. Everyone has challenges, but I'm in trouble. Even if I get my life back, I have no transferrable skills from the mill," Viv said. "I started working there in high school, so I have no other job experience."

"You have people skills and more. Pete can help you polish a resumé and show you online places to post it."

"My life is here on Shell Island. I'm not moving."

"Who says you have to move? Pete is a corporate turnaround specialist. He'll evaluate your strengths and point you in the right direction."

"If you say so." Viv paused for a moment, sniffing the air. "I hoped for commiseration, pity, and lunch."

"I can help with one of those." A buzzer sounded inside. "There you go. Lunch is ready if you want to join us."

"I do. Thanks." She shot me another glance. "No chance of pity?"

"Pity takes time and energy away from helping friends."

"Gotcha."

Viv followed me inside and had munched halfway through her lasagna when Pete joined us. We caught him up, and he agreed to mentor her job search project. "We'll start next week at your convenience," he said. "Today River is prepping for a catering job and I'm helping her serve."

I beamed and squeezed his hand across the table. "Thanks."

"What're you making?" Viv asked.

"Mini crab cake appetizers, pan-seared red snapper with mango salsa, roasted asparagus, sourdough bread, and a tomato and cucumber salad."

"Sounds super healthy. What about dessert?"

"Peach supreme a la mode."

"Now we're talking. I could eat some cobbler right now. Any chance you doubled the recipe?"

"Tell you what. We'll celebrate with peach supreme when you and Doug are cleared."

Viv drained her iced tea. "You've ruined me for regular food, woman."

"Good to know. I need to get over to the commercial kitchen to stay on schedule."

"I'll catch these dishes," Pete said, rising with a stack of plates.

"Thanks for lunch," Viv said, padding outdoors with me.

I hugged her. "Hang in there. We'll keep asking questions and turning over rocks."

"My arrest and incarceration changed me," Viv mumbled. "I'm too scared of trouble to visit my normal haunts so I stay home. I don't know who I am anymore."

"You're my friend, and you'll get your life back."

As she drove off, my arm hairs snapped to attention and a shiver rippled through me. I stilled. That nervy sensation of being watched hit me again. Feigning a long stretch and a yoga-like neck roll, I scanned the woods bordering my property. Nothing looked sinister. No faces in the shadows, no glints of gun barrels.

Which should be a relief.

Except my intuition shouted another message.

Someone was out there.

Chapter Twenty-Six

With time in short supply, I needed to focus on tonight's event, but my brain wouldn't cooperate. As I pulled out the frozen sourdough loaves and parked two sticks of butter on the counter, I realized I should heed my biofeedback. Several times now I felt someone spying on me, but I had no proof.

However, I trusted my instinct. It never steered me wrong in the past.

The window over the sink beckoned, and I stared into the yard, seeing and not seeing at the same time. Several possibilities sprang to mind. Earlier, I'd verbally sparred with new client Dylan Barresi, but he seemed too direct to sneak around. It seemed likely the watcher might be Curtis Marlin's killer or the food thief. Both perpetrators were sneaky, and spying fit their wheelhouse. Or maybe a master lockpicker had gained admittance to our home the other day.

While the sheriff didn't mix and match cases, I had no trouble imagining a furtive connection between the homicide, a food thief, a maybe housebreaker, and now a sense that someone lurked in the shadows. But only two of those concerns were facts. Curtis was dead. Someone was stealing food. Cops dealt in facts, not speculation.

With a start, I realized I'd been standing here doing nothing for ten minutes when I had a busy afternoon on tap. I had to pull it together. I couldn't disappoint Lizzie Collins tonight.

I turned away from the window and walked over to my to-do list. The mango salsa would stay firm all day. I peeled and cubed a large mango, and then mixed in cucumber, onion, lime juice, lime zest, cilantro, and salt before sealing it in a labeled container and refrigerating it. I'd been thawing red snapper filets in the refrigerator since yesterday. A quick touch of a fillet gave the right amount of fleshy yield, so they were thawing on schedule.

Mini-crab cakes were next on the list. With clean fingers, I combed through a pound of lump backfin crabmeat, discarding the few shells I encountered. In a small bowl, I beat an egg and then added mayo and seasonings. Last I added panko breadcrumbs and patted out bite-size crab cakes. To make sure they held their shape in the oven later, I refrigerated the pan of uncooked crab cakes.

Next, I measured the remoulade sauce ingredients into a bowl, stirred them, and stashed the labeled container in the fridge. Too soon to roast the asparagus, so I washed the spears to allow them time to air dry.

I was working on the cobbler when Pete appeared with the vanilla ice cream I'd requested from Island Creamery.

"They give you any trouble?" I asked as I stored the carton in the deep freeze.

"They were happy to see me," Pete said. "The server remembered you'd made this request before and went right along with the plan. We should buy stock in that place as often as we visit."

My suspicion mounted. "Pete Merrick, did you eat ice cream and ruin your dinner?"

He grinned. "I may have partaken, but I had an ulterior motive."

I stilled and gave him my full attention. "Do tell."

"I lingered to ask Owen about job openings. He said it never hurt to talk with the manager, so I set up an appointment."

My eyebrows peaked at my hairline. "You wanna scoop ice cream?"

"I'm interested in a food service business, but first I want a handle on their foot traffic and sales. The Island Creamery should be raking in cash, but they only seem moderately successful."

I understood his caution after he'd been burned by the North Merrick deal earlier this year. But the ice cream shop seemed small potatoes in scope compared to the corporations he used to fix. Only, Pete's attitude conveyed seriousness, and I needed to get on board. "And the why is important to you?"

"Absolutely, but importantly, the shop has the Village location I want. It'd be the toehold I need to get started down there."

"Small problem. All those shops are occupied."

"Everything is for sale at the right price. I'll buy a business or purchase a building. I'm still crunching numbers. Enough about my business plans. Your catering gig is at six. You need anything else from me before we leave at a quarter to five?"

"Yes. It's a personal matter." I steeled my nerve and forged ahead. "I've been hesitant to mention this before, but I can't ignore this feeling any longer. I believe we have a problem."

He studied me in a vacuum of sound, his expression unreadable. "This sounds ominous."

Pete trusted me. He'd understand my rationale for complaining about a feeling. I hoped. Nothing to do but blurt it out. "Someone is spying on me."

"Did you see them?"

"No. That's the maddening part. I've felt this sensation a few times now. The feeling won't go away. The new locks are a good first step in our home protection, but I want to know who's out there. What would it cost to install security cameras?"

He breathed easier and nodded. "Not as much as you think. I got this. I'll check prices right now so we can discuss options after your event."

~*~

Lizzie Collins and her husband Wesley wore flowing neutral clothing for their dinner party, in contrast to their neighbors, Emma and Blake McDonald who glittered like a Vegas floor show act.

After taking social media photos of each other and the crab cakes, they wolfed down the appetizers and drained two bottles of wine. Pete and I filled the dinner plates in the kitchen while the cobbler warmed in the oven. I sent him out with the water pitcher with instructions to ask the McDonalds if they'd ever been in show business.

With everyone engaged in conversation, I carried two plates to the hutch and went back for the other two. While Blake and Wesley commiserated about the good old days, I served the festive meal.

Amid their gasps of delight and another flurry of social media photographs, we slipped into the kitchen to eat our own supper.

"Delicious," Pete said around a mouthful of red snapper.

I nodded, intent on finishing my portion before they needed us again. Normally I waited until we returned home to eat, but today's edginess took a toll and I'd been stress eating all afternoon.

"Any progress with security cameras?" I asked softly between bites.

"The DIY ones I prefer are in stock over at the mainland big box hardware store. We can be up and running tomorrow afternoon, if you're in agreement."

Practicality raised its ugly head. "What if you find the perfect house for us the next day? Are we wasting our money?"

"That's the beauty of this system. Undo a few screws and it's portable, like the devices the feds used at the Christmas Tree Farm last month."

The tension in my shoulders eased. "Sounds perfect."

"We'll be covered soon. Also, we can practice some take-down moves so you won't be defenseless."

No way did I want to strike, kick, or fight Pete, who'd had barely a month of healing after being on the losing end of a bad guy scuffle. My personal philosophy on self-defense included awareness and prevention, which is why I was happy about the cameras.

Pete wanted to protect me, and I wanted to protect him. "I don't want to hurt anyone, least of all you, but I understand the value of preparation. If someone came at me and all I had was my keys, I'd palm my keys in my fist and hammer that fist down using the keys as a weapon. And yell. Yelling is good. I'm a firm believer in using what's at hand to protect myself."

Admiration filled his eyes. "That's my girl. You've got the right mindset."

His praise made me blush. "I, uh, took a few self-defense classes while you were in California."

"I'm glad."

We ate quietly, the delightful aroma of decaf coffee blending with cobbler's cinnamon. "Valerie Slade had an idea the other day," I said. "She suggested I offer gourmet lunches, for delivery, one day a week."

"Not a bad idea, but it would be expensive to run all over the island making deliveries. What about take out?"

"Ola Mae and Valerie said they'd be regular customers and the bridge ladies might glom on too as the word spreads. If I did it, I'd cap it at twenty lunches, but to be economical, it would have to be chicken or a vegetarian meal."

"The gourmet lunch crowd wants upscale meals. How about selling a month of Wednesdays to each customer, with a vegetable meal one week, chicken the next, a beef dish following, and a seafood something to round out the package. You could add a 'special' for fifth Wednesday months."

"Hmm." I rolled the idea around in my head as I lifted the bubbling cobbler from the warm oven. "The nice thing about your strategy is it keeps my prices and entrée selections in the catering realm."

Pete carried our dishes to the sink and watched me transfer peach cobbler to the fancy china serving bowls I brought with me. "You have contact info for your past customers," he said. "You could email them to see if they want to hear more about the idea. That would be an inexpensive way to determine demand for a subscription service."

I checked the ice cream. Ready to serve, but I wouldn't add it to the cobbler until we removed the dinner plates. "Maybe. I'm feeling less panicked by the idea now."

The rest of the event passed swiftly. Wesley Collins gave me 10 percent extra as a tip and Blake McDonald insisted on taking five business cards for his friends.

Driving home in the dark, Pete said, "I wonder if Ty Carvell is still in police custody."

"Haven't heard any news from Deputy Franklin this afternoon or evening," I said, automatically glancing at my watch for the time. Shoot, too late to call him. "There's always tomorrow."

Chapter Twenty-Seven

Sunday rolled around with church in the morning, followed by a flurry of installing security cameras. In my spare time, I started a list of people who might be interested in a gourmet lunch program but after a good night's sleep, my hesitation returned full force, and then some. This plan sounded like a first step toward opening a restaurant, and I didn't want that path. Needing a distraction, I tried Deputy Franklin again. Unlike my earlier calls, Franklin answered this one.

"Ms. Holloway. What can I do for you?"

His voice sounded strained. Had I called too many times? I should be as brief as possible. "Several things. First, did Ty Carvell reveal anything new about his pal's murder?"

"The Curtis Marlin homicide is officially closed and, before you ask, Ty's still in police custody."

"He's a violent man with a temper."

"True. Doesn't mean he'd use poison to kill someone."

Not what I wanted to hear. Disappointment seeped through my body, souring my mood.

"On another note," Franklin continued, "The sheriff is interested in the poker guys. Pete thought anymore about wearing that wire for us?"

I swallowed hard, not wanting to admit I'd signed a catering contract with one of those men. "Pete refused. Said he got on the wrong side of people like Gino before and it didn't go well."

"Circumstances change, so let me know if he changes his mind." He paused. "Anything else on your list?"

Seemed like everyone knew about my habit of making lists. "We spent the afternoon installing security cameras. I'm certain someone's watching me."

"Sorry to hear about that. Let me know if you get a clear image of anyone."

"Will do."

~*~

Doug and Viv joined us for burgers on the grill and strawberries with whipped cream over pound cake at dinnertime.

"I'm stuffed and loving it," Viv said, pushing back from the table with an armload of dishes. "Ever thought about opening a restaurant?"

I rose with more dishes and followed her to the sink. "Funny you should mention a restaurant. Valerie Slade suggested I offer a gourmet lunch on Wednesdays. And, not too long ago, Jerry and Dasia Allen asked me to create a specialty crab cake called River Cakes to market exclusively through their shop. I've resisted tangents in the past, but now I wonder if my vision for Holloway Catering is too restrictive."

"I see." Viv began loading plates in the dishwasher. "None of these ideas appeal to you?"

Her question sent my thoughts into a tailspin. "Each idea has merit and income potential. I'm the hold up. I can't make that mental leap. At the core, the ideas feel wrong to me."

Viv didn't respond as she rinsed and loaded the last of the big bowls. In the sudden quiet I reflected on what I said. My vision of Holloway Catering only stretched so far. If I thought outside that box, I felt anxious.

"When did I get to be so narrow-minded?" I asked.

"You really want to go there?" Viv asked, drying her hands and propping one hip against the counter as she faced me. "When your mom got sick, your life changed. You stayed in this house and took charge of her and Doug."

143

I squared my shoulders. "That's what family does."

"The thing is," Viv began slowly, "you took on those personal challenges, but your business couldn't grow with the limited time you had available. It's my opinion you kept your dream alive by catering infrequent events due to your time constraints."

A hot retort sprang into my throat but it ebbed just as quickly. She had a point. I didn't like hearing I had self-limited my business. I would prefer to blame someone else for not being a smashing financial success. I loved Holloway Catering, but I couldn't risk it by going all in on someone else's idea.

"I suppose so," I admitted.

Viv edged closer. "These business options sound scary because you can't evaluate them from a disaster mode mindset. From that perspective, any change feels like a threat."

Her words echoed my thoughts, but it was hard to hear them from someone else. I'd dropped anchor when Mom got sick and I hadn't set sail since.

My expression must've flickered. Viv nodded. "You see it."

"I do." I swallowed around the knot of emotion in my throat. "That's insightful. I hadn't realized how afraid I am to vary from booking single events."

Viv laughed. "If only you knew a primo business expert to help evaluate expansion opportunities."

My thoughts veered to Pete, deep in conversation in the dining room with my brother about surf fishing. "You're right. I have the best of all worlds right now. My business is growing. People want more access to my cooking. And I have a hotshot business consultant living under my roof."

"Ask Pete about your options. If you keep the same business model, fine, but at least you can make future decisions from an objective perspective."

Viv's insights opened my eyes. I'd gone into survival mode when I became Mom's caregiver, Doug's surrogate parent, and a business owner. Since then, with Mom's passing and Doug's successful business launch, my perspective should've shifted out of disaster mode.

"I'll think about it, Viv," I said. "I didn't make that connection before but you're absolutely right. I need to let the past go."

"The past has long arms," Viv said glumly. "Look at the fix I'm in."

Her comment sobered me instantly. While I worried about business options, Viv grappled with an unfounded murder charge. "Let's discuss a related topic. What drew you to Curtis?"

Viv studied her hands for a bit. "He made me feel like the most desirable woman in the world, but once he lured me into his web, his tactics changed. He used a push-pull of degradation and praise, and I never knew what would upset him. The constant drama wore me out, so, in the end, I walked away."

My dislike for Curtis intensified. "I had no idea he treated you like that. You should've said something."

"Hard to admit you've been a fool," Viv said quietly. "He stole my pride and made me feel second-rate. I endured the verbal abuse because I wanted to party with Mr. Cool. I didn't want to be a boring adult. I loved being party-girl Viv."

"Yikes. No wonder you pegged my avoidance behavior. You've been engaged in extensive self-analysis."

Viv's cheek twitched. "Amazing the things you consider while penned in a cell."

"We'll find out who killed Curtis, and you won't go back. By all accounts he had a good thing going on Shell Island, living in his grandmother's house, having a crew of former teammates who practically worshipped him and gambling buddies who let his debts ride. What inspired Curtis to go to Alaska?"

"He claimed he'd get rich quick out there. He wanted all of us to go with him, but I had no intention of going to Alaska. Since he went alone, I'm guessing the guys opted out of the trip too."

"He died owing everyone money, so he didn't strike gold up there. Do you know when he left?"

"We broke up before he went to Alaska so I never knew his travel dates. The gossip around the bar hinted Curtis lost his shirt in Alaska. Which is why I never understood how he got my brother so fired up to go there. Once Darry caught the get-rich-quick fever, he lit out for glory. He was more excited about this trip than the camping trip we took on the Altamaha River to see all those big gators."

My heart welled with sympathy. "Any word from the Alaska State Troopers?"

"Nothing good." She grimaced. "His supposed address led nowhere. The rooming house manager said Darry stayed there one night and left. There are no other leads. Darry vanished. I should've paid attention instead of living large. I'll never make that mistake again, but I awakened too late to help my brother."

Viv needed the truth about her brother. One way or another, I'd help her find it. "Once we get you and Doug cleared of these charges you and I will go to Alaska and find your brother."

"Deal."

Chapter Twenty-Eight

Monday morning's security footage starred one black cat. Major had an uncanny knack for being where the cameras aimed because his treks across the backyard and around the front of the house tripped the motion-sensitive cameras repeatedly.

"I'll adjust the camera angle." Pete sat back in the dining room chair, looked away from his computer monitor, and massaged his temples before turning to me. "Otherwise all we'll see is your cat patrolling the yard."

"Patrolling?" I set aside my paperwork and studied the array of cat videos.

"Look at the time stamps on these images. About once an hour he visits the front yard and then the back. Something has him on alert."

"I did good in giving our kitty a soldier's name then."

"I'm glad we have the cameras. If you and the cat are right about a trespasser—"

"We are," I interrupted.

"The cameras will catch whoever is spying on us."

"Good."

Pete cleared his throat. "Moving on, you and Viv stayed in the kitchen fooling with the dishes a long time last night. Everything okay?"

"She convinced me I've been operating in fear mode when it comes to my business. I don't want to be self-limiting, and at some point I'd like you to help me weigh my options."

"Anytime."

"We also talked about the case. Viv told me Curtis convinced Darry to go to Alaska. Darry's officially missing, by the way. The Alaska State Troopers can find no trace of him."

Pete whistled softly. "If the cops discover Curtis orchestrated Darry's disappearance, that strengthens Viv's motive for killing Curtis."

"They won't hear it from me."

"Not even your pal, Deputy Franklin?"

"Not even him. Speaking of the deputy, I need to call him."

"Careful what you say. You might accidentally cut short your brother's freedom."

"It strikes me as interesting that both Viv's brother and mine have shadows hanging over their heads. But whereas Doug is innocent and I'll go to the mat to prove it, helping Viv find her brother might be impossible."

"You told her you'd find him?"

"I did but it has to wait until we find Curtis's killer. I'm spread thin with this investigation and Holloway Catering. Seemed like I careened from one thing to another all weekend. I forgot to mention something I overheard during my limo ride with Dylan Barresi. His driver Vince told him a package had gone missing. What were they talking about?"

"You think I speak mob?" He grinned. "Maybe I picked mob-speak in California. It could be a physical package they're moving or a person."

Ghostly tendrils brushed my face. I shuddered. "Glad you're out of that life."

"I'm worried you're getting sucked into that life. We know nothing about Dylan Barresi. I checked and he has no social media or internet footprint."

"Just because he's an extremely private man and a jerk is no reason to condemn him. He backed down when I called him on his crap. I trust him."

"I understand your position, babe, but you're my world. I don't want to lose you. I love you and don't want anything to jeopardize our future."

"Understood." I kissed him. "By the way, I'm having lunch with Peggy from the Wine Bar today. If there's dirt on Heavy D, Ty, and Eggs floating around the night life scene, she'll know it."

"Where are you meeting her?"

"Aunt Ida's down in the Village. Want to join us?"

He grinned. "Thought you'd never ask."

~*~

Aunt Ida's décor blended the look of an old-fashioned diner with a seafood shack, and locals loved it. I ordered a grilled shrimp salad while Peggy and Pete opted for the bacon burger with battered fries.

"This place has the same retro vibe," Pete said, "but the furnishings and menus have been updated since I last ate here. Very appealing upgrades. Even with so many dining options in the Village, this place is humming."

Peggy looked confused. "Uh-huh," she said noncommittally.

"Please excuse him," I said. "He's focused on business analysis these days."

"Right." Peggy crossed her arms and glared across the table. "Just so you know, the Wine Bar is not for sale. Both owners are happy about the business and its profits."

"They're telling employees that?" Pete asked.

"Yep. Last week they held a staff meeting at shift change to make sure everyone knew our jobs were secure."

"That place is a cash cow. One thing you should know about a lucrative business in a primo location."

"What's that?"

"Sharks circle when the living is easy. They want a piece of the action."

"The only shark I see is you," Peggy said.

"You're on target." He grinned. "I inquired about purchasing the Wine Bar. Every place is for sale, if the price is right."

"Thought so," Peggy said with a self-satisfied smirk. "You two should go into business together. With your hustle and her cooking, you'd make history."

"Holloway Catering is doing fine," I added quickly. "I'm happy with my laidback business style."

"Exactly." Pete signaled the waitress to refill our drinks. "We have different goals and strategies. River loves the pleasure of hands-on cooking and Southern hospitality. I plan to make money hand over fist."

"Speaking of different goals, let's change the subject." I leaned in. "What can you tell us about Curtis Marlin's relationship with Heavy D, Eggs, and Ty?"

"Curtis and the guys became tight in high school. Now that Curtis is dead, his crew is scattering. Ty's in jail for aggravated assault and can't bond out. Heavy D hasn't been seen in days, and according to gossip Eggs is hiding from the repo man."

"I want to know more about all three. Start with Eggs and the repo man."

Peggy nodded. "Eggs is late on child support for his two kids by two baby mamas. They garnished his wages at the store where he worked, but he quit that job a month ago. He's been crashing with friends in the interim, but his only asset is his fancy ride, hence the repo man is after him."

So much for his adamant claim that Curtis and his posse had a condom clause since high school. "How old are his kids?"

"His sons are twelve. Good athletes. Eggs used to flash their pictures at the Wine Bar and brag about their track wins."

The repo man angle prompted more questions as did two children by two different women. "Why'd Eggs quit his job?"

"Don't know."

"Hmm." Obviously Eggs had personal baggage unrelated to Curtis. Dodging child support wasn't in the same league as murder, but I couldn't eliminate Eggs as a suspect. Rats. "Why is DeAndre out of circulation?"

"Nobody knows."

I tried my last lifeline. "Did Ty's assault victim leave the hospital?"

Peggy shrugged. "Rumor has it Ty and this guy were in a love triangle."

"Who's the third party?" I asked.

"LaShaundra Delight."

"Oh, my." The clatter of people eating and talking faded. I hadn't heard that name in years. LaShaundra Delight made quite a name for herself singing as a drag queen in Savannah clubs for years. With her prowling stride and husky voice, people loved watching her entertain. Mystique surrounded the entertainer because of her involvement in a high profile murder case, then she abruptly retired. I'd heard LaShaundra moved here, but I'd never seen her on the island.

If Ty got involved with a drag queen and another man, perhaps those rumors about his sexual preference were true and Curtis used it against him. A former basketball star might shy away from being salacious front page news, though by getting in a brawl he'd done exactly that.

"Where does LaShaundra live?" I asked.

Peggy shrugged again.

"My guess is two people might know. Either Ty or his assault victim," Pete added with a pointed glance at our font of information.

"Johnsy Hubbard," Peggy said.

"I know Johnsy, or I did," I said. "Same school bus back in the day."

Our conversation drifted to non-case topics and lunch arrived. After we ate, we stood on the sidewalk outside, ready to part ways, and Peggy said, "I know you enjoy solving puzzles. Did you see today's paper?"

I shook my head. "It's been a busy morning. What's the news?"

"A single mom with six children wrote an editorial thanking her anonymous benefactor. A stranger paid off her overdue rent, electricity, and water bills. She had a couple of weeks in a row where she couldn't work because a virus went successively through her kids. She'd get one healthy and another one got sick. Anyway, she was two days away from living in the family minivan."

I caught Pete's eye. "That is interesting."

"Don't you wonder who's being so helpful?" Peggy asked. "Plus, an anonymous person paid Viv's bail. What's going on?"

"I wish I knew."

"The newspaper called it an Angel Donor. Who can spare so much money?"

Both of us looked at Pete.

He shrugged. "Not me."

Peggy made an empty-handed gesture. "Me either. Thanks for lunch. Catch you two later."

Pete and I strolled toward the pier. "I'm not the Angel Donor," he said. "I put my money to work. I don't give it away."

I stopped and faced him, a balmy sea breeze stirring my hair. "Suppose this is missing cash from the money laundering operation in my last case? Now two islanders have benefitted from the anonymous action of a stranger."

"Perhaps."

"If the Angel Donor has that missing drug cartel money, he'll operate in the shadows. Otherwise, the cartel would find him." What kind of person used stolen cartel money so openly? Wouldn't he or she fear reprisal? Not something I could investigate now, not when my brother and Viv's freedom were on the line. I tamped down my curiosity. "Interesting, but I have to stay focused on the case. Let's find LaShaundra Delight."

"I saw her in Savannah during her heyday. One hell of a show," Pete said.

"Imagine being her age and being attractive enough that grown men fight over you."

He kissed my brow. "I'd fight men for you, now, fifty years from now, and everything in between."

My heart warmed. "Good to know."

Chapter Twenty-Nine

I fumbled for the buzzing phone on the bedside table Tuesday at first light. My brother's name showed on the lighted display as I padded barefoot down the hall and answered.

"The cops found Curtis Marlin's car in the woods near that old battle memorial," Doug said without a hello or anything. "They asked me and Viv to come in. What should we do?"

"The car doesn't incriminate either of you." I halted in my kitchen, breathing in the familiar spices and willing my racing heart to slow down. Doug expected advice.

Common sense would be a good place to start. "If it were me, I'd comply with their request. If not, deputies may come for you in an unpleasant way."

"That's what I thought." Doug's voice broke. "I wish we'd never gone to Curtis's house that night."

"We can't change the past. I wish I knew who killed Curtis. At first I thought Heavy D, Eggs, and Ty set you two up. They have a history of being manipulated by Curtis, but no matter what I learn about them, I can't clear them from suspicion or prove them guilty."

"Yeah, Viv told me how Curtis messed with his friends. That's low."

"He told lies about his basketball pals and owed his poker friends megabucks. Both those suspect pools have strong motives for revenge. So why did the sheriff file murder charges against you and Viv instead? Either of you ever piss off the sheriff?"

"I've never met the man." He paused. "River, I'm scared. Viv cried herself to sleep last night. Nothing I said made it better. She's exhausted this morning. I don't want her alone in that interrogation room, and we can't afford to be out of work."

I sagged against the island counter, wishing I could be Doug's hero. "I share your frustration. The more I learn about Curtis, the more people I find with reason to hate him."

"Don't blame yourself. I made this mess. I didn't want to go to his place that night. Viv did. I caved because I wanted to be Mr. Agreeable. I should've trusted my instincts."

"You have good instincts," I said, meaning it.

"Having your support matters to me. Keep digging for the truth regardless of what happens today."

Doug had lost hope. I couldn't let him give up. "Remember you did nothing wrong. The cops must have new questions because of finding the car." I gazed out the window at my statue-still cat who returned my intense stare. "It's odd how my mind works. In the last case I worked, the cops confiscated the victim's vehicle right away to search for clues. When Curtis's car wasn't parked at his place, I mistakenly jumped to the conclusion that the cops had the car, same as they took the vehicle in that previous investigation. That'll teach me to assume. Did you know about the missing car?"

"I never thought about it. Three cars were outside his place when we arrived. I assumed one belonged to Curtis," Doug said.

"That's a point in your favor. Maybe they'll drop the charges against you today. You might come home from this chat a free man."

"Spoken like a true optimist." He gave a small laugh. "Actually, I'm calling for a pessimistic reason. Viv and I are driving my truck to the Law Enforcement Center. If they hold us, will you and Pete fetch my truck and keep it at your place?"

"Of course. Let me know how it goes."

The call ended and I puttered around the kitchen, making coffee and a pan of sweet rolls for breakfast. When I started frying bacon, Pete joined me in the kitchen and gave me a kiss. "It smells good in here."

"It's been quite a morning already." I shared the news about the car and Doug and Viv's summons to the sheriff's office. "I wanted Heavy D, Eggs, or Ty to be guilty either individually or as a group, so Viv and Doug would be cleared. Unfortunately, I can't rule those guys in or out. Detecting is tough work."

"You're too hard on yourself, love." Pete filled two mugs with coffee and handed me one. "You found the poker angle. The cops didn't know Curtis gambled or that he convinced Darry to go to Alaska. From all accounts, Darry loved exploring nature and partying. Being on an offshore fishing boat with a group of guys would be an irresistible lure for him. Keep doing what you're doing. You'll get there."

"I hope so. Doug and Viv's freedom is a ticking time bomb. I need a quick answer, and I don't have one."

"Allow me to distract you." His smile reached all the way to his gem-green eyes. "I believe you wanted to find LaShaundra this morning."

"Yes. Let's focus on something we can do."

~*~

The hospital coordinator I spoke to on the phone said Johnsy Hubbard, the guy that Ty had fought, had checked out, so I moved on to Plan B. I remembered where Johnsy lived in Windward Oaks. Armed with a bag of white chocolate macadamia nut cookies, Pete and I drove over there after breakfast. The Hubbard house sat at the end of Mermaid Lane, and it looked vastly different.

Two stories now, for one thing. The adjacent cottages were gone and the acreage transformed into showcase gardens. "Wow. I wonder if this is still Johnsy's place," I said to Pete. "Might as well ask since we're here."

A pleasant looking dark-skinned woman answered the doorbell. She looked older than me, but by how much I couldn't tell. Her abstract jewel-toned dress fit like second skin while a matching turban adorned her head. Mule-styled slippers in a deep turquoise graced her feet.

"Yes?" she asked in a voice that sounded like it belonged to a heavy smoker.

I noticed she kept the security chain on the door. "Good morning, ma'am. I'm River Holloway, and this is my fiancé Pete Merrick. We're looking for Johnsy Hubbard. He used to live here when I rode the school bus with him back in the day."

"Johnsy just got out of the hospital."

"I heard about the fight, and I brought him these homemade cookies."

The woman's eyes narrowed. "Wait here." She closed the door in our faces.

Pete's lips quirked. "His girlfriend?"

"She's beautiful."

He beamed. "Guess who?"

My eyes widened. "LaShaundra?"

He nodded. "In the flesh."

"Wow."

"She still has charisma. She must've made millions in her entertainment career."

"Wow," I said again, feeling like an idiot for repeating myself. On the street, I wouldn't have pegged her for a man. No way, no how.

The door opened wide. Instead of LaShaundra, a man with his arm in a sling greeted us. His scowl thinned his swollen lips. "Who the hell are you people and what do you want?"

I stated our names again. "We want to talk with you about Ty Carvell."

"Is this about the civil lawsuit I intend to file? Because I'm suing him to kingdom come and back."

"I believe Ty and his friends set my brother up to take a murder rap. I want to compare notes and learn what you know about him."

"I don't have time for this."

"Let them in," the woman called from the other room. "River Holloway is a caterer with five-star reviews. Those cookies will melt in my mouth."

Johnsy glared at me. "You're the scrawny white kid with pigtails, third row on the bus?"

I nodded and held my breath.

"All right. You can come in, but not for long. I don't want to waste my time talking about that loser."

He waved us through to a sunny den. Every area in the house looked like a spread from an interior design magazine. Plump cushions lined deep, inviting sofas, with glass sculptures and striking art adorning the walls. Rich colors everywhere added to the warmth of the rooms.

"You've met my girlfriend, Shea," he said, slumping into a leather recliner.

"Why yes, just now," I said, sounding like the fool again as Pete and I perched on the sofa, my cookies placed on the table between us. "Your home is beautiful."

"Oh, for goodness sake, Johnsy, they know who I am," LaShaundra said. "You'll have to forgive his dark mood. He hates Ty."

"Ty isn't my friend either, ma'am. He visited Curtis Marlin's house with Heavy D and Eggs the night my brother, Doug Holloway and his girlfriend, Viv Declan, stopped over. Curtis died that night, and the cops arrested Viv and Doug. They didn't kill him. Someone framed them."

LaShaundra chucked at that. "You think hotheaded Tyrone Carvell could be the mastermind of a frame job? He's too volatile. His friends used his temper as a weapon his entire life, winding him up and pointing him at their enemies."

Silence echoed in the room. "Excuse me? His friends? Not just Curtis?"

"DeAndre and Egbert are as guilty as that other snake." She shuddered. "Thank you, Jesus, that Mr. Evil got dead and won't bother us no more."

"What's this about?" I asked, turning to talk with her.

"Personal business," LaShaundra drawled. "I'm sure you understand."

"Where does Ty fit in?"

"He doesn't get along with Johnsy."

"Everyone is aware of that now."

"I saw you sing in Savannah," Pete said, "and you held the audience spellbound. Sorry to hear you've retired."

The chanteuse studied Pete for a long moment. "Life is not kind in equal measure. It's best to go out at the top of your game."

"Are you in a relationship with Ty?" I covered my mouth, appalled at my outburst.

"You might say that," LaShaundra said with a naughty grin as she reached for the cookies. "He's my baby brother."

Chapter Thirty

Pete and I were still marveling over our superstar encounter when Doug and Viv dropped by after lunch. "Everything good?" I asked.

"I am so done with cops. I need sugar, caffeine, and a shower," Viv said with a big yawn. "Then I need to sleep for a million years."

"You came to the right place for food." I fixed her a plate of sweet rolls and poured tumblers of sweet tea for everyone.

"I like." Viv dug into my offering and moaned in delight. "These are delish."

"Did either of you eat lunch?" I asked.

"We came straight here from the cop shop," Doug said. "I'll have what she's having."

"Okay, but I also have a fresh batch of shrimp paste. I can spread some on a croissant in a red hot minute."

"I want both," Doug said, "but the shrimp paste croissant first. Please."

"Me too," Viv said. "I'll eat another sweet roll after I have your shrimp paste."

"Can do." I set about fixing a meal for them. Pete circled and handed me things as I needed them, a topnotch assistant. "Thanks," I said with a kiss.

"Inquiring minds want to know what they grilled you about," I said, depositing the plates on the kitchen table.

"More of the same except for a few pointed questions about the car," Doug said. "At first they didn't believe me when I said I never knew what he drove. I told them the truth, same as I did the night they arrested me. There were three cars in the driveway when we arrived."

"Odd. What did he drive?"

"An older model Mustang. The three vehicles we saw belonged to Heavy D, Ty, and Eggs, as it turns out."

"That's even odder," I said. "Why would three friends drive separate vehicles, especially if they were drinking and spending the night together on the town?"

Doug had just taken a big bite of his croissant and held up a finger that he'd talk in a minute. Viv jumped in. "Exactly. I thought nothing of his Mustang not being at his place because it was always in the shop. The cops didn't mention his car was missing before. Now they think it's a Big Hairy Deal the Mustang turned up near Overlook Park."

"Did he loan it to a friend?"

"Unlikely. His friends were there."

"Did someone take the car without permission?"

Doug shrugged. "Sheriff Vargas alternated between my interrogation room and Viv's. I hope he saw how innocent we are. A deputy I'd never met before, Deputy Jenny Zillo, questioned me. She drilled me over and over."

"Deputy Z's aggressive, results-oriented, and bucking for a promotion to undersheriff." I studied my brother. "You look good for several hours of interrogation."

"I had nothing to hide, and I told the truth before. My answers lined up, so they booted me to the lobby after forty minutes. Viv, on the other hand, endured a longer session."

"Deputy Franklin was mean," Viv said with a sour face. "He asked the same question so many ways I got confused and upset. Then I cried. There were no tissues, and he said I couldn't leave the room. I sat there sniffing for hours."

I grimaced. "It sounds horrible."

Viv mirrored my expression. "Awful and exhausting. I feel bad Curtis is gone. He didn't deserve an agonizing death. He had moments when he acted like a gentleman, but few people saw

160

that side of him. It's like he'd been tempered in a hot fire and only showed his snarky, manipulative, world-hardened side."

"That's his real side," Doug added. "He only turned on the charm for the ladies but he couldn't maintain that degree of suaveness for long. Snarky and ugly defined him, hon. One of these days you'll admit it."

"No way," Viv said, leveling a finger at Doug. "I'm not a poor judge of character. I saw good in Curtis, that's why I dated him. He had inner demons, and I believe he orchestrated that scene of me finding him with another woman to encourage me to break up with him. I'd been clear I wanted a committed relationship, and he couldn't handle that."

Her insight rang true. "That's a spin I hadn't considered before. It explains how he avoided you and didn't talk to you for months. He hurt both of you but in his way, he still cared for you."

"His brand of caring felt like a knife in the heart." Viv said. "Doug and I connect on so many levels."

"I'm happy for you, and I hope you get the future you want. Our root question remains. Who killed Curtis?"

"I wish I knew," Doug said, "and I wish this was over. I have so many plans. Uh, speaking of the future, I have a request." He leaned forward to catch my eye. "I'm doing okay with small jobs and my one-man shop, with labor assistance from Anita and Viv, but I can't bid as a sub on bigger jobs, like total rehabs or new homes without heavy duty equipment. Can you help me with that?"

Pete stirred beside me. Under the table I put my hand on his leg, letting him know I had this. "What did you have in mind?"

"Could you loan me the money for the tools? I'd pay you back as I got the jobs. It'd probably be about twenty grand."

To my credit, my jaw didn't drop. "You want to discuss this in front of Pete and Viv?"

"Yeah. I need the money."

I took my time answering. "I want you to be successful, and steady work is a great start. Your business future looks bright."

Doug's gaze narrowed. "I sense a *but* coming."

"I don't have twenty grand to loan you, and even if I did, the terms you proposed aren't good. Interest, fees, and monthly payments go hand-in-hand with loans. Did you ask a bank for a loan?"

He looked away, color staining his cheeks. "Didn't think they'd take a chance on a one-time car thief turned handyman, not with this murder charge hanging over my head. I can't make regular payments because my work is erratic."

"Catering isn't a nine-to-five job either, but I make it work. Now's not the best time to expand. Clear your name first and build your clientele. Once you have a year of income production behind you, you'll know what level of loan payment you can afford."

Doug flopped back in his chair "That's too long."

"Welcome to the real world." Tough love tasted like sawdust, but I stood firm. No more of big Sis swooping in to save the day. "Let's change topics. I have news. You'll never believe who Pete and I met this morning."

Viv tapped her finger on the table. "Do tell."

I paused until I had their complete attention. "LaShaundra Delight."

My gaze panned from Viv to Doug, both of whom sat slack-jawed. "Not only did we meet her, we learned she's Ty's big brother."

Viv punched me in the arm. "Get out! Are you serious?"

I rubbed the sting from the not-so-playful tap. "Yep. Turns out Ty got mad at Johnsy Hubbard for taking advantage of his sibling. LaShaundra renovated and expanded the Hubbard homeplace by annexing two adjoining parcels to create an estate feel. In Windward Oaks, if you can believe that."

"I'm in shock that someone so famous lives on Shell Island. How come I've never seen LaShaundra Delight out clubbing?"

"If she wasn't in drag, would you recognize her?" Pete asked.

"Good point. Hmm. How is this related to the case?" Viv asked. "If Ty protected his sibling, is he more or less likely to be a killer?"

I'd wondered the same. "His temper exploded when he realized LaShaundra lavished money and attention on Johnsy."

Viv reached for a sweet roll. "Johnsy doesn't do relationships. Hook ups are more his speed."

"Perhaps Ty got mad because Johnsy cheated on his brother." That thought vanished and another chilling one took its place. "Any chance Johnsy dated Curtis?"

"Oh, my," Viv said. "If it's true, it gives Ty a stronger motive to kill Curtis, payback for hurting his brother."

"Curtis dated men?" I asked.

"Not sure but sometimes he fawned over guys in an over-the-top kind of way."

Pieces of the puzzle snugged together in my head. "I'll run this possible lead past the deputy."

Chapter Thirty-One

"Ty Carvell has an alibi for the night of the murder," Deputy Franklin reminded me when I phoned him later about the possible love triangle motive for Ty killing Curtis. "Stop wasting my time."

In the ensuing silence, the kitchen wall clock ticked off moments of my aggravation. I had to keep trying to break Ty's alibi. "The house party he and his friends went to? They drove separate cars. Ty could've slipped out for a few minutes and they'd never notice. Even so, I think the gin was poisoned before the party, so Sully's party doesn't alibi the guys for time before Curtis's death."

"It's possible Ty could've slipped out unnoticed. The individual vehicles are of interest to us. As for when the bottle got dosed, the simplest answer is usually the best. It happened when all five of them were with Curtis."

He was listening! I warmed to my theme. "I respectfully disagree. Alibis are needed from those suspects for the time frame prior to Viv and Doug's arrival at Curtis's house. That gin bottle could've been doctored with antifreeze much earlier. Heavy D, Eggs, or Ty could have swung by that house earlier that day or week and left the poisoned gin."

"Poison is traditionally a woman's method of killing. Using the same logic you laid out, Viv could've doctored the gin prior to the party."

Not the direction I wanted him to go. "Did you canvas liquor stores to see who purchased that brand of gin in the last month?"

"That bottle of Beefeater's Gin could've been purchased any time prior to the murder, and perhaps bought elsewhere."

"Curtis drank daily, and with gin and tonic his choice of alcoholic beverage, gin had a short shelf life at his place."

"The sheriff stands by his case against Viv Declan, who coincidentally is the only female suspect. Plus, she cracked under interrogation today."

"She got flustered and upset." My grip tightened on the phone. "You were tough on her."

"That's how we treat criminals."

This side of Deputy Franklin didn't mesh with the man I'd come to know. His uncaring attitude made me reach deeper. "Viv isn't a criminal. Neither is my brother."

Franklin sighed. "The sheriff may drop the accessory charges against Doug but don't hold your breath. Vargas refers to them as a modern day Bonnie and Clyde."

No way were they gangsters. "This is total garbage. I have no law enforcement training, but Sheriff Vargas should know better. Maybe I'll run for sheriff next time."

"That'd be a waste of your cooking talent, ma'am, since you belong in the kitchen, but I take your point. From your perspective it looks like we're sitting on evidence. Appearances can be deceiving. Solid policework takes time. We require a body of evidence for convictions."

His comment hit one of my personal tripwires. Sure I loved to cook and that happened in the kitchen. But if he thought all women should be in the kitchen, I had a problem with that. "What do you mean by that kitchen crack?"

"You one of those militant females that takes offense at every little thing a man says?"

"Only the sexist and discriminatory remarks," I said.

"Apologies, then. No offense intended. I complimented your cooking but it got lost in translation." He paused a moment. "The official investigation remains closed. The follow-up interviews today were prompted by the discovery of the victim's car and another antifreeze jug, nothing more."

"But you have new information that has bearing on the other suspects. The sheriff's laser focus on Viv and Doug is limited in scope and imagination. You can tell the sheriff I said that too."

I ended the call abruptly, so restless and irritated I had to do something. Pete went into town right after Viv and Doug left, so I was alone. Not entirely, I thought, glancing out the window to where Major sat on the hood of Mom's old Buick. The black cat wanted a ride, and that suited me fine.

I grabbed my keys, locked the house, and hustled over to the carport. Major bounded inside as soon as I opened the car door. I drove to the beach and sat on the warm sand watching the surf pound the shore. I'd left all the car windows open for the cat, but he made no effort to join me. Waves kept rolling, cresting, and breaking. I tried to work out the tension in my shoulders but beach therapy didn't work today. I couldn't stop thinking of how tightly the sheriff had locked on Viv and Doug as suspects. To help them, I needed a different approach, so I visited case locations.

The area where Curtis's abandoned car had appeared, Overlook Park, had a certain charm with centuries-old oaks forming a vast canopy and framing a stunning marsh view. This marsh once ran red with blood during a Revolutionary War battle between the English and Spanish. No blood or visitors here today.

"Nothing here to see," I told the cat as I circled the empty lot and motored over to Curtis's place. Nobody here and no crime scene tape. Hmm. Dare I see if I could get inside?

I turned the car off and stared at the porch, seeing the worn-out rockers. Wait. Something looked different. I got out of the car, with the cat darting around me. I glanced at the bare eaves. The dreamcatchers were missing.

Someone had been here. Curiosity drove me up the steps, where I knocked on the door. "Anybody home?"

No answer. I tried the knob. Locked. Might as well check the back door. I circled the house, found the door open. Literally, wide open. I called out again. "Hello?"

I breezed into the kitchen. Fingerprint dust coated the counters and exposed dishes. Chairs were upended, the garbage can on its side. Boy, would Grandma Talley be furious about this mess.

Major stayed with me as I walked through the shabby house. I didn't know what I sought, but mess and spindly furniture dominated the interior. The cat yowled. I turned quickly and stubbed my toe.

"Ouch!" I limped over to the denim clad sofa and sat. Major vaulted up to patrol the back of the sofa as I massaged the ache from my foot. "What are we missing here, kitty?"

The wall over the fireplace mantle looked oddly pristine. Correction, a rectangle over the mantle looked pristine. I limped over to examine the space. About three by two feet. Like a picture had been there.

A rustling from the kitchen got my attention. Major and I crept forward. The cat's back arched and he stayed beside me, hissing, as I stood on the threshold. Nothing looked different. No people or critters in sight, no wind to stir threadbare curtains. I drew in a shallow breath and waited. Then I heard it again. A scratching sound. Under the sink.

I crept forward, inching my way through the debris-filled floor, picking up a broom along the way. After what seemed like three eternities, I reached my goal. Standing to the side, I opened the cabinet door. A gray streak galloped out the door, feet barely touching the ground.

Raccoon.

I looked under the sink and found an empty bag of dog food. No dog and now no raccoon. "Coast is clear," I said to Major, who sniffed the cabinet.

I walked through the house one more time, hoping something looked out of place, but everything looked broken, and sad. Except for three ironed dress shirts, one pair of khaki slacks and a navy blazer, Curtis Marlin's clothes looked too worn for a secondhand store. I shook my head at the wasted life.

Major scampered out, and I locked the door behind us. Other than missing dreamcatchers and the faded imprint of a missing picture over the mantle, I didn't learn anything new.

Next, I drove straight to Sully's house, the place where Heavy D, Eggs, and Ty allegedly hung out after they left Curtis's house that fateful night.

The trip took ten minutes and included navigating a traffic circle, two stoplights, and busy roads. Sully lived in an older section of beach cottages. Once highly desired as two-blocks-from-the-beach rentals, these places had gone to seed. Three vehicles in various stages of disrepair dotted Sully's yard. With the houses here on small lots, I wondered if the neighbors complained about Sully's party that night.

Yet another question for Deputy Franklin.

Wait a minute. Were those dreamcatchers hanging on his porch? They were. Could it be coincidence? Another thought for Deputy Franklin.

I shifted into park and hurried over to knock on the door. Sully answered. I knew him on sight, though we'd never spoken to each other. He wore a Georgia Bulldogs red shirt that barely covered his paunch, black shorts, and flipflops.

"What?" Sully asked.

"Hi. I'm River Holloway and I was driving by—"

"I know who you are, lady."

"Right." I managed a smile. "I saw your dreamcatchers just now. I've been looking for something like that for my fiancé. I'm hoping you bought them locally."

"No."

"Oh, well, would you tell me where you bought them? They are just the right size."

"Got 'em from a friend. Don't know where he got them."

"I see." I nodded emphatically. "Sorry to have bothered you."

I walked away, thinking this stop had been a waste of time, except for Sully lying about the dreamcatchers he'd lifted from Curtis Marlin's front porch.

Sully's voice turned snide. "Your brother's going down for killing my friend. You're nuts if you think I'd help you. Now, get off my property or I'll call the cops."

~*~

Too stirred up to go home, I cruised the island, looping through Seashore Park and lapping the pier. Sully's animosity kept circling my brain, and I couldn't make it stop. I needed to be around people, so I headed for the one place I knew there'd be people and gossip. The post office.

Ola Mae and her sister were collecting a neighbor's mail. Seems like they lived at the post office these days. "You hear the news?" Ola Mae asked. "Four houses got hit last night."

"Dear me. Where?" I asked, my concern genuine.

"Windward Oaks. Three regular-sized homes and one palace in the back."

A palace? "The Hubbard place?"

"That's the one. John Boy must've come into some money."

"It's Johnsy and he did come into money, sort of."

"I heard he's playing house with someone. These kids today." Ola Mae tsked. "They think nothing of their legal situation until everything goes south. Money can't make you happy, but it makes the world turn."

Technically, Pete and I fell in the playing house category but we were engaged. I guess that gave me a pass in her eyes. "That's their business," I added before she started talking about the good old days of monogamy and alienated everyone in the post office. "Did the thief steal food again?"

"Yes. It's the darnedest thing. Apparently he prefers canned goods and bakery items."

Made sense to me. The canned goods were precooked, the bakery items a treat. "He has a sweet tooth."

"Something like that," Ola Mae grumbled. "He can't get in our place. Our handyman installed new locks a few days ago. Valerie and I are protected."

The wink she sent my way made me think she had guns at the ready. I didn't have the heart to tell her that most folks who knew her rumored "Black Widow" history wouldn't spend a second under her roof, much less steal a crumb of her food.

"Good to know," I said.

"I'm surprised he hasn't hit your place," Valerie chirped. "He could live for weeks or months on whatever's in your freezer. Course, you'd probably ruin him for canned goods."

I nodded toward the black cat sitting on the hood of Mom's old Buick. "I have a watch cat. The thief probably can't get past Major. He's always on duty."

"That cat sure took a shine to you," Ola Mae allowed.

"My feral cat allows me to pet him now and a few times he's jumped in my lap. Sometimes he sits on Mom's Buick and won't budge until we take a car ride."

"You're a cat charmer, dear," Valerie said, echoing Pete's assessment. She patted my arm before she turned to her sister. "I'll wait in the car. My feet hurt today."

Ola Mae watched Valerie shuffle off. "I'm worried about her. She's losing ground."

"What does the doctor say?"

"Neither of us has seen a doctor our whole lives."

Her answer stunned me. "Not even for a flu shot or an annual physical?"

"Don't need that stuff. If you fight germs naturally, you build up immunity."

"I see." I held my tongue because Ola Mae wouldn't change her mind. "Well, I should be going."

Ola Mae nodded. "Keep your doors locked, your guns handy."

~*~

Pete returned home at suppertime, his face wreathed in smiles. "I got the job."

I wiped my hands on a dishtowel and turned the burners off before turning around. "Oh?"

"Yeah. It isn't much of a managerial job, but I'll learn the ins and outs of the place. This birds-eye view is step one in implementing my master plan."

He'd been making noises about his business plan, but I'd not paid as close attention as I should've. "The ice cream place?"

"Yes. I'm the new manager of Island Creamery."

"Wow. I'm delighted you got the job. You love that place."

"I know, right? It's perfect." He kissed me and then popped open a cold beer. "That's good."

"Tell me more."

"Real estate is a limited resource on an island. Shell Island is poised on the verge of change. A generation of people are retiring and want the good life. They'll come here. I recognize the pattern of growth. That entire shopping area near the pier will be golden with the right oversight."

Knowing how he thought led me to an incredible conclusion. "You're buying the entire Village?"

"I plan to buy the Island Creamery, and I'll create consortiums to buy the rest as they come on the market. It'll be fantastic."

"Wow. Your plan is off to a great start. Awesome. Good for you."

"This will be great for us."

During dinner, I heard more about his dream for the Village. I understood Pete's bone-deep passion for business because I felt the same way about Holloway Catering and my family. Pete and Doug were my family. I'd do anything to protect them.

By contrast, Curtis Marlin hurt people deliberately. Now his death threatened my family. Though the cops believed Viv and Doug poisoned Curtis, my leads circled back to those former basketball stars, Heavy D, Ty, and Eggs.

They knew more than they were telling.

Chapter Thirty-Two

"River."

I turned from the pan of Canadian bacon on the stove. Pete's dour expression implied he had a killer toothache. "What's wrong?"

"I reviewed last night's security footage." He set his laptop on the kitchen table and gestured toward it. "Someone *is* watching the house."

My hand covered my heart. "This sounds dumb, but I hoped the cameras would validate an overactive imagination and prove we were safe here in the woods. This is terrible news. Are you sure?"

"Absolutely sure a man stood in the woods watching this house yesterday. There are several images of him."

"Who is it?"

Pete shook his head. "I don't know. Perhaps you'll recognize him."

I crossed the kitchen to his computer but Pete gestured to the stove.

"Oh, dear. I'm rattled." I moved the sizzling pan and cut off the gas.

Moments later, we viewed grainy black-and-white photos. The man wore a dark ball cap pulled low over his face, a black long-sleeved t-shirt, jeans, and dark shoes. Each frame captured a side of his face or him walking away from the camera. Wisps of hair feathered over his ears.

"He needs a haircut," I said on the second viewing of the still shots. "He has a solid build and appears muscle-bound from lifting weights."

"Not someone we want to meet in a dark alley," Pete said.

I stared at the image in vain. "I don't recognize him. I can't tell his height, eye color, or hair color. His face shape is round, and there's no facial hair."

"I duck under that branch that he walked under, but you don't need to at your shorter height. He's probably between five-six and five-ten."

"No glasses or backpack."

"He doesn't fit the description of a spindly food thief. But if it is the food burglar, he could've stashed his pack near the road or left it wherever he's staying."

"You know this how?"

Pete shrugged. "It's what I would've done. That way, his stuff would stay safe."

I didn't care who spied on me. I just wanted him gone. "I'm calling my deputy friend."

~*~

"You eat like this every morning?" Deputy Franklin asked as he pushed back from his empty plate. "Those are the best sweet rolls I've ever tasted."

"I like cooking." I carried the dishes to the sink. I'd added omelets to our menu when he said he'd be right over.

"Lucky dog," I heard him say. Pete replied in a similar low voice and both men laughed.

"Let's show him those images now," I said, joining them in the dining room.

We gathered around Pete's laptop as he scrolled through the snapshots.

"Doesn't match the description of the food thief," Franklin said. "I don't recognize him. You're sure he didn't get inside?"

"The system Pete installed would've picked up an intruder."

"Good job catching him in the shrubs. How'd you get the right camera angle?"

"Easy," Pete said. "Few vantage points offered cover. I set up motion sensitive cameras on those areas, along with doorbell cameras that focus on the front and back entries. This guy never approached the house."

Franklin asked for a replay. "Looks like a Caucasian male, husky build, and shoulder-length hair."

Pete gave him his height assessment rationale.

Franklin listened attentively and jotted down the data. "Make me a copy of these images. Y'all ever think about getting a dog?"

"We've got Major," I said. "He lets us know when something's amiss."

Franklin gazed at Pete.

"The stray cat," he said, handing a flash drive to the deputy. "He's smart, but I agree. A dog would be better."

"A dog would be into everything and animals aren't allowed in commercial kitchens," I said. "Don't get me started on the tribulations of puppy training."

Pete held Franklin's eye. "We'll consider getting a dog."

"Check the pound for owner surrenders," Franklin said. "Often, perfectly good pets land there when their owners move to a nursing home."

My resolve melted at the thought of older abandoned animals needing a home. "I don't know the first thing about taking care of dogs."

"I do," Pete said. "What about retired police dogs that need rehoming?"

Franklin appeared surprised by the question. "I can ask around."

"Thanks. If we go the dog route, I want one that's had training."

I liked animals on the smaller side, Major's size. However, dog shopping had no place on today's to-do list.

"Where do we stand on the investigation?" I asked the deputy.

"The burglar is at large. As for the Marlin homicide, the department is not actively investigating that case."

Rats. "Is Ty Carvell still in jail?"

He hesitated, then shook his head. "Out on bond."

"I'd hoped you'd question him about his last days with Curtis. We never knew Curtis's state of mind. He might've put the antifreeze in the gin."

"I've only read one case in the literature when someone took antifreeze on purpose. It's a painful death. Death by antifreeze is drawn out and agonizing. This was homicide, and the killer wanted Curtis to suffer."

"Curtis treated friend and foe with disdain, a fact borne out by dismal attendance at his funeral. Only a few hardy souls and his great uncle came."

Franklin shifted in his seat. "Funny you mentioned the uncle. The funeral home contacted us when his check for the funeral bounced. Left the ashes there too."

"Curtis's remains are at the funeral parlor?"

"He'll stay there for now, which is best for all involved." Franklin stared at me for a few moments. "There's a new wrinkle in the case. Viv is the beneficiary of Curtis Marlin's life insurance policy, which further cements her guilt in the sheriff's mind. It isn't much money, a whole life policy for ten grand someone bought years ago in better times."

IIow odd. Viv profited financially from his death. "Does she know?"

"Doesn't matter. The insurance company won't pay since she killed him."

"She allegedly killed him." I stared at the painting on the wall. The beach scene faded as my thoughts churned. Franklin had claimed the Marlin case was closed, but despite this, he'd listened to my leads all along. I had to continue looking into the other suspects. "I drove to Curtis Marlin's house yesterday to time the drive to Sully's. In the process, I noticed the dreamcatchers from Curtis's porch were missing and that Sully's porch has identical dreamcatchers. Anyway, the run from Curtis's house to Sully's house took ten minutes. At night, it would be faster. No one at the party would notice someone's absence for twenty minutes."

"Good to know," Franklin said agreeably, "but you made a valid point about the poison being in the bottle before all five of them met at the house." When I started to speak, he raised a cautionary hand. "However, that doesn't clear your friend or

175

brother. If anything, it gives them a broader window to sabotage his booze."

"What about the dreamcatchers?"

"I can ask Sully where he got them, but if they belonged to Curtis we can't prove it. In any event, they have no bearing on the murder."

"Huh." The dreamcatchers I saw at both homes looked like tourist trinkets, definitely not valuable items. "What if a painting is missing from the house? I noticed a white rectangle on the wall above the fireplace mantle. Art theft might be a motive."

"I can check into it, but truthfully, there were several such rectangles on the walls. It looked to me like Curtis sold anything he could to survive."

Heat steamed up my collar. So much for my detecting skills. I met the deputy's level gaze. "You ever feel like you're shouting in the wind? That no matter what you do it isn't enough?"

He nodded. "Evil stays on the attack. Once we close a case, another one opens. People do terrible things to each other, and homicides are often committed by someone the victim knows, someone you wouldn't consider a killer." He rose. "Thanks for breakfast and the burglar pics. I'll keep you posted."

Pete helped me with the dishes, then checked his phone calendar. "It's Wednesday. Let me check with Father Ben to confirm our appointment at four."

While he did that, I sorted laundry. "Are you available for counseling right now?" Pete asked from the doorway. "Father Ben has another conflict in late afternoon, but he's clear before then."

"Sure."

~*~

Father Ben welcomed us into his study. He placed a printed list on his lap as we took seats across from him and he then opened with a prayer.

The next two hours passed in a blur of questions about our spiritual journey, love, commitment, family, and finances. Pete squirmed when Father Ben grilled him about the North Merrick debacle in California and the former rift in our relationship. I fielded other uncomfortable questions about setting priorities with regard to work and family.

Pete and I walked out of the session shell-shocked. "Very intense," he said on the short drive home. "I didn't expect such pointed questions. I thought it would be a pat on the back and selecting the service readings."

I waved the form Father Ben handed me on the way out. "That's our homework." I shot him an anxious glance. "You want to revisit anything we just said?"

"Give me a second," Pete said as we neared the turn off for our place. "It's hard to be dialed all the way into this conversation and drive."

A few moments later, he parked the truck and took my hand. "I'm certain that I love you and that I'll take care of you. I've always known we were meant to be together, and I'm sorry for nearly breaking us when I went to California. I learned my lesson and thank goodness you forgave me when I came to my senses."

Talking about last year made me sad that I didn't push harder for our relationship at the time. "You've always been the one for me, love, and I won't lie. It felt awful when we drifted apart. I never want to do that again. On the other hand, I'm equally guilty of letting work and investigating absorb my time. We are two independent people. What if we put our individual needs first after we're married?"

"Our independence is a strength, same as our togetherness is a strength. We'll find the right blend. It would be great if no relationship hiccups occurred going forward, but life isn't a polished book like that. There are strikeouts and edits and revisions. I want you by my side as we face life together. I am 100 percent committed to you, never doubt that again."

"I don't doubt you," I said as the tide of marriage concerns ebbed. "Yes. We're stronger together."

Chapter Thirty-Three

What with ordering the food for Dylan Barresi's Friday afternoon event, I didn't leave to tell Viv about the life insurance policy until five. Pete messaged me that he had to close tonight. His delayed arrival at home meant we'd eat a late dinner after eight, so I didn't need to rush my visit with Viv.

Doug dozed on the sofa when Viv let me in. "What's up with Mr. Sleepyhead?" I asked as I followed her to the kitchen.

"Long couple of days." Viv rustled up two glasses of water, and we sat at the table. "Today we finished a home repair job for a bridge lady. Doug did the hard part, interfacing with the client. I painted, a much easier task."

"How's that going for you?"

"Good, I think." Viv brushed a few blonde strands of hair behind an ear. "I love seeing tangible results. When you paint walls, you get tired, but you made something better."

"I hear you. I get satisfaction from creating delicious food, and I enjoy seeing happy smiles after a meal." I traced a finger around the rim of my water glass. "I have news related to the homicide investigation." I told her about burglar pics, the life insurance policy, and the missing dreamcatchers.

"I'll be." Viv's face wreathed in smiles. "Curtis named me his beneficiary? How sweet."

Her surprise rang true, and I breathed easier. "Unfortunately, it strengthens your motive to kill him. I need more information about Curtis and the guys. What secrets did Curtis have?"

178

"Curtis didn't confide in me, but a time came when he was adamant about locking his doors. After he locked himself out three times, I suggested he hide a key in the yard. He used the same fake-rock-key-hider that we both use, and presto, problem solved. He seemed less paranoid after that."

"First I've heard about problems with locked doors. What did he fear?"

"He didn't say, but he belittled, demeaned, and conned money out of everyone in his vicinity."

"I need specifics. Did anyone threaten him when y'all were together?"

"No, but he never admitted any deficiency to me. His personal firewalls kept me at arm's length. When he cheated on me, I dumped him. Given that I walked out, I'm shocked my name is on his life insurance policy."

"Sounds like Curtis never accepted the risk of being vulnerable."

Viv gazed at the wall. "I told him I loved him, but he never said the words. Not once. His cutting remarks took a toll on my confidence and emotions."

"For what it's worth, I believe he cared in his own way. Heavy D said he'd drink himself into a stupor when you left the bar with any guy."

Viv's mouth dropped. "Why didn't Curtis say something?"

"Maybe he couldn't. When Pete moved to California, he thought he protected me by concealing his struggles. I felt broken the entire time, like a huge part of me went missing. Maybe Curtis, like Pete, thought he knew best."

A storm of emotions crossed Viv's face. "Then why'd he sleep with another woman in our bed knowing I came home at that time every day? If he loved me, he shouldn't have sabotaged our relationship."

I raised my hands in surrender mode. "Perhaps he wanted better for you long-term, and he gave you an out. Maybe he loved you enough to let you go."

Tears spilled down Viv's cheeks. "Don't mess with my head. Not now. He was a jerk."

"Agreed. A decent person wouldn't act that way."

"When I think of the angry energy I burned afterward, I get steamed all over again. Don't get me wrong. I'm glad we broke up. I'm in a better relationship now. Curtis exhausted me."

"You and Doug are good for each other." I sought another way to focus this conversation on Curtis again. "Let's talk money. How did Curtis handle his bills?"

She snorted and shook her head. "He tossed them out unopened. Wait. That's not entirely true. In the beginning he had income from Grandma Talley's estate and paid his bills, but that didn't last long."

Viv gazed up for a moment, then looked away. "No judgements, please. For a few months I paid his bills because I felt sorry for him. He never offered to repay me. It sounds naïve in retrospect. Guess on some level I thought I could buy a supercool boyfriend."

She stopped for a few deep breaths. I waited and when she didn't speak and enough time had passed, I tried another tack on the same topic. "What about paintings on the wall? I noticed there used to be a large framed picture over the fireplace."

"Grandma Talley is missing? Curtis loved that oil portrait."

"Did he sell it?"

"No. Said he'd rather starve than part with it." She fell silent for a few moments. "If it's gone, perhaps that relative from Alabama took it for sentimental reasons."

"Could be." I had to find a new lead. "What about employment? I know about his restaurant and bar jobs. Did Curtis work at the mill or elsewhere?"

"Not that I know of. He talked about Alaska constantly. Thought that trip would land him on easy street. He went after we broke up, and nothing changed when he returned. Same car, same clothes, same rundown house."

Hmm. The much-hyped trip turned out to be a bust. "I wish I knew more about his time in Alaska."

"I wish he'd never talked my brother into going there."

"Nothing yet on Darry's whereabouts?"

"No one's seen him there, and he's not here. They checked Alaska morgues and hospitals. No sign of him."

More dead ends. "Did you call Darry's boss in Alaska?"

"Never knew his name. Darry supplied few details about his trip. He didn't know anyone in Alaska, and while he was scratching his traveling and partying itches, he could've easily trusted the wrong people. I'm worried he got into something illegal, and now he's locked in prison for smuggling guns or drugs."

Illegal activities? Darry gave his mother fits with DUIs in high school and drunken beach trips in Florida. He'd once been caught on camera when kids dared him to steal a teacher's car during class. He'd spent many after school hours in detention and in community service for that mistake. While Viv met challenges head on, her brother had a history of self-indulgence and poor judgement.

I more than understood Viv's anguish. For many years I'd feared my brother might not outgrow his free-ride mentality. Finally though, Doug had turned his life around. Viv's brother was still a question mark in the maturity column, and his sister, my friend, had valid concerns about her brother's safety. "Should we fly there and look for him?"

"I can't go anywhere because of my legal situation. What a mess. For so long, Darry's been like a cat with nine lives, landing on his feet after every hare-brained stunt." Viv sighed deeply. "Considering the length of time he's been out of touch, I know something's truly wrong. Someone should've remembered seeing him. A Southern drawl like Darry's would stick out in Alaska. He's either dead, has amnesia, or switched identities."

A sobering trifecta. I studied my friend in a new light. "You've given this some thought."

Viv stared into her water glass like it held the secrets of the deep. "Darry and Anita have had personal differences through the years but they worked them out. He loves Anita and his kids. He wouldn't willingly abandon them. He wanted extra money and another fine adventure."

"Why?"

"He said he wanted money for the kids' college fund."

I chewed on that for a moment. "It feels like we're missing something. Alaska is a beautiful but harsh environment. What really drove Mr. Good-time Curtis to Alaska and then persuaded Darry to follow in his footsteps?"

"It's sad that I barely knew Curtis, and it appears I barely knew my brother." Viv chewed her fingernail. "One shallow relationship is easy to dismiss, but two is a pattern. I went through the motions of life for years. I see that now."

My phone rang. "Excuse me." I pulled the mobile phone out of my bag to mute it and saw Geneva Walker's name.

"Take the call," Viv said, rising. "I'll check on Doug in the other room."

I listened to a fast-talking Geneva. She wanted Holloway Catering under retainer for specialty events at Ocean Crest Plaza, and more to the point, she needed me for an event this Sunday evening.

"This isn't the first time we've had double bookings," Geneva explained. "Two groups booked our banquet service at the hotel. Previously, we jockeyed things around with early and late sittings for dinner. Otherwise our staff is overtaxed. Neither party will change their time."

"You could hire more staff," I offered.

"Not realistic. These double bookings occur a few times a month. I can't justify the expense of double kitchen staff right now and your catering service is a perfect alternative. You cook offsite, so there are no in-house kitchen conflicts. You'd have access to our staging kitchen adjacent to the banquet room. We'll prep the tables and clean up. All you do is provide the prepared meal for our smaller function."

"I'm interested," I said, making a snap decision. "I have availability this weekend if we can come to terms."

"I'll email you a contract right now," Geneva said. "We're talking fifty women and a pre-set menu. The price I'll pay you for Sunday is firm."

The rosy glow of a contract faded. "I appreciate the offer, but I have to price the job before I agree to anything."

"Our clients paid when they booked their event package at the hotel. If what I'm offering doesn't suit you, say so and I'll hire someone else."

Hopefully she'd charged her clients enough money up front. "I'll review the contract and get back to you, Geneva. I can't operate at a loss."

"I've got two dozen more events already double booked."

My mental calculator whirred. Eight months left in the year and two dozen events came to about three events a month. Having a regular client like the hotel would be a godsend financially, and Geneva wouldn't stiff me on the payments.

"I'll review the terms tonight and contact you in the morning." I ended the call, ramifications tumbling in my head. Geneva Walker's approval went a long way on the island.

So did her disapproval.

Chapter Thirty-Four

My plan to rush home to read that contract had a fatal flaw. A knife hilt protruded from my front tire. Outrage with a strong backdraft of fear careened through my body. I glanced around Viv's modest apartment complex, hoping to catch someone watching me. Plenty of car traffic in the lot, but no one made eye contact. I scanned the area for security cameras. No help there either.

Who did this? I wanted to scream in frustration, but I'd probably get arrested for disturbing the peace. I wrestled my emotions under control and regrouped. I needed to go home and to do that I needed four inflated tires. I could change a tire, so I approached the rear-mounted spare.

Another utility knife stuck out of that tire.

Two knives was too many for me. I whirled and sprinted for the safety of Viv's apartment building. Deputy Franklin answered my first call for help, Pete my second. My fiancé arrived first.

He drew me into his arms with an iron grip. "You're okay?"

I melted against him, shaking with emotion, needing the comfort he offered. "I'm fine. But somebody hates my tires."

"Tires can be replaced, but we're documenting this vandalism with a police report."

When Deputy Franklin arrived, I stood beside Pete and gave the cop the short version of the tale. "You notice anyone suspicious?" he asked.

"No. After I saw the first knife, I scanned the lot. No one paid me or my van any attention. The second knife in the tire spooked me. I raced inside until help arrived."

"I checked on my way over and there's a baseline of petty crimes in this neighborhood. This is the first tire slashing incident, so it doesn't follow the pattern. You in an argument with anyone?"

I rubbed my arms, willing my jumpy stomach to settle. "The cops. You arrested my brother for a crime he didn't commit."

Franklin paused. "Noticed you didn't mention Viv Declan just now."

"She's innocent too. An oversight on my part."

The deputy snapped photos of the knives in my tires, put on gloves, and bagged the knives as evidence. He surveyed the lot and pulled me aside. "This sabotage doesn't feel like a cop. By nature, we're direct people. If a cop came after you, you'd know it."

Pete watched me intently and I made a hand motion to let him know I could do this. "Are cops spying on me?' I asked Deputy Franklin. "If so, you know who damaged my tires."

"You aren't under surveillance. The obvious source of a potential dispute is the Curtis Marlin case. Someone resents you nosing around."

"Someone better get over themselves. I'm doing this for my brother. He's innocent."

"River, stop for a moment. This type of anger tends to escalate." He stared pointedly at me. "You could be next."

"Is this the guy spying on my house? Did you ID him?"

"No ID yet. This warning is serious. Treat it as such."

I barred my arms across my chest and glared at him. "I am taking it seriously. I reported the threat. Do your job and find this creep."

"I'm advising you to leave investigating to the pros."

"We're deadlocked because Doug and Viv didn't murder Curtis. I can't stop investigating. You wouldn't either if your brother got slapped with a murder charge."

A tow truck arrived while we talked and it hauled my van away. Franklin left with a stern admonition to my fiancé to "keep an eye on her."

Pete drove us home in strained silence. I mulled over the deputy's remarks, understanding his message but knowing just as strongly that I couldn't stop asking questions now. My brother needed help.

"Are you headed back to work?" I asked.

Pete kept his gaze on the road. "Adele will close. I'm not leaving you alone tonight. This case is heating up."

"Something like that."

"Did you find a new lead?"

"I quizzed Viv about Curtis and got nowhere. Viv didn't know about inheriting Curtis's life insurance. Turns out, Viv and Curtis had lousier communication skills than we did. Worse, Curtis never got over Viv."

"That's unfortunate as it sets up a love triangle motive for Doug to kill Curtis."

I stared at my fisted hands. "Doug didn't do it."

We motored through a congested area. "So Viv and Doug are a solid couple now?" he asked.

"Seems that way. She's his assistant handyman, and they share a bank account."

"If not for the murder charge, I'd say that sounds promising."

"Something else came up. Viv and I wonder why the two Alaska trips are shrouded in mystery."

"Curtis traveled there twice?"

"He went once and Viv's brother went once. Now Curtis is dead and Darry is missing."

"Never looked at the case that way before. Perhaps there's more to this Alaska business."

"Maybe that's why we can't make anything stick to Heavy D, Ty, or Eggs. The murder came from a different direction."

"We have no proof Alaskan activities or a vengeful friend caused Curtis's death. We're striking out everywhere."

"I hate feeling stymied."

Pete patted my leg. "You'll figure it out. You always do."

"Speaking of figuring, Geneva Walker called. She wants Holloway Catering under contract for her overflow events. She emailed a contract and I have to respond by morning because the first event is this Sunday."

When Pete pulled into the drive, he parked behind Mom's old Buick. "I'll review the contract terms, if you like."

My spirits lifted. "I like."

"All right then. Contract review and dinner."

"And tire repair. I need my van for transportation tomorrow."

"My car guy will replace your tires and save an old tire for your new spare."

"Can't we patch them? New tires are expensive."

He shrugged. "You need tires. And if you book the hotel overflow gig, you'll have money in the bank. But we should take a note from Viv and Doug and merge our bank accounts. I've got a steady job now, and investment funds in North Merrick are on the way."

"Will merging accounts complicate tax time?"

"Possibly. We'll meet with an accountant and make an informed choice about our finances, since our overall financial picture with two businesses is more complex than Doug and Viv's. As for the other issue, it's my choice to replace the tires, so I'll cover the expense."

"If you're sure."

"I am."

We exited the truck and Major the cat darted over to greet me, mewing loudly. I hoped his distress had to do with a late supper. I couldn't take one more thing going haywire today. Everything looked fine though, the house was locked, no one lurked in the bushes.

As I pulled dinner together, my thoughts settled. Someone wanted me to stop investigating. I was asking the right questions now.

Chapter Thirty-Five

The financial terms of Geneva Walker's contract looked generous until I read the fine print. At Pete's advice, I changed meal pricing terms to include fair market prices of fresh food. I didn't like the caveats that my staff had to wear the hotel server uniform and that I couldn't promote my catering business.

I hand-delivered the amended contract to her at nine the next morning, while Pete waited in the lobby. Despite the plush carpet and the dainty feminine desk, the absolute silence within the slate gray walls made me feel like I sat in the principal's office. Geneva's cloying perfume weighed me down as did the piercing looks she shot my way over the top of her reading glasses.

I rose in protest when Geneva began lining out my changes. "This is a standard contract," she said. "There's no room for negotiation."

It felt like I stood in plough mud and couldn't break free. Thank goodness I didn't sign that document. This woman may be a force, but she wouldn't bully me. "Food prices vary by season," I stated, matching her crisp tone. "I can't commit to a flat rate for food."

"Nonsense. We'll tag your food order onto our commercial kitchen's food order. That will lend stability to your costs. I'll clear it with our chef."

It would be nice to take advantage of their bulk pricing. "When are those orders made?"

"We have a standing order every week. Our head chef oversees it personally."

"Were Sunday's raw ingredients included in your regular order? Or can that order be placed today?"

Geneva pursed her lips. "Let me check with our head chef. Have a seat."

I eased into the delicate guest chair across from her and waited as she made the call. Her face gave nothing away during the brief conversation. All the while, my feelings waffled wildly. Did I want the head chef to order my food? I'd have to rely on them getting all the ingredients right and then they'd have to be separate from the hotel order. If even one thing went wrong in the acquisition chain, I'd be screwed.

Geneva fixed me with a glare. "Chef Lorraine can't accommodate this food order on short notice without incurring a rush fee from our usual vendor. You must source the menu items locally. This particular second banquet is a last minute favor I booked yesterday for a personal friend."

So I had to supply the food for her menu in a hurry. I had to wear a hotel uniform, and I couldn't promote Holloway Catering. I didn't like these terms.

I rose and shouldered my purse. "No, thank you. I decline the opportunity to cater your extra banquets. I appreciate your consideration, but this doesn't work for me."

"You're leaving?" she asked.

"I am."

"But you can't expect me to find someone on such short notice."

"Last night you agreed to hear my response this morning. I arrived promptly at nine."

"I thought you'd take the deal."

"You're better off with a caterer who accepts your terms. I prefer working for myself."

"I need you on this job."

"Your terms favor the hotel. I'm not even assured of breaking even the way you wrote that contract. I can't commit to terms like these, especially one that demands booking preference over my schedule. I already have events booked on my calendar. I might reconsider if we narrow the scope to one event."

"Please reconsider," Geneva said. "You must sign a contract before you leave this room."

I waved off her request. "We're deadlocked. You won't budge. I have other commitments."

"Forget the deal for the year. Just sign a contract for Sunday night."

Pete said she might go for a short-term fix. I exhaled a long breath. "I'm listening."

"I can't negotiate on the hotel uniforms, but I'll pay you cost plus 15 percent."

This job might pan out after all. I could do steely gazes too. "If you sign my contract and up the plus to 20 percent, we have a deal."

Geneva's mouth moved but no sound emerged. She regarded me steadily. "I didn't expect this from you, River Holloway. You have me over a barrel."

Must be the free cookies that gave the impression I was a softy. "Those are my terms."

Silence pulsed like jellyfish tentacles.

"All right," Geneva said. "You win."

I pulled a pre-priced contract from my bag, itemized to the max, clearly specifying who provided what. "Because I knew the number of guests, the menu, and didn't need to rent dishes, I itemized the contract last night. I need a 40 percent deposit before I leave this room."

Geneva signed her name without reading a single word and printed out a check. "Done."

~*~

I crowed with delight as Pete drove me to the tire shop. "You did it," he said. "You slayed the dragon."

"I wouldn't have had the nerve without your help last night. I've never had so many details in a contract before. And best of all, I'm not locked in for weeks on end. We signed just for the single event."

"I'm proud of you for sticking to your guns."

"Will she consider me for the other events after this? Or am I too much trouble?"

Pete tapped his fingers on the steering wheel. "I bet you anything, she'll try another caterer first, but the quality won't compare. She'll be barking at your door again."

"I want to grow my business, so I'm grateful for the booking. She's lucky I had an opening."

"I'm happy for you, but it's wise to go slow in these situations. With this event, you can observe the hotel's work environment. If it doesn't suit you, you have your answer for future events."

"I hope it works out."

An hour later I had most of my Sunday ingredients ordered from my bulk food supplier. I headed to my favorite fresh market on the mainland for the rest of the items I needed when Viv phoned. Her news startled me. I made a U-turn on the causeway and headed directly to her place.

Darry was showering at Viv's apartment. He'd come home.

~*~

With Pete at Island Creamery and Doug estimating a new job, it would just be me, Viv, and Darry at her place. After my tire vandalism yesterday in her parking lot, I hesitated to park at the apartment complex, but I felt lucky to find a spot close to the building, and close enough that if vandalism occurred it would be on the building security camera. The Alaska connection puzzled me. I needed to know when Darry returned and why he'd been off the grid.

I hurried inside to Viv's second-story apartment, hugging her as she welcomed me. "Is he all right?" I whispered.

A door opened down the hall and Viv gestured that way. "See for yourself."

A haggard man ambled out of Viv's bathroom, wet hair slicked behind his ears. I recognized the baggy shorts and t-shirt I'd bought for Doug. But I wouldn't have known Darry Declan if I passed him on the street. He'd shed at least fifty pounds and the cheeks on his sallow face pinched in. I wished I had cookies in my van to offer him.

I smiled at him. "Welcome home, Darry. We've been worried about you."

"Good to be home," Darry mumbled as he tightened the shorts drawstring. "Good to know someone cares about me."

"I never stopped caring for you," Viv said. "I got mad because you didn't call your wife and kids. Or me. But I never stopped loving you. You're my brother."

"Everything went wrong." He shuddered. "Alaska went south from the get-go."

"Let's sit at the table," Viv said. "I'll fetch some tea. You want another sandwich, Darry?"

He waved off her offer. "I'm good. I don't eat much anymore."

I followed them to the kitchen, questions brimming in my head.

While Viv filled beer glasses with tea, I dragged an extra chair into the kitchen. I couldn't wait to hear Darry's story. Was there a chance the Alaska connection related to Doug and Viv's sad plight? "Tell us what happened, Darry."

"I made the biggest mistake of my life." His dull eyes heated as he glanced around the room, reminding me of a trapped animal. "Curtis lied to me about the excellent adventure waiting for me in Alaska. There was no 'job' waiting for me, just thugs who shanghaied me onto a fishing boat. My captors stole my phone and my suitcase. I wore the same clothes for weeks at a time and endured harsh conditions because they said they paid workers twenty grand a month. Instead, they stiffed me."

"Why didn't you go to the cops?" I asked.

"Crew boss said I was a dead man if I talked to the cops. He said they would kill my entire family."

"Omigod," I said, recoiling. "Are the kids safe?"

"Yeah. I kept my mouth shut. But my silence cost me my health and my family."

"Why didn't you call me to send you a plane ticket?" Viv asked.

"I'm the breadwinner. I couldn't slink home with nothing. I thought I could recover my health and land a job with a legitimate crew."

"Did you stay in a shelter?" Viv asked.

Darry visibly trembled. "I tried it for two days because it's freaking cold there. I couldn't take being cooped up inside. I needed fresh air after being locked in that boat hold every night. I felt miserable until I decided to come home. Thank you again for opening your door to me, Viv. I have no right to ask for your forgiveness and kindness but I'm a broken man."

"You are welcome here. I had no idea you were in trouble," Viv said. "When you left, you said you would be fishing for months at a time with no phone service. You raved this would be an adventure of a lifetime. That's why I didn't look for you sooner. I would've come for you."

"I stumbled into hell to help my family." He paused until his breathing evened. "Curtis played me. He knew my weakness for adventure and that I dreamed of feeling invincible again. I was stupid to fall for his line of crap, but I bought what he was selling. Anita and I were financially underwater. We needed thirty grand to pay our bills. It wasn't about the kids' college funds like I told you. I should've filed for bankruptcy last fall, but pride held me back." He nodded to her small balcony. "Can we sit outside? I can't breathe in here."

"Okay. I'll grab another seat," Viv said.

A few minutes later, Darry and I rested on the loungers and Viv perched on a wooden stool. The narrow balcony overlooked a parking lot and faced west. Must be blinding out here at sunset.

Darry had endured a terrible ordeal and somehow managed to travel home. While I admired his fighting spirit, the journey had exerted a terrible toll. The man beside Viv had no spark of his former personality. If not for his familiar voice, I'd declare this man an imposter. I desperately wanted more information. Would he answer pointed questions? I had to try.

"I'm not sure I understand, Darry," I began slowly. "You lined up a paying job before you left home, reported for duty and did the work, but they kept your wages? That's against the law. The cops should've helped you."

"The paymaster said it went on account. I thought that meant deferred payment when my hitch ended, but they never intended to pay me. When my back gave out four months later, they left me for dead by a dumpster. A homeless vet saw what they'd done and took me to the place where he squatted. I got better after a few days of rest, then we got rousted and I tried the shelter."

Forced labor. No pay. Bad back. Not good. "Must've been March by then," I said. "How'd you survive the Alaskan winter?"

"That boat changed me. I'm not the brother, husband, or father who left here with stars in his eyes. I felt exhausted, sick, and so cold I couldn't get warm in a heated room. I've never been any place before where I didn't know a soul."

Darry paused for a swig of iced tea and then launched into a coughing spell. He stared at parked cars until his breathing steadied.

"Why Alaska?" I asked.

"Money," he groused. "I never should've trusted Curtis or his easy money stories. He made his trip sound like a cakewalk, but he lied. The work broke me physically, and the crew were cottonmouth mean."

"That's horrible," Viv said. "Curtis knew the working conditions there. Why'd he steer you wrong?"

Darry flinched in the bright sunlight. "You still with him?"

"Curtis is dead," Viv said.

"Dead?" Darry blistered the air with swear words. "Soon as I got my strength back, I intended to teach him a lesson. My hate for him kept me warm many a night."

Darry's situation in Alaska sounded gut-wrenching. I couldn't imagine being alone, broken, and adrift in such an unforgiving climate. Yet, somehow, he survived terrible conditions and limped back home.

"Did they get him?" Darry asked. "Is that why he's dead?"

"Omigosh." Dread edged Viv's voice. "You don't know."

Darry wrenched his gaze from the horizon. "What?"

"Curtis died from poisoned gin. My fingerprints were on the tainted bottle, but I didn't know about the poison. I'm charged with killing him, Darry. Me and my boyfriend, Doug Holloway."

Darry swore some more. "If I'd gotten a better-paying job around here or accepted a government handout, none of this would've happened. Curtis Marlin screwed us both, in life and death. Getting even with him kept me going on the way home. Now somebody screwed me out of my revenge. I'm pissed."

His anger pulsed through the air. Who could blame him? Curtis owed both Declans more than an apology.

"This may be hard to hear," Viv said, pausing until a motorcycle cleared the parking lot below. "Though your anger toward him is justified, you have to let it go. Someone poisoned Curtis and framed me for murder. I have nightmares about living in prison. The cops are certain I'm guilty. River is my only hope of beating this wrongful charge."

"Pete and I are turning over rocks, trying to clear Viv and Doug," I said, feeling comfortable about easing into the conversation again. "Curtis treated his friends as poorly as his enemies."

"I've moved to the enemy camp," Darry said. "I'm glad he's gone."

Darry's pronouncement sobered me and seemed to have had a similar effect on Viv. When I couldn't take the silence any longer, I asked the question that seemed the most obvious to me.

"What about Anita, Darry?" I asked. "Why didn't you go home to hug your wife and kids?"

"I tried." His lower lip quivered. "She wouldn't let me in. Wouldn't let me explain. She said I abandoned them. You're all the family I have left, Viv."

"You can stay here with me and Doug," Viv said. "You need time to heal, but you also have to pull it together in due time and move forward, whatever that looks like."

Darry shuddered. Tanned skin framed his sunken cheeks, making it clear he'd sported a beard for months. "I need my job back at the mill. Will you put in a good word for me?"

"No can do. After my arrest, I got fired from the mill. You're better off bagging groceries at the supermarket."

"I've got more to offer than that."

"Here's the thing, Darry," Viv said. "I respect you've been through an awful ordeal, but once you are feeling better, say in a few weeks or so, you need to get a job and it shouldn't matter who hires you. A job is a job. Everybody has to work."

He gave her a quick glance before looking away. "You have changed."

Viv grinned. "For the better. I want a home and a family."

"With Doug?"

"If he'll have me. And if I don't rot in prison for a crime I didn't commit."

"Some mighty big ifs there."

"I dream big now that I'm hanging out with positive-thinkers."

He nodded and held his peace for a few long minutes. "I'll see about a job. I want my family back too."

Sensing an accord, I rose. "I have to go. Thanks for the tea."

"Thanks for coming," Viv said, following me out to the building's internal corridor. "Keep me posted on the investigation."

"I wish you didn't live under this dark cloud, Viv, but I'm happy Darry's alive."

"I feel better now that Darry is home. The tide is finally turning in our favor."

I said the right things to leave, but as I drove away I had a stunning realization. Something about Darry Declan didn't sit right with me. I couldn't quite put my finger on the wrongness. Truthfully, I'd never spent much time with him before, but the air around him felt disturbed, as if his misfortune roiled the atmosphere.

Then it hit me. He didn't make eye contact when he spoke. That avoidance posture put me on notice. I didn't know why he looked away as he spoke but most people looked at the people they conversed with. Maybe I should be more generous. He was probably ashamed of being duped by Curtis. He'd made a terrible mistake in going to Alaska.

The experience changed him. I kept coming back to that. Fun-loving Darry had turned into a vengeful wreck of a man. Having a place to recover should have given him a spark of hope. I didn't see anything like that. In fact, he made me nervous.

Bottom line, I didn't trust a single word Darry said.

Chapter Thirty-Six

Early Friday morning, I hustled to purchase the locally-sourced ingredients for Sunday night's hotel banquet. Once I stowed those supplies, I began cooking for today's event, the Dylan Barresi tailgate gathering.

Time passed swiftly as I prepared the chicken wings, spiced pecans, broccoli salad, ham and cheese sliders, and cornbread muffins, as well as the chilled and peeled boiled shrimp with cocktail sauce. The melon balls and strawberry cheesecake I'd prepared last night.

For this carry-out meal, I used disposable containers, bagging the hots together and the colds separately.

Promptly at three, Vince arrived, clad in a tuxedo. He handed me a thick envelope, which I stowed in my apron pocket. "What is it with your boss and cash?" I asked.

"It's how we do business. Cleaner that way."

Vince appeared to be a few years younger than Doug, surely he used mobile banking. "Most bill-pay systems are electronic these days," I said. "It must be challenging to use cash for your monthly bills."

He glared at me. "You have a problem with cash?"

I raised my hands in surrender mode. "I love cash. No problems here."

He muttered something, so I asked, "What's that?"

"Your food better be good after all this trouble."

"My food is always good. You can take that to the bank, or, er, the safe, or wherever you keep your cash."

He pointed to the four large foil hot/cold bags behind me. "That's Uncle Dylan's food?"

"It is. May I help you carry them to the car?"

"I've got this."

And he did. He had no problem carrying four bags to a little black sportscar in the driveway. I gave him a few minutes head start, then I darted out to bank my cash earnings.

Did I have a problem with cash? The question lingered in my head. Dylan Barresi paid on time and tipped generously. His cash worked at the bank, so that passed muster. I wasn't thrilled about his possible mob ties, but truly how much did I know about my other customers?

Once again in my commercial kitchen, I started on the Sunday banquet meal for Geneva Walker. To pull this off, I needed to mix the marinades and sauces today. Since this meal featured baked chicken, I used the rubbed chicken recipe from Melanie's wedding.

When I reached a stopping point, I drowsed in a lounger on the back deck before I cooked our dinner. Not long after I sat, my brother appeared with a lost-boy look on his face. "Got your message," he said, "so here I am."

I had questions for him, but I needed to be gentle. "Will you join me for milk and cookies?"

His eyes lit with enthusiasm. "Oatmeal raisin with walnuts?"

"Coming right up." I pulled a baked cookie tub from the deep freeze, zapped a handful in the microwave, and then filled glasses with ice and splashed in milk.

Major purred beside Doug's lounge chair. "Didn't know you liked cats," I began.

"Didn't know I did either, but this one and I have an understanding. I told him to guard you a few weeks ago and here he is."

"Really?"

Doug lit into the cookies like he hadn't eaten all week. "Yeah. We were on a job, and he stalked up like he knew me. I told him you needed a friend and that he should find you and watch out for you. He's a smart cat."

"He's very serious about mealtime and every now and then he demands a ride in Mom's Buick. A couple of times he's warned me of danger. For whatever reason he's here, I'm delighted Major became my cat."

"Glad it's working out for both of you. I wish I had another almost-tame wildling for Viv. She's thrilled about her brother's homecoming. I'm happy too, happy that she stopped worrying about his fate. But. Darry Declan is a piece of work."

I set my milk glass down abruptly. "You too? I don't trust him. He endured a terrible ordeal, but why didn't he phone Viv once he saw daylight? Why didn't he call the cops?"

"Funny you should mention that."

"Why?"

"I asked him the same questions, pointblank."

"And?"

"He yelled at me to mind my own business. So frustrating. I'm afraid his dirty laundry will blow up in Viv's face. She has enough trouble on her plate."

"Can't you and Viv convince Anita to take him back? I feel uneasy with him living in the same apartment with you. He may be dangerous."

"Not happening. Anita is furious. Even before Darry surfaced, she called out of work this week. I asked another buddy of mine to fill her spot. Joel helped yesterday and this morning. He's working out fine, plus I don't have to listen to Anita's troubles all day. As for Darry being a threat, time will tell. If left to his own devices, he sleeps all day."

I braced myself against the chair arms as I filtered what he'd said. "Wait. Back up a minute. That makes no sense. Anita called out of work before Darry showed up at Viv's place today? How odd."

"I thought so too, especially since she desperately needs income. Even if Viv pressures me, I won't hire Darry. He's more like Curtis than Viv, and I don't trust him."

"That could be tough on your relationship. Speaking of work, can you and Viv help me with catering Sunday evening?

Yesterday I signed a contract with Geneva Walker for a hotel banquet."

"Sure. Text us the time. Are we helping you set up and clean up or just serving?"

"If one of you helped load the van at five and then the other met me at the Ocean Crest Plaza thirty minutes later, that'd be awesome. This is a buffet, so we need to keep the food station replenished and the dishes cleared. Should be easy money."

"Why isn't the hotel doing it?" Doug asked.

I gave him the background. "Geneva said double-booked banquets are infrequent but catch them shorthanded every time."

"She wants you to save her bacon, in other words," his voice awash in disdain.

"Yes, she does."

"She's a user, River. She used you to get her daughter married."

"I didn't mind. The missing groom added extra zest to that day. This hotel catering arrangement has long-term implications, but I signed for the one meal. I'll see how it goes."

"Always a good idea to test the waters before diving in." Doug cleared his throat after finishing his milk. "Getting back to Darry Declan. He told his story several times this morning and contradicted himself repeatedly. He jumps at the slightest noise. I wonder if he has a mental health issue. Did you know him well before?"

"I didn't. He kept busy with sports in school. After high school, I had my hands full between taking care of Mom, launching my catering business, and helping parent you. I didn't see Viv much during that time, and I never saw Darry. Anita got pregnant in high school so she married Darry, and he started at the mill. That's all I know about Darry."

"That's my take on him as well." Doug gazed off into the trees for a moment. "It's just...and I hope this comes across the right way...I'm so glad Viv and I are hitting it off. She gets me and I really like her. I don't want Darry fouling the waters."

"He'll smooth things out with Anita, or he'll get a place once he has a job."

Doug frowned. "I'm not sure he can work. Truly, he seems broken to me. Sometimes he shakes."

"Like a dog?"

"Like an old person. He needs a doctor, but he won't go."

"Give him time. By all accounts, he's been through hell. Viv deserves the happiness of having her brother return home. At the same time, I'm thrilled you and Viv are hitting it off. Mom would be happy for you too."

He sighed. "Viv and I have a shot at happiness, long as neither of us goes to prison."

"Working on it."

Chapter Thirty-Seven

Darry Declan's homecoming and his tale of hardship occupied my thoughts Friday evening and into Saturday. Finally, I couldn't take it anymore. I pulled my lemon tart filling off the stove to cool and phoned Deputy Franklin. "Did you know Darry Declan is on the island?"

"News to me," he said in a disinterested voice. "Alive or dead?"

"Alive and staying with his sister." I said, standing by the window and feeling relieved all the shadows looked normal. "He's lost so much weight I didn't recognize him."

"Ms. Declan failed to notify me of his return. Since you've seen him, I'll cancel the missing persons alert. Anything else?"

His terse answers implied he cared little about Darry or his story. "Darry shared a harrowing story of his time in Alaska. Captors held him prisoner on a fishing boat for four months, stiffed him for his labor, and dumped him ashore when he could no longer work. Darry claims Curtis set him up."

"Unless he makes a police report, my hands are tied."

I didn't appreciate the brush off. "I'm concerned for Darry, and also for Doug and Viv's safety. Darry claims he just arrived, but what if he's lying? My intuition tells me something is off about him. Can you do a welfare check on them? Don't you need to personally verify he's alive?"

Profound silence filled the line. A chair squeaked. "One minute."

I heard footsteps and a door closing, making me wonder about his location. Every day, Deputy Franklin patrolled the island. Had I interrupted him during a staff meeting?

"I can talk more freely now, but I'm on the clock. Look, River, I appreciate your safety concerns for your brother and friend, but I can't help you. I'm on desk duty because Sheriff Vargas found out I continued to check leads on the Marlin homicide. My job is on the line."

Oh, no. I'd brought this punishment down on Deputy Franklin. "The sheriff is wrong to close the murder case and wrong to sideline you for doing your job."

"He's the boss."

"Not if we vote him out," I said. "I've had it with his cavalier attitude and so have others. I won't vote for Sheriff Vargas again, and I'll tell my clients he's closeminded. We need a sheriff who doesn't leap to conclusions."

The deputy took his time answering. "Your best bet today is Deputy Z. She's on island patrol while I'm riding the desk. Gotta warn you though, she's pissed at her exile. She prefers the mainland where, according to her, all the action is."

While I empathized with Franklin, I needed to keep my investigation moving forward. "How do I contact Deputy Zillo?"

"You don't. Call dispatch, report Darry's reappearance, and request a welfare check. Be sure Darry's in residence and that someone opens the door at Viv's place. If anything's wrong with him, Zillo will pick up on it."

Rats. If Darry had something to hide, he wouldn't open the door to a cop. "Then I better wait until Doug and Viv get off work this afternoon."

"Good idea." He paused. "Any more strangers spying on your house?"

"Nothing on the camera feed."

"Three witnesses came forward about your tire incident. All three said two men in hoodies did the damage. However, none of the descriptions matched."

"Great. So now I have two men after me?"

"Stay safe. My cop intuition says something's up on the island, but right now I don't have the luxury of investigating."

"I apologize for getting you in trouble."

"No need. I made the choices that got me benched. I must make better choices now. My daughter and ex-wife rely on my financial support."

If the sheriff fired Deputy Franklin, I'd make a stink. Franklin listened to my ideas and followed up on most of them. "Doug and Viv are innocent. Otherwise, I wouldn't bother you with my leads."

"You did what any concerned citizen would do, and I did my job. Do me a favor and text me a recent photo of Darry Declan."

"Soon as I see him again, I'll snap a pic." The implications of my actions hit hard. "Viv will be furious with me for ratting out her brother, and by extension, my brother will be upset too."

"If you want to be popular, stick to giving out cookies. Investigation is a lonely field."

My spirits rose. "Are you calling me an investigator?"

He chuckled. "I'm missing your delicious cookies."

"Oh."

"To be fair, you have a nose for gathering information."

His praise warmed me to my toes. "We'll learn what really happened to Curtis, and there will be cookies on that desk."

I ended the call and then prepped, marinated, and cooked for the rest of the day. Not knowing what equipment I had to work with at Ocean Crest Plaza, I decided to run over and take a gander. Better to be prepared than caught short Sunday afternoon.

When I went to leave, Major stared at me from atop the Buick. I smiled. No reason I couldn't drive the car to the hotel. "Good idea," I told my independent pet. "Road trip."

I unlocked the car door and opened it, and Major scampered inside. Instead of jumping in the back, however, he claimed the passenger seat. I climbed in beside him, careful not to make any sudden moves. He circled on the fabric seat and lay down like he'd done it a million times.

Well, imagine that. He trusted me as his chauffeur. We exited the driveway and merged onto the main road. The heavier island traffic on the weekend made for a slower drive. The leisurely pace didn't bother me. Or Major.

I left the windows open when I parked. A nice breeze blew in off the ocean, and surely Major liked fresh air. "I'll be back in a few minutes," I told the cat. With the temperature in the low seventies, he'd be fine in the open car.

Shouldering my purse, I entered the hotel and asked a clerk for directions to the banquet area. He pointed me toward a corridor to the left. Lush hedges trimmed to perfection bordered the arched windows.

The double doors to the ballroom stood open wide, and thirty tables for ten dotted the floor. I paused to observe the hotel staff busily adding tablecloths, centerpieces, and place settings to the tables, then I continued on to the Frederica Room. The closed doors gave off a keep-away vibe.

Undaunted, I opened a door and stepped inside. Instead of a hub of activity, this room felt abandoned and forlorn. A rack of five round tables and two hanging racks of folding chairs slumbered near the door. Guess the staff would stage this smaller function after finishing the larger room. A dais with a podium stood at the opposite side of the room. I saw the service door near the podium, walked through it into an internal corridor.

I found two support rooms nearby, one nicely sized and the other much smaller. Banks of counters with warmers and a large walk-in refrigerator lined the inside of the larger room. "Perfect," I exclaimed.

"Not so fast, missy."

I turned and saw a fireplug of a woman in an immaculate double breasted chef's jacket with a toque on her head. Her aggressive stance and narrowed eyes reminded me of a pit bull. I walked toward her offering my hand. "Hello, I'm River Holloway of Holloway Catering. I'm catering a function here tomorrow evening."

The woman glared at my hand. I hastily withdrew it.

"I know who you are," the woman said. "This is my domain, and I say what goes in these rooms and the kitchens."

"You must be Chef Lorraine," I said, gutting it out. "Nice to meet you. Ms. Walker signed me to cater a meal in the Frederica Room tomorrow. Should we speak with her about your concerns?"

Maggie Toussaint

"I don't like what she did. My staff can handle two events."

How awkward. "I came by to get the lay of the land for tomorrow. This staging area works nicely for my event."

"Think again. This area supports the ballroom. The smaller prep area is for Frederica."

I nodded my understanding. "My mistake. I'll check out the amenities, find out where I'm to unload, grab some uniforms, and I'll be out of your hair."

"We're not finished." Chef Lorraine blocked the exit. "What's your angle here? You after my job?"

Now I understood her irritation. "Absolutely not. I turned down this gig at first. I like working for myself and cooking my menus."

"Why'd you take the job?"

"Oldest reason in the world. I need the money. Working for yourself has its ups and downs. Right now, catering is slow."

"That woman wants a second chef in here."

"Ms. Walker explained the burden on current staff when double bookings occur," I stated calmly, though I felt irritated. "For your information, I declined the opportunity to contract for more than one event."

"You did?"

"Yeah. I'd rather create smaller meals in intimate settings. I prefer cooking a variety of foods. I can do mass production, but I'd rather not."

"So you say."

"You're awfully suspicious."

"I don't like other chefs horning in on my turf."

"First, I'm not a chef. No formal training. I've learned this trade through the school of hard knocks. Second, I'm a caterer. A different lane altogether."

"But you're attempting to perform to my high standards."

Not a dig but I took it as such. "My food is delicious. Ask anyone on the island."

"I know your reputation," the woman repeated, "but I question your intention."

"My intention is to do a good job and pay my bills."

"Your competition charges less."

My chin lifted. "Their customers get what they pay for."

Chef Lorraine harrumphed. "I suppose I have no choice since the big boss okayed the hire. Let's get the items you need."

~*~

On the way home, I swung through the parking lot at Viv's place. Doug's truck sat in one numbered slot, but Viv's car was gone. It would be good to get that photo now for Deputy Franklin so I wouldn't have to keep remembering it. I parked in the general parking area near the front again.

"Take care of the car. I won't be long," I told the cat who purred contentedly on the seat. Again, I left the windows down so he could get out if he wanted.

I entered the building, climbed the steps to the second floor, and knocked on the interior door. My brother waved me inside, a worried look on his face. "Glad you're here," he said. "We were about to call you. Come on in."

I followed him to the living room. "What's going on?"

Viv's tear-stained face rose over the faded floral sofa as I approached. "I never should've trusted my brother, that's what."

I sat next to her and took her trembling hand. "It can't be that bad."

"He stole my car today. No note, no nothing."

"Maybe he's running errands. Have you called him?"

"He doesn't have a phone."

Right. "How long's he been gone?"

"Don't know. We didn't wake him when we went to work this morning. We knocked off early so I could hang out with Darry. We've been home an hour, and he hasn't returned."

"Did you try his place? Maybe he reconciled with Anita."

"This time of day she's busy with the kids."

"I'll call her," I said. "This is important."

Anita picked up after a few rings, loud shrieks of children playing in the background. "Hey, River."

"Hi. This is somewhat awkward, but Darry returned to Shell Island and he has Viv's car. Have you seen him?"

"He left me high and dry, and I never want to speak to him again."

"There were extenuating circumstances. He got shanghaied and forced to work under terrible conditions."

"Don't believe a word out of his lying mouth. He promised things would improve if he went to Alaska, and it's been a nightmare. I appreciate you and Doug helping me get back on my feet, but never mention Darry to me again. As soon as I can hire a lawyer, I'm divorcing his sorry hide."

"I didn't mean to upset you. Viv is a mess too. The two of you should compare notes."

"Viv is my friend, and I'll work with her, but her brother is off-limits for conversation."

The phone clicked in my ear. I turned to face Viv and Doug. "She hung up on me."

"She does that," Viv said. "She hates my brother now."

I sank down on the sofa on Viv's far side, feeling the need to share what Anita said. "She plans to divorce Darry."

"Can you blame her?" Viv said. "He barely provided for them before he left, and then he abandoned her and the kids. She has every right to hate him."

"I wish I understood why your brother thought Alaska would fix his financial problems."

"Curtis must've dazzled him with tales of riches. Nothing else makes any sense. Darry never said a word about Alaska before Curtis started talking about it."

"What about your missing car? Will you report the theft?" I asked.

Viv's eyes squeezed shut. "No, I can't do that. He's my brother. He doesn't need a criminal charge on top of everything else."

Darry had problems with Anita, Viv, Curtis, and Alaska. You'd think no money and poor health would be reason to stay put, but he'd skipped. Did he have a secret agenda?

Regardless of Darry's issues, Viv needed help. "I'll ride the roads and look for your car."

"No need. Doug and I will do it. Gimme a few minutes to pull it together."

"Understood." Doug had his arm around Viv, and I felt like a third wheel. "Let me know if there's anything I can do. Come to dinner tonight."

"No, thanks," Viv said, sniffing back her tears. "We'll be busy changing the locks around here."

Chapter Thirty-Eight

Despite its less than auspicious beginnings, the Sunday night catering gig at Ocean Crest Plaza Hotel went like clockwork. I served dinner on time and the guests raved about the food. Viv and Doug helped with everything, and I felt grateful for their help because Pete had a work conflict at the last minute.

"Thanks again," I said as we hauled the last cart of equipment back to my van. "I don't know what kind of ice cream shop emergency detained Pete, but I couldn't have managed without your help. Thanks for all the hustle today."

"Doug and I are a great team," Viv said in the hotel's employee lot. "This size crowd kept us hopping, but we managed. By the way, more than one person wanted seconds on dessert."

"Thanks for the feedback. My lemon tarts are popular with ladies. Wish I could've handed out business cards."

"Wish I knew where my brother is. I'm starting to waffle on calling the cops, and I really don't want to do that."

Doug hustled up behind us with a food warmer in his arms. "While we're sharing wishes, I wish I had jobs booked solid for the next three weeks. I started out like gangbusters and now work slowed to a small job or two a week."

"You'll make it," I said. "Construction is cyclical, so you'll need to save for the slow times like I do. And Viv, are you sure about putting your brother on record as a car thief?"

"No, I'm not sure of anything. I'm worried and upset with him. He isn't thinking clearly, and he needs medical attention. I need to make that happen."

I understood her perspective and shared her reluctance to involve the police. Sometimes we all needed a diversion. Perhaps she'd like to share mine. "I need a beach day tomorrow. How fun would it be to kick back and do nothing all day?"

"I'm in," Viv said. "Shall we meet at our favorite spot about eleven?"

"Works for me."

~*~

After I unloaded the van, I headed to the house on a wave of adrenaline. Despite cooking a menu I wouldn't have chosen ordinarily, tonight's success boosted my morale. Pete waited for me in the kitchen, a dozen red roses and flickering candles gracing the table. "Welcome home!" he said.

"What's all this?" I asked, gesturing widely.

"Can't a guy do something special for his one and only?"

"What are we celebrating?"

"I've held some big news for a few days because of your hotel event. You're looking at the new owner of Island Creamery."

"Congratulations!" My smile widened. "What a surprise. I never dreamed your plan to buy the ice cream shop was so far along."

"I signed the papers on Friday afternoon, but the former owner invited all of his family down from Atlanta for a private party today, so the actual hand-over happened at close of business, when it should have been hours earlier as we'd agreed upon."

Pete chewed his bottom lip. "I couldn't leave until after they did because I had a locksmith standing by to change the locks. I hope you'll forgive me for leaving you shorthanded today."

Inside me, emotions swirled and arced like heat lightning. How was it possible to be irritated and happy and anxious at the same time? "I didn't appreciate the late notice but we managed.

211

I'm more upset that you felt you couldn't share your news with me."

"I didn't mean it that way." He didn't say anything for a long time. Finally, after what seemed an eternity, he spoke. "I'm sorry my plans went astray. The hotel gig was a big deal for you. My intent by omission was to shield you from any distraction my news might cause."

Pete did it for my own good? I stood toe-to-toe with him. "I want to marry a man who's honest with me. I don't want to be taken for granted or kept in the dark."

He raked his fingers through his hair. "I didn't mean to hurt you. If everything happened on schedule, I could've done both things today, but my time wasn't my own. I wanted to be there with you."

He meant it. I knew he did. And I knew that sometimes my catering jobs ran long or that there might be occasions when I couldn't leave an event at a set time. "It's okay. I understand schedule conflicts will arise."

"You're not mad at me?"

"Pete, I love you for you, the man inside. I love sharing sunrises and sunsets with you, talking with you, doing things with you. Mistakes will happen, on both sides. We're fine as long as we both remember we're part of a team. That means we share our news and concerns."

"I've focused on building my portfolio for so long, it's hard to rewire my thoughts to a team mindset. What if I screw up again?"

"You won't." I took his hands and drew them to my hips. "Let's start this celebration over again."

~*~

At the beach the next day, I shared the news with Viv. "Pete bought Island Creamery. I knew he planned to buy it, but he didn't tell me he actually bought it until afterward."

Racked out in her lounger, Viv made a comforting sound, so I kept going. "My emotions flared because he excluded me. My reaction surprised both of us."

Viv turned toward me, shading overtop her glasses with her hand. "Hmm. Sounds like a relationship speedbump but no damage was done."

"I hope not." The hubbub of blaring radios, circling gulls, and cresting waves filled my senses. I watched a series of waves crash onto the sandy shore. That rhythmic give and take of water over sand seemed so natural, so effortless. Why couldn't interpersonal relationships flow so easily?

Viv rolled a towel and placed it under her head. "How goes the wedding plans?"

"May 10 is the wedding date."

"And our gowns?"

The sun came out from behind a cloud and the steely glare blinded me. "You and I should visit the bridal shop on the mainland. I'm going with a traditional white gown, but you can select any style maid of honor dress."

Viv nodded. "Let me know when you want to go. My schedule is flexible. Any other details decided yet?"

"Father Ben of St. Luke's will marry us there. That's as far as we've gotten."

"Umm." Viv drowsed in the sun for a while. I had drifted off to my happy place when she asked, "Any progress on project baby?"

"Sadly, nothing to report. I'd rather not go the route of charts and thermometers, but it may come to pass. It's hard to conceive at thirty-two."

"Doug and I want kids. We'd like to both have steady income first. Look at Anita. Her kids are great, but she's in a deep financial hole. You may as well know, Darry and Anita have always argued about finances, so their money problems are old news, only I don't know why they didn't turn things around this time."

"First, you'll make a great mom. I've always known that." I glanced around to make sure no one could overhear our conversation. "As for Anita, she helped create the debt load. Darry didn't bankrupt his family by himself. Like you, I feel sorry for her, but only to a point."

"Agreed, and it irks me how she won't let Darry see his kids. Anita claims he lost that right by abandoning them. He looks so lost now. Those Alaskans broke his body and maybe his mind. I'm concerned for him."

"With good reason. He's lost so much ground."

"Darry's broken in many ways, and he's burned bridges with Anita, but I forgive him for taking my car."

"Did you find the car?"

"No car and no Darry."

Our conversation lagged as we drowsed under clear skies. Two teenaged girls in suits smaller than Viv's sauntered by, fixated on their cell phones.

"Times have changed," I said, pointing a thumb their way.

"Everything is easier with the latest technology, especially indulging in vices. Over the course of a weekend with Curtis, he checked a phone app repeatedly. When he took a bathroom break, curiosity got the better of me. I peeked, expecting to see porn, but saw online betting. He gambled on his phone. That threw me for a loop."

"You could lose money fast that way."

"Heads up!" someone shouted.

I turned and narrowly missed being scalped by a red Frisbee. A teen darted past, sand flying from his bare toes. "Sorry about that, ma'am," he said.

"No problem," I told the kid.

"Or win big, which is how Curtis thought," Viv said, plowing ahead. "Any chance at instant riches got his attention. By then, I realized Curtis wore secrets like a second skin."

Calls, messages, and internet search histories were stored on mobile phones. "Where's his phone now?"

"Must be in the case evidence box. No one mentioned his cell phone to date."

"Can't your court-appointed attorney request a list of the evidence inventory?"

"I didn't think to ask." She scowled. "Truly, I expected my hotshot sleuth to clear my name by now."

"I wish I had progress to report, Viv. Getting back to that phone, the cops should've subpoenaed his phone records. Your lawyer needs access to that information to build your defense." I cleared my throat. "Moving on, I hope you get your car and your brother back."

She pulled down her over-sized sunglasses to glare at me. "Now we're talking miracles."

The weight of Doug and Viv's fate bore down on me like a rogue wave. I wanted answers, but everything churned in circles in this case. All lines of inquiry led to a central figure: Curtis, a dead man. Suspicion abounded, but I wouldn't give up. I couldn't.

I summoned a breezy smile. "We need a miracle or two."

Viv settled back in her lounger, shielded by those large lenses. "You got that right."

Chapter Thirty-Nine

When I returned home that afternoon refreshed from sunbathing, I texted Deputy Franklin about Curtis using a phone app for online betting. He called, saying, "I have news."

Hope stirred as I walked toward the back door carrying my beach bag and lounge chair. "About the case?"

"Yes. Early on, I put out feelers about Marlin's Alaska trip and the request got buried until today. Turns out Curtis Marlin left Alaska owing over thirty grand. His landlord filed a police report, as did the bar near his former lodgings. Alaska State Troopers tracked down the fishing boat Marlin crewed on. They had no problem with him and said someone else paid his outstanding debt. Guess who?"

My feet stopped. I only knew two islanders who'd traveled to Alaska, one living and the other dead. Instead of relief, the answer filled me with dread. "Darry Declan. Curtis sent him to Alaska to settle the gambling debt he owed."

"Righto. The boat captain didn't elaborate and cast off when he unloaded his catch. The hasty departure made the trooper curious. He asked questions around the dock about the two men from Georgia. People remembered Marlin but nobody knew Declan. No one recognized his photo at the nearby bars and restaurants."

I dropped the lounger and hurried inside, needing the security of my home. My fears for Darry mushroomed, and I felt sick to my stomach. I slid into a kitchen chair and gazed out, half expecting bad guys to be coming after me the way they came after Darry in Alaska. Such a flight of fancy and not a reasonable thought at all.

"Perhaps Darry blended in or used cash instead of credit cards," I said.

"More like he never saw the light of day on dry land," Franklin said. "That's what the trooper thinks. Historically, a few fishing captains walk a fine line between slaver and crew boss. The cop's checking into it further."

My shoulders sagged in empathy for Viv's brother. "That fits with Darry Declan's claim of being prisoner on a fishing boat for four months of unpaid labor. Once his back went out, they left him for dead by a dumpster."

"We need to find Declan." The line fell silent for a few beats. "You spoke with the man. What's his state of mind?"

"Not good. He left Shell Island in mid-November, vibrant and hopeful. None of that bounce and swagger returned with him. He lost weight and is incoherent at times. He startles at noises and loses track of conversations."

"Is he on drugs?"

"He can't afford them. It appears he bummed his way across the country."

"A drug addict finds a way to get what he or she needs."

On some level, I knew that but it stunk. "I hope he isn't hooked on drugs. Nothing else accounts for his mental lapses?"

"I haven't seen him but given his alleged trauma he might have PTSD."

"His account sounded harrowing, for sure. Seems very likely being held prisoner and robbed of your belongings in a place far from home would trigger post-stress trauma. A person enduring that ordeal would have to process it later."

When Deputy Franklin didn't reply, my grip tightened on the phone. "What's the treatment for PTSD?"

"Counseling to cope and some meds. Even if Declan ends up with a PTSD diagnosis, it might not help him. Some sufferers won't seek treatment. We interact with plenty of untreated PTSD people in my line of work."

"Thank you for that ray of sunshine."

"Cops see a lot."

"Dare I assume that you're starting to believe Viv and Doug are innocent?"

"I wouldn't go that far. However, while I cooled my heels on desk duty, I kept digging in Heavy D, Eggs, and Ty's backgrounds. Each guy has baggage and made mistakes, but they come up clean as a whole. They didn't do it, River."

Depression seeped through my pores, sapping my hopes for Doug and Viv's exoneration. "Where does that leave us for suspects?"

"If we eliminate those three men, Viv, and Doug, then we reboot from scratch. Darry Declan's tale is unusual, and he allegedly worked with shady individuals. We haven't verified his return date to Georgia. He's a possibility, as are any unsavory types Curtis Marlin burned or offended in Alaska and here."

"If you saw Darry, you wouldn't think he could manage more than getting himself dressed in the morning. He didn't kill Curtis. You mentioned other people Curtis offended in Alaska. Given that we're dealing with shady folks, wouldn't they stand out on the island?"

"Perhaps. However, a pro would use an expedient means of death like a gun or knife. Poison is a signature that red flags easily. The Marlin homicide feels personal. Someone wanted him to suffer. Since we believe Darry suffered because of Curtis, he'd be on my suspect list if the case were reopened. Even someone with a mental deficit has moments of clarity. Perhaps he used poison because of his physical condition."

"He suffered all right, but the only time I saw him react strongly occurred upon learning somebody else killed Curtis," I added, watching seconds tick off the day. How many more minutes of freedom did Doug and Viv have? "Darry suffered, but so did his wife, who got stuck at home with two small kids and no income."

"I don't see her dragging the kids with her on a booze-poisoning run."

His sarcastic tone rubbed me the wrong way. "Once we learned about her troubles, Doug and I helped Anita. I kept her kids one afternoon so she could work for Doug. I feel sorry for her, but I don't understand why she didn't seek help sooner. If I'd been abandoned with kids, I wouldn't have sat around and waited for my guy to return. Unless she's been reaching out to various friends at different times to get by."

"Is she a people user?"

The users I'd known had taken full advantage of me. I trusted easily, a trait others saw as naivete. "I can't say. I wish she'd give Darry a second chance, and they could try again. After all they've both been through, I want a happy ending for them."

"Cops don't deal in happy endings, but we follow leads. Which begs the question, why didn't Darry get a job around here?"

"Darry worked at the mill, but their family of four couldn't make ends meet on his salary. Curtis talked him into the Alaska gig. Convinced him this golden opportunity would pay off his debts and then some."

"Instead, the opportunity squared Marlin's debt. That guy had all the charm of a rogue alligator. I wish your brother steered clear of his orbit."

I drew in a quick breath, aware the deputy had strayed from fact.

He quickly countered with, "Not that my opinion matters. I will do everything in my power to put away the person that killed Curtis Marlin."

I smiled to myself at his deft recovery. "That's what I thought you meant."

The call ended and the constant ticking of the clock now reminded me of the late hour. Dinnertime approached. I'd better start sautéing those soft-shelled crabs.

Chapter Forty

Pete and I were in bed that evening when the phone rang. "Turn on the late news," Viv said. "The Savannah station. They interviewed Anita and are running her 'Deadbeat Dad' segment right after the commercial."

"What? How'd a Savannah TV station hear about Anita and Darry?" I asked, reaching for the remote and queuing up the correct channel.

"Got no idea, but this is terrible," Viv said. "He'll be furious she aired their dirty laundry."

With Viv on the line, I sat in mute disbelief as the news segment rolled. Anita's barbed words and flashing eyes telegraphed fury. If she wanted nothing to do with him, why'd she wait around to take action? Her infant, cute little Zoey, slept through the tirade in Anita's arms. Her toddler son, Harry, pushed his cars and trucks across the floor behind her.

The reporter tried to bring the interview around to agencies that helped people like Anita, but Anita kept spewing vitriol about how she'd been victimized. When she stopped for a breath, the segment cut to the reporter standing outside of an agency and wrapping up the segment.

"Oh my God," I said when the story ended. I had to unclench my fingers from the sheets. "I had no idea she could be so vicious."

Pete began massaging my back and I leaned into his touch.

"Mom tried to warn Darry in the beginning," Viv said. "Anita's mother thought the world owed her and now Anita carries that torch. She must've been bashing Darry behind closed doors the whole time they were married. No wonder he went to Alaska."

"Darry's actions led to her desolation, and I have sympathy for her," I said, rising to her defense. "She protected herself and her kids because he didn't. Regardless of his rationale for the Alaska trip, Darry hurt his family by leaving. Somehow Anita survived and cared for their kids."

Viv sniffed a few times. "I wish I'd known her dire straits in November. You're right, Darry wronged Anita. After he left, I invited her over and offered to take the kids overnight, but she always refused. Eventually I quit asking."

"Wonder how she made ends meet all those months."

"Who knows? While I have sympathy for what happened to her, I can't forgive her for shunning Darry. He expected his wife to shelter him as he recovered. She locked him out and won't let him see his kids. That's wrong."

Tough enough for couples to deal with pressures of careers, money, religion, and the like without being married to someone who hated your guts. It sounded awful. "Darry suffered from his choices, but he has legal rights regarding his children," I said, hoping that eased my friend's hurt. "He'll turn up, and we'll sort this out."

"I sure hope so. Thanks for listening to me vent."

"Any time."

I ended the call, switched off the TV, and lay down beside Pete. "Anita's furious."

Pete settled into his pillow and reached for me. "That came across loud and clear."

I snuggled into his arms. "I understand her anger, but I won't jeopardize my business with a hot tempered employee. I'm lucky she didn't mouth off the time I did use her."

"Be ready for backlash," Pete said, stroking my hair. "She's not a turn the other cheek person."

"I'll explain why she's not on my call list if she asks why I don't call her for future work."

"Sounds like a plan." He gave me a slow smile. "But now that we're wide awake, another subject has arisen."

"I noticed."

Chapter Forty-One

Tuesday dawned under gunmetal grey skies with an ominous sense of foreboding. Even the cat refused to stay outdoors. He darted inside when I opened the door to carry out his food. Thunder rumbled in the distance.

"Good choice." I set his food and water dishes in the kitchen and shut the door. "Your breakfast awaits."

Pete and I ate cheesy scrambled eggs before he left for work. The sky opened a few minutes later, and a steady drizzle followed. The dreary weather and thick humidity made it harder to see outside and breathing became labored, even for a coastal native like me.

However, I needed coffee, so I dashed to the supermarket to buy more. Returning to the van, I saw a missed call and voice mail from Viv. Her tearful voice shared the news that her brother crawled home an hour ago, beaten to a pulp. An ambulance hauled him to the hospital, and that's where Viv and Doug were headed now.

I called her. Viv picked up but shouting and commotion on her end drowned out our conversation. "Darry just lost it. I'll call you back," Viv said.

My thoughts raced as I pocketed the phone. Windshield wipers swept the steady rain to the side. I swung by Island Creamery to tell Pete the news. "I need to go to the hospital," I told him when I'd finished. "Do you want to come?"

"Appreciate the ask, but I'm in the middle of optimizing the new payroll system. I'd be in the way while you offer moral support to Viv and Doug, and that's exactly what you should be doing. Mind if I sit out this trip?"

"You're good. Darry is a mess. Viv is worried about him."

"I'm glad you can help your friend. Take my truck, okay? It's our safest vehicle in bad weather. I'll drive the van home after we close today."

By the time I reached the causeway, the sky opened again. Heavy rain pelted the truck and left large puddles on the road. I slowed and crept resolutely forward. Finally, I parked at the hospital, dashed inside, and texted Doug and Viv that I'd arrived. Doug texted that he'd come down to show me the way.

The gift shop drew my attention, and I stared into its glass walls wondering what a visitor bought for a PTSD victim who doubled as a thief and possibly a killer. Flowers, balloons, and cards seemed wrong.

"River," Doug said from behind me. I turned and saw his usually tanned skin looked ashen.

"You're all wet," he said. "Glad you got here safely. Thanks for coming. Darry freaked when they tried to put in an IV. He's beat to hell and back. Looks like someone tried to break every bone in his body."

"Oh, no. Any idea who attacked him?"

"He's mostly incoherent and angry."

Doug clung to me, trembling all over. I reared back enough to look him in the face. "You all right, Doug?"

He retreated, rubbing the back of his neck and staring at the tiled floor. "I'm upset at Darry for taking advantage of Viv, and I'm appalled at his injuries. Now he's belligerent and talking crazy, and I'm afraid of his strength and foul mouth. This is hard. I've never seen anyone in this shape before, and I'm ashamed I want to run from it."

"You didn't do that, brother. You stayed to support Viv through her family emergency. That's what people in love do for each other." I squeezed his shoulder in sympathy. "He's in pain, Doug. He needs time to mend. Y'all did right to get him to the hospital."

Doug's hands fisted. "He keeps yelling they're coming back to kill him. Viv can't stop crying, and I can't make the madness stop. If this were a TV movie, I'd be riveted to the drama unfolding. To be living it is horrible. I can't comment on Darry's behavior without Viv defending him."

"I understand. You're doing fine, considering. Darry will calm down. The doctors will treat his issues. Our compassion won't fix Darry, but it will comfort Viv. Let's join her, okay?"

I accompanied him down a maze of corridors and up a limited elevator. As we walked, I asked, "Did anyone notify Deputy Franklin he'd been found?"

"Yes. He's in the cubicle."

"Is his presence upsetting Darry? We could ask the deputy to return when he's calmer."

"Too late for that. The deputy requested a tox screen along with medical treatment. Darry lost it when they tried to draw blood. They restrained him, took the blood, and administered strong pain meds. He's still complaining, but he's no longer screaming and writhing in agony."

"Has anyone said what's wrong with him?"

"The doctor said his lungs are clear but X-rays will reveal his tally of broken bones. That's where Darry is now, getting those scans. It appears his right arm is broken and maybe both his ankles."

I winced. "Poor guy."

The elevator door opened to shouting. I cringed at Anita Declan's shrill voice. Once again she held baby Zoey in her arms while Harry raced cars on the furniture.

"This man abandoned his family to go on a fishing trip in Alaska," Anita shouted. "He didn't send home any money for months. He's a deadbeat dad."

I whispered to Doug, "How'd she know his whereabouts?"

He shrugged. "Viv filled out the intake forms with her as his relative. Maybe Anita is listed on a previous visit as his next of kin. If so, the hospital notified her."

"Oh." I respected her anger, but it made me uncomfortable. "I wish she would go home."

"Ma'am," a male nurse said. "You're disturbing the patients. Calm down or security will escort you from the premises."

I hurried to Viv's side and hugged her. "Sorry I'm damp," I said, "but I'm here to help."

Viv returned my hug woodenly, her gaze locked on her sister-in-law.

Anita stomped her foot and gave a horse snort. "I got every right to be here, voicing my opinion, and seeing after the welfare of my legal husband."

Deputy Franklin darkened the corridor and waved off the nurse. "Mrs. Declan, I have questions for you about your husband. We'll move over here where we have privacy."

"I got nothing to hide," Anita said in a normal voice, her chin rising. "Ask away."

Viv, Doug, and I stood mute and statue-still.

"Your choice," he said. "Did you beat your husband last night?"

"You think *I hit him*? That's rich. If I beat him as payback for all the crap he put me through, he'd be dead. Worse than dead. Unrecognizable."

"Where were you last night?"

"Same place I am every night. At home taking care of two kids, all the while that sucker lived the high life. He went on vacation for months without a single word. Now he thinks we can be a family again."

"Mrs. Declan, are you aware your husband claims imprisonment in Alaska for months?"

She brushed away that comment same as she would a pesky house fly. "He made up a story so people felt sorry for him. Feel sorry for me. I walked the floor at night to figure out how to feed my family on no income."

"Be that as it may," Franklin cut in, "someone brutally assaulted your husband and the police want to catch the person who did it. Who has a grudge against him?"

"He has no friends or enemies. He does what I tell him."

Her words shocked me. And they made no sense. Darry had a mill job before he went to Alaska. Why couldn't they make that work?

"You told him to go to Alaska?" Franklin asked.

Anita glared so fiercely at the deputy I thought he might incinerate. Viv trembled violently, so I guided her over to the loveseat so we could sit together and still be within earshot.

"Not hardly. For once, that miserable twerp showed some backbone. I told him to stay gone if he went to Alaska, but he left anyway and then came crawling back. Doesn't work that way in my family."

While Anita spoke, the color drained from Viv's face. A sheen broke out on her forehead. "Excuse me," Viv mumbled as she rose. "Bathroom."

I followed her to the restroom, waited outside as her stomach emptied. Doug looked my way and I shook my head. Water ran, and Viv reappeared. "Sorry. Every time Anita berates my brother, I want to scream. She makes me livid. I can't deal with her today."

"You don't have to. Let's wait in Darry's room until he returns from X-ray."

Doug followed us in and sat on the other side of Viv, holding her hand.

Meanwhile, Deputy Franklin escorted Anita and her kids to the elevator and none of them returned. In moments, the craziness factor fell from 100 percent to zero. A helpful male nurse brought Viv ginger ale, and her color gradually improved.

"What now?" Viv asked. "Darry's in big trouble."

"Did he say anything to you?" I asked.

"Nothing that made sense. He kept saying 'they're here.' I don't know who he's talking about."

I considered that for a moment. "Worst case scenario is that someone from Alaska followed him home."

"Two someones," Viv said, brushing tears from her cheeks. "He used the word 'they.'"

"Assuming his captors found him, they didn't kidnap Darry again. They gave him a terrible beating. Why?"

"Because he escaped?" Viv sniffed and blinked back more tears.

"Perhaps. We need more information. I'll tell you one thing though."

"What?"

"We'd better be on our guard. If the killer who framed you and Doug for murdering Curtis is connected to the men who assaulted Darry, they'll stop at nothing. We could be dealing with stone-cold killers."

Viv shook her head. "The timing doesn't work. Darry just arrived."

"We don't know how long it took Darry to hitchhike home. If his captors flew, they would've arrived in a day."

Viv clamped both hands on her forehead, her eyes wide. "Oh. My. God."

Chapter Forty-Two

By Wednesday afternoon, Darry had been admitted to the hospital's psych ward and had responded well to medications. Deputy Franklin recorded his sworn testimony about being held captive in Alaska and forced to work four months for no compensation. Viv relayed the information after insisting on being present in the hospital room when Franklin questioned her brother. The deputy agreed and brought in Deputy Zillo as backup. They talked and listened to the patient until the doctor threw them out of Darry's room, saying the man needed to rest.

I spent the day doing chores at home and helping my friend Rosemarie clean a new client's house later in the afternoon. I'd just finished the client's kitchen when my phone rang. Geneva Walker, the display said.

I silenced the phone. "You can stop to take a call," Rosemarie said, brushing her purple and white streaked hair behind her ears. "I'm not that much of a control freak."

"I'm not ready to talk to her. Geneva wants me to be a substitute caterer for Ocean Crest Plaza. I did an event for her on Sunday, and she wants me under contract for the remaining twenty-something events she's already booked."

"For a gig like that, you could name your own price. You'd be rolling in the dough too."

"Except Geneva expects her hotel booking to have preference over my pre-existing customers."

"I understand, but, River, you need the money—"

"I do. Need the money."

"Then show her your calendar of recurring events and say those dates aren't available to her."

"Geneva Walker expects to get her way. She's a force."

"So are you."

~*~

After depositing my housecleaning income in the bank, I drove to Seashore Park to watch the waves for a few minutes. Fortified, I listened to the voice mail from Geneva. She praised my work and asked to me to come in at my earliest convenience to sign another contract with her.

My long-term customers didn't pre-book events with me. They'd become spoiled by my mostly open calendar. Rarely did I have a scheduling conflict. If I went with Geneva, conflicts were guaranteed. I'd work every weekend, possibly every night. As a rule, I avoided back-to-back large events. Taking this job might lead to burn out, and then where would I be?

On the other hand, I could call my repeat clients and invite them to commit now. I could offer to hold their preferred date for a month without a deposit. In my calendar I made a note of the recurring occasions. Anniversaries, annual fundraisers, holiday parties, graduation parties—those I could book now. That would ensure that I satisfied my preferred clients.

I liked that idea.

One problem solved. Everything would be easier for the Declans if Anita acted like an adult. Could I convince Anita to cut her husband some slack? I drove to Anita's place and knocked on the door. Her across the street neighbor, a woman, waved, and I returned the wave.

Anita answered, holding baby Zoey. "River. I didn't expect you."

"I'd like to talk with you. Is this a good time?"

"Sure. Come on in. I owe you apology for my behavior last night."

"I understand your anger at Darry's extended absence. His behavior hurt your family." I glanced around at the tidy home. "Where's Harry?"

"Playdate. Give me a second to put Zoey down for her nap. Make yourself at home."

Bedding rustled, water ran in the kitchen, and Anita returned with two drinking glasses. "Ice water?"

I took the glass she offered and set it down on the nearest end table. "Thanks. This is awkward for me. You've been through an ordeal and so has Darry. I hope time will heal your anger and maybe even your marriage."

"I can't believe you'd say that to me." Her chin jutted forward. "Everyone believes Darry's captivity story, but nobody asked about me during that time. I was a captive too."

The hair on my neck prickled. Anger freighted her every word, and I glanced toward the door. "What happened, Anita? Should I call Deputy Franklin?"

She came closer, waving a finger in my face. "He's not interested in my story, but I have to tell someone." Her gaze slid to the floor for a long moment. When she spoke again, her voice sounded thin. "Promise you'll keep my secret. I'd be embarrassed if it became common knowledge."

"Of course." My promise came without hesitation.

Anita took a quivery breath. "Once Darry left, Curtis demanded intimate privileges in exchange for news about my husband. I turned him down, of course, and called Darry, but Darry didn't answer. I held out for two months, but I needed news about Darry. Next time Curtis visited, I let him in the house and more."

I wanted to say something, but I sensed she wasn't finished. My instinct was to offer a hug, but maybe she couldn't tolerate anyone's touch after submitting to Curtis. She needed professional help, same as Darry. How much bad news could one family bear?

"I didn't like the way Curtis acted or how he manipulated me." Anita stared out the window before she continued. "When pressed for details about Darry, he bragged he'd know immediately if Darry wasn't fishing because his Alaskan friends

231

were keeping an eye on Darry for him. I swear I didn't know they'd imprisoned him on a fishing boat. Curtis must've laughed himself to sleep every night over destroying our family."

Despite my intent to encourage Anita to welcome Darry home, I realized it wouldn't be a simple fix. Both Darry and Anita suffered deep emotional trauma for months. Poor Anita. My blood boiled at the atrocity she'd suffered. "Curtis had no right to play on your vulnerability. I'm sorry this happened to you."

"Curtis continued coming over until someone killed him. I kept phoning Darry, but he never answered. Then his phone stopped working, and I couldn't even leave him a message. I couldn't see any way out of this mess. The bills kept piling up. My sister helped some, but I couldn't keep borrowing money from her. All I could do was keep going for the children."

"It was wrong and hateful and abusive for Curtis to take advantage of you this way." I stopped to gather myself, needing to dial back my anger. "I recently learned Curtis had a reputation for lying and manipulating people. From my perspective, Curtis took advantage of you and Darry."

Anita burst into tears, sobbing as she spoke, gradually regaining her self-control. "Curtis badmouthed Darry constantly. Then someone killed Curtis and nearly killed Darry. My thoughts are upside down. No wonder I melt down in public."

Moved, I gave her hand a comforting squeeze. "You've been traumatized, Anita. You should see a professional counselor, so should Darry. You've both been through hell."

She pulled back, wrapping her arms around her belly. "I can't afford counseling, can barely afford to feed my family. I'd be homeless by now if not for you and Doug. I'm sorry I showed my tail at the hospital yesterday. I couldn't hold that anger inside any longer, then I just couldn't stop shouting." She shuddered and her face flamed red. "I'm ashamed of my behavior, ashamed that I don't want my husband to touch me."

"Telling someone is often the first step to healing. However, Doug, Viv, and Darry need to hear what you've shared. I'm barely involved."

Her head bobbed up, and a militant spark flashed in her eyes before she glanced away. "You're more than that. You're the matriarch in both families. Doug and Viv listen to you. You're also the nicest of the bunch, so I thought I'd start my apologies with you."

All I'd ever done is try to set a good example for Doug. He'd always looked to me for solutions, and now by virtue of this situation, Viv fell into the same category. But matriarch? Not so much. However, Anita's perceptions had been influenced by her recent experience.

"Your ordeal was as harrowing as Darry's. I get why you're upset with him," I said. "He disappeared and left you to the mercies of a sexual predator. I have no training as a counselor, but as a woman I'm appalled at what happened to you. It's a wonder you can stand to be in a room with any man. You survived. That's important, so cling to that triumph as you heal."

Anita's shoulders straightened and she stood tall. "Thanks, and I mean that from the bottom of my heart. Telling you helped me begin to process what happened. Now I have the courage to face the others."

"They need to know you were a victim too."

"I will tell them, but I'll do it in my time."

"I understand. And hopefully, you and Darry can mend fences."

"No. He's not welcome here."

A sigh slipped out. "I get that you're still upset with him."

Her fists clenched by her sides. "It's not going away. He hurt me."

"For the children's sake, I hope you find some middle ground." I left then, uncertain if I'd made things better or worse. Anita had been wronged, violated, and traumatized by Darry and Curtis. Another realization dawned with icy clarity. She had a strong motive to kill Curtis. I wanted to tell Deputy Franklin this latest development, but I'd promised to keep her secrets.

What a pickle.

~*~

Due to his full daily schedule, Pete requested the remainder of our premarital counseling be moved from four to six p.m. As the appointment approached, he rolled in, collected me, and off we went.

"Thanks for accommodating our time change request," Pete said to Father Ben as we settled in the circle of three chairs.

"It's a pleasure to meet with you two at any time." Father Ben withdrew a sheet of paper from a folder and joined us.

His office always looked like a tsunami rolled though, but Father Ben knew exactly where everything was. Our session began with prayer, and he asked us if we'd discussed finances, how our children would be raised, and wills for inheritances, adding a plug for including the church in our wills.

Fortunately, we had created wills.

He cleared his throat. "Now all we have left to cover are the readings and to confirm the date of May 10."

I handed him the sheet I'd tucked in my purse. "Here are the readings we selected, and yes, we did them together."

He nodded in approval. "That's a great habit to cultivate. And the date? We're still good on that?"

"Definitely here at St. Luke's on May 10 at four," Pete said. "We've asked River's brother, Doug, and Viv Declan to be our attendants. River and I want a small, private ceremony."

"Good, good," Father Ben said as he made notes on the page and in his phone. "That does it on my end. I'll see you two on May 9 to run through the staging and such. Let's use four as the time for that too. We'll have paperwork for you to sign. But you're in charge of getting the marriage license from the courthouse. No license, no wedding."

"We're on it," I said.

Chapter Forty-Three

On Thursday morning, I begged out of tutoring to accompany Viv to the hospital. After hydration and stabilizing meds, Darry Declan appeared calm and collected, though he was busy when we arrived. We were only allowed to peer in his room where he worked with a police sketch artist. The officer outside his room said we'd be allowed a brief visit after the sketches were complete.

We padded to the waiting area and sat. "Did Anita find you last night?" I asked in a soft voice to ensure privacy.

"No, we didn't see her, and I'd slam the door in her face anyway." Viv's eyes flashed fire. "She's a miserable excuse for a human being and I hope you treated her like the enemy she is."

I chewed my lip. Viv didn't know of Anita's troubles, and I couldn't tell her. Could I soften Viv's attitude toward her and keep my promise? I had to try. "I went to see her yesterday, and I understand her over-the-top behavior now. Something awful happened in Darry's absence, and she couldn't tell anyone."

"Right. If you believe her, I've got top dollar swamp land to sell you."

"Granted, after her earlier behavior, being civil to her didn't come easy, but I listened to her. She intends to apologize to you, Doug, and Darry."

Viv's eyes closed for a long moment. "She had a difficult time financially when Darry left. I don't know how she managed. She

235

doesn't have to like me, but her hard heart toward Darry is unforgivable. He got caught up in something horrible."

"I hear you. From your perspective, her behavior seems cruel, but there's another side of the story. Her experience is shattering. Should she approach you, please hear her out, and then if it suits you both, begin a dialogue. No matter what the future holds, she's the mother of your niece and nephew, and she'll be in your life."

Viv's cheek twitched and she glared at me. "What tale of woe swayed you to her side?"

"That's for her to say. I promised to keep her secret."

"Ha! I don't trust a word out of her mouth."

"People bashing is not allowed," Deputy Franklin said, coming up behind us. He focused on Viv. "How's Darry holding up?"

Viv lifted a shoulder. "We haven't spoken yet, but his appearance and energy level seem higher. He's made a big improvement over yesterday."

"That's my impression, too," Franklin said. "He needs to stay in the secure psych ward until his medicines are optimized. Did he have pre-existing medical conditions before Alaska?"

"Nope. He's perfectly healthy. I mean he was healthy. Now he's not all there. I'm very concerned about the trauma to his ankles."

Franklin gentled his stern gaze. "He's young, and young bones heal."

"You sound like River. She sees a half empty glass as half full."

Franklin nodded. "Happens when you hang out with optimists."

"Is the sheriff okay with you being an investigator again?" I asked.

"Sheriff Vargas wants to win the next election, and case closure is his guiding force these days. As of this morning I am officially working this case."

Darry's door opened and a thin, lanky man wearing a crossbody bag strolled out. In each hand he carried a sketch. "Got 'em," the man said to the deputy.

Franklin studied the drawings. "These are great." He showed me the images of two men, one was labeled Simon Sharpey and the other was Jaxson Glass.

My breath stalled at the dark menace portrayed in each man's eyes. No wonder Darry feared these thugs. Even though these men had rounded faces, dark hair, and dark eyes, their similarity ended there.

Jaxson Glass looked sturdier, more muscular. His unforgiving square jaw accented the slashing scar below his left eye. His dark hair, striped with blond highlights, hung limply over his ears.

The other man, Simon Sharpey, looked slim by comparison. His crooked nose and slicked back long hair reminded me of stereotypical bad guys on TV. I would not want to meet either of these men in a dark alley or on a sunny beach.

My gaze drifted back to the first sketch. I tapped the image. "I've seen him before. Not sure where. Maybe at the pier or driving around the island."

"Try your surveillance camera," Franklin said in a wry tone.

Recognition hit with the snick of a key fitting into a lock. "You're right. This man, Jaxson Glass, snuck around my yard. No wonder I felt uneasy. Jaxson watched me. I want him arrested for being a Peeping Tom and trespassing and whatever else you can get him on."

"We'll add those charges, along with assault on Darry, but if you're right about the Alaska connection to the Marlin homicide, we can charge him with a more serious crime. That would be good news for Viv and Doug."

"Find them," Viv said. "These men nearly killed my brother."

"I'll upload the sketches and check their criminal records. Maybe one of them used a credit card to rent a car. Meanwhile I'll issue a BOLO on both men, and patrol will pick them up if spotted."

I translated BOLO in my head automatically to "be on the lookout" and felt a mixture of relief and dread. We were getting somewhere. If these dangerous men had framed Viv in addition to assaulting her brother, Doug and Viv got their future back. Catching Sharpey and Glass before they inflicted more harm would be key.

"What should we do?" I asked.

"Stay together and keep watch over each other. Gauging by what happened to Viv's brother, the violence is escalating. I requested an extra deputy to come watch your place, but I can't guarantee we'll get the approval for another overtime officer. Twenty years on the force says this will be over soon."

"There's more room at my place," I said to Viv. "You and Doug can stay with us."

"Good idea." Viv turned to the deputy. "What about Darry's wife and kids?"

Her question caught me off guard. Maybe my words to her about Anita's troubles made a dent in her wall of anger towards her sister-in-law.

"Deputy Zillo is parked out front in a patrol car," Franklin said. "She'll stay the night with Anita."

"Why are we on Sharpey and Glass's radar?" I asked. "They had issues with Curtis and Darry. Why spy on me or Viv?"

"Because you're determined to prove Viv and Doug didn't kill Curtis," he said. "They're violent men who operate in the shadows. I'll text these sketches to your phone, River. Share them with the others. With all that's happened, Sharpey and Glass are living on borrowed time. If they intend more harm, they'll act soon because the longer they stay on Shell Island, the greater their risk of capture. I'll schedule extra patrols past your place, and we'll guard Darry at the hospital."

I nodded, sobered by the thought of violent criminals coming for me. Could I survive a brutal beating like the one Darry received? It looked excruciating. Like Viv and Doug, I wanted my planned future with my fiancé. All of us deserved a chance at happiness.

"Okay if I see my brother now?" Viv asked, breaking the brittle silence.

"Sure." Franklin nodded toward the door. "River, a word."

Viv darted in to see Darry, who had nodded off in the wheelchair. From this distance, the stark evidence of his brush with danger showed in his blackened eyes, heavily bandaged feet, and the broken arm in a cast. I reminded myself that Darry had police protection tonight, and so did his wife and children.

I turned to Deputy Franklin. "What is it?"

"Making sure you hear this message. The situation is serious. No errands alone to the grocery store today. No walking alone to your commercial kitchen. These men cased your place and know the layout and vulnerabilities. The four of you must stick together and be vigilant."

"Okay." The word dragged out in my thoughts. Safety sounded like house arrest. Pete and Doug would hate being told they had to come home from work today. I still had to decide about that hotel contract and no telling what Viv had scheduled this afternoon.

"River, snap out of it," Franklin said. "These men threatened to kill Darry's entire family if he didn't submit to them. They use family members as leverage. You want your family to be safe? Circle the wagons."

"For how long?" I asked.

"Until it's over."

~*~

Pete, Doug, Viv, and I lunched on vegetable soup, grilled cheese sandwiches, and pear slices. Or at least three of us did. Viv hardly ate anything. "I apologize for dragging you into this mess," Viv said. "I'm sorry everyone put their lives on hold today."

"Don't stress, Viv," Doug said, patting the gun he wore on his hip. "We've got this covered. Those Alaska boys won't know what hit them if they come around here."

"I don't like guns," Viv said. "Someone could get shot."

My thoughts exactly as I refreshed everyone's tea and served cookies.

"Men who break into homes aren't paying social calls," Pete said. "You saw what those thugs did to Darry. We're not letting that happen to anyone else."

"I've got an idea." I hurried to a kitchen drawer and returned with a handful of vintage pocketknives. "Help yourself. Make sure you can open the knife you select."

239

Doug's eyes lit up. "My pocketknife collection! I'd forgotten about it. Dibs on the red handled one."

Pete took the largest knife with a variety of blades. Viv and I each took a lightweight one-bladed knife that opened easily.

"I doubt they'll come during the day," Pete said, "but in case they're brazen, we'll take lookout shifts starting now. I'll watch the first two hours, then Doug. Also, we should finish dinner before dark. I don't want house lights giving away our positions."

"I can feed us early," I said. "What else? Close the blinds and curtains?"

"Not yet. Stay away from the windows, but we need to see outside in addition to the real-time video feed from the security cameras. Doug and I will check door and window locks. No one goes outside or opens a door unless it's the cops."

"What about the cat?" I asked.

"The cat can damn well take care of itself," Pete said. "Our security system's doorbell cameras give us a fish-eye view of the area. If the cat needs to come in and no one is visible outside, fine, the cat can enter. But no one opens doors or windows for any reason or without at least one other person present, agreed?"

A chorus of "agreeds" followed. Viv went upstairs for a nap, and Pete and Doug rechecked the door and window locks.

"We're good," Pete said, joining me in the kitchen. "What's that you're making?"

"A chocolate cake. We'll need sugar and caffeine to stay awake tonight."

He wrapped his arms around me for a backward hug. "You're the best. Chocolate cake is my favorite."

I tipped my head back for a quick kiss. "Where's Doug?"

"Napping with Viv." He waggled his eyebrows. "Say, when I'm off-shift from lookout duty in two hours, wanna nap with me?"

"Good idea. If we're staying up all night, we'll need our rest."

"We'll rest too. Meanwhile, what can I do in the kitchen?"

"I need half a head of cabbage grated for dinner prep."

"On it."

~*~

The afternoon passed uneventfully but my nerves wouldn't settle. I tried not to stare outside the whole time, but my gaze kept drifting to the window. Was someone out there?

Doug kept watch from two to four, and then Pete took watch duty again. All during the afternoon watches, my cat prowled the front porch and then the back deck. I "rested" for a bit with Pete during Doug's watch, but I couldn't relax, so I focused on dinner preparations.

With the wild-caught shrimp already in my kitchen freezer, I'd make tortillas and sriracha sauce and we'd dine on a simple feast of shrimp tacos. I thawed, peeled, and deveined the shrimp under running water and then stored them in the fridge to cook later.

I fiddled around the house with the duster, ran two loads of wash, but those everyday chores felt surreal. Would clean laundry matter tomorrow?

When reading a book didn't still the jitters, I pulled out Geneva Walker's contract proposal. Couldn't focus on it either. I paced the house, pausing by Viv who'd settled on the sofa with a magazine.

"I wish this would happen already," I said. "I can't stay still. My spine has that creepy-crawly sensation that something bad is fixing to happen."

"I don't want them to come," Viv said. "I'm practicing denial. It's a reverse mentality from the movie *Field of Dreams*. If I don't think about it, they won't come."

"How's that going?"

She showed me her fingernails, chewed to the quick. "Not good. Even so, this is like when pink slips appeared at the mill. The entire place felt edgy. We never knew when or who'd get the axe until it happened."

"The mill sounds like a harsh environment."

"Wasn't that way when I started, not that it matters now. I wouldn't work there again even if they gave me backpay for wrongful termination, even if they begged me. I'm digging my handyman's-assistant lifestyle."

My lips turned up. "You and Doug are good together. I'm happy for you."

"Me too," Viv said. "Now all we need is a future to go with our fresh starts."

I circled to the kitchen, threw together the sriracha sauce, then I started cooking dinner. My shrimp were on the small side so I plunged them into salted boiling water with lemons until the shrimp curled into circles. Then, I doctored the drained shrimp with spices and set them aside. The last part involved making soft flour tortillas from scratch.

Since I had four hungry adults to feed, I doubled the recipe. Mixing the flour, salt, oil, and water came first, then I kneaded the dough and let it rest for ten minutes. While I waited, I set the table. I had divided the dough and flattened dough balls into tortillas when Major pawed frantically at the kitchen door.

I called Pete from the front of the house. "Come here, please. The cat wants in."

My fiancé hurried in, ignored the frantic cat, and studied the tree line. "See anything suspicious?"

I hovered behind him. "It's eerily quiet. The whole house feels like a circling shark about to strike."

He nodded. "I feel that brooding heaviness too." Handgun at his side, he cracked the door, ushered the cat inside, and quickly relocked the door.

Major sniffed the air, stalked over to the covered trash can, and parked on the floor beneath our cooked shrimp. "Cover the shrimp," Pete said, "or the cat will eat our dinner."

I moved the thick glass bowl into the microwave. "On it."

Pete went back to watching the front while Major kept one eye on the microwave and the other on the back door. Each tortilla took a quick minute in the frying pan.

Despite our best efforts at conversation, dinner was a solemn, though tasty affair. Shadows lengthened, dusk thickened, and night flooded in, relentless and all-encompassing. One question lodged in my thoughts. Would we see Friday's sunrise?

Chapter Forty-Four

The men gave up the pretense of shifts once darkness settled around us, prickly and uncomfortable. Doug and Viv covered the front while Pete and I watched the back. I placed soft nightlights in the hall and bathroom, and each of us carried a small flashlight.

"Would you wear your engagement ring tonight?" Pete asked.

I generally wore the diamond solitaire on a chain around my neck to keep it safe. The perfect fit ring loosened under cold water, enough for the ring to slide around and cause concern.

"Sure."

Pete brought my ringed finger to his lips and kissed it. "That looks great."

In the twilight, I admired my hand. It looked amazing.

"I'm sorry the sheriff didn't approve another deputy for us," Pete said. "Are you upset about that?"

"I'm upset at every bad decision the sheriff makes, and this is a bad decision. Deputy Franklin said this was coming to a head and I agree."

"Doug and I will protect you and Viv."

"We're all protecting each other," I said. "Let's switch subjects and catch up on the wedding plans. We've got Fr. Ben on May 10 at the church. Anything else ceremony-wise needing our urgent attention?"

"I looked at flower arrangements for bouquets and instantly realized you should pick those. I have photos of some choices I thought you might like in the truck," Pete said. "Thought we'd swing up to the Bridal Shop in Savannah this week for gowns and tuxes."

"Viv and I talked about visiting that bridal shop on the mainland. Let's try there first."

"Good deal."

The security system pinged. An intruder. Our worst fear come true. "I'm scared." Instinctively, I clung to Pete. I didn't want anything to happen to us.

The darkness shifted in the hall doorway. "Someone with a flashlight is approaching the front of the house on foot," Doug said quietly. "Not a deputy or there would be a cruiser in the drive. Safe to assume this is Sharpey or Glass. With a frontal approach, I assume they're coming in through the front door. Viv should stay here with River while Pete and I deal with the threat."

"Right," Pete said in an urgent but soft tone. "That's our plan. You ladies take flank. Doug and I have point."

Moments later, Viv and I huddled alone in the faint starlight of my kitchen. "I don't know about you," I said, "but even though I'm so scared my hands are shaking, I resent being sidelined."

"No worries here," Viv whispered. "We're the second wave should one of them get past Pete and Doug. Let's see. We've got pocketknives. What else should we use for defense?"

"I've got cast iron frying pans," I said.

"Perfect," Viv said.

We each grabbed a frying pan and crouched behind the kitchen's center island. My heart thundered in my chest and strained against my ribs. All too soon, glass broke and punches landed. Groans and grunts rose to a fever pitch.

I heard guttural noises, more heavy breathing. No gunshots, thank goodness, but I couldn't tell if Pete and Doug needed help. Mom always said to face my fears. That's what I'd do. I wouldn't cower in the dark.

"Stay here and call the cops," I said to Viv as I sprinted across the kitchen, stopping beside the hallway doorframe, cast iron pan held firmly in both hands. I strained to see in the darkness.

Hearing was my only link to the melee playing out in my front room.

"Stop or I'll shoot," Pete yelled.

A shot rang out.

Paralyzing fear gripped me.

Someone might be hurt. Don't let it be Pete or Doug. It couldn't be Viv, safely tucked behind the island, and I felt no pain. An invader got hit, that was the only reality I accepted.

I heaved a sigh of relief, and the world became fluid again.

More glass broke in the other room.

Wood splintered.

A thud shook the floor.

I gripped and regripped my frying pan, cocking it over my shoulder like a baseball bat. Sounds of the cage fight in the other room intensified. Men grunted, but another sound caught my notice. Footsteps. A thin shaft of light lanced the hallway.

Someone walked this way. Someone who didn't announce his presence. Doug or Pete would know we'd go after anyone who came through unannounced. A familiar board creaked. I held my breath, counted to five, and swung the frying pan with all my might, smacking flesh that wasn't there a second ago.

The impact ricocheted up my arm, jarring my right shoulder. The intruder fell to the floor. The cat shrieked as I cocked my arms for another strike.

"Hit the lights, Viv," I said. "I got one of them."

The overhead lights came up fast, and I blinked against the flood of brightness. The man on the floor wore a black ski mask and black clothing. Major stood on his chest, staring at the man's face, claws out. The man still held a gun in one hand. Instinctively, I stepped on the hand and grabbed the gun.

Viv crept over, frying pan in hand. "Who is it?"

"Don't know. Grab the cable ties from my junk drawer by the fridge and let's immobilize him. Did you call the police?"

Thuds and groans continued in the next room.

"Not yet." Viv set her pan down and hurried over with the cable ties. "It happened too fast."

"Sure did." I nodded at his legs. "Feet first. Then we'll cinch his wrists. He so much as twitches and I'm shooting him with his own gun."

Viv knelt and made quick work of his feet. She slipped a band around each wrist, including the one I had my foot on, then she looped his hands together with a third tie.

"Remove his mask," I said.

Viv yanked it off the unconscious man. "Jaxon Glass," she said upon viewing the stocky Alaskan with collar-length hair, square-jaw, and a scar below his left eye.

To my satisfaction, blood flowed from his nose in a steady stream.

"Is he dead?" Viv asked.

"He's breathing. Here, hold the gun. I'll call the cops." Hand-off completed, I punched a number on speed dial.

Franklin answered on the first ring. "What?"

"They're here." I said. "Jaxon Glass is unconscious on my kitchen floor. Simon Sharpey is fighting Doug and Pete in the front room. Someone fired a gun. Don't know if anyone caught a bullet."

"On my way. Three minutes, max. I'll request more units and a bus. Hang tight."

I glanced at Viv. "You got this?"

"Yeah," Viv said. "Glass isn't going anywhere. If he gives me any reason, I'll shoot his ankles for the beating he gave my brother."

I grabbed my frying pan and crept toward the living room. With the element of surprise gone, I flipped on the lights.

Pete and Doug sat atop another masked intruder who lay face down. Blood stained the carpet beneath the man in black. "Cops are on the way," I said.

"We got him," Pete said. "What about the other guy?"

"Got him too," I said. "Jaxon Glass walked right into my frying pan and hasn't moved since."

"Ouch."

"With Glass in the kitchen, this must be Simon Sharpey."

"He's a helluva wrestler. Took both of us to hold him down, even with a bullet hole in his shoulder."

"You want cable ties?"

"Nah," Pete said. "We'll wait for the handcuffs."

"How'd they get in?"

"Popped the front door lock in seconds. Even though we knew they approached, they came in quick and fought hard."

Pete had a few scrapes on him, but nothing bad. I glanced at my brother. Swollen eye, possible shiner on the way. Heavy breathing but no gushing wounds.

"Hang on, Doug," I said. "I hear the sirens."

I glanced around my living room. The coffee table, two chairs, and three lamps would never be the same. The wall beside the mirror sported a round hole. Guess the bullet that hit Sharpey went clean through and struck the wall.

Seconds later, Deputy Franklin and a deputy I didn't know stormed the house, entering with guns drawn.

"Both intruders are secured," I said. "We've got Jaxson Glass in the kitchen. This is the other Alaskan, Simon Sharpey."

Franklin kept his gun aimed at the injured man while he nodded to his associate. "Cuff 'em."

The first hand cuffed easy, but when the deputy tried to move the second hand, the man groaned and cursed vigorously. "That hurts," he yelped.

"Too bad." The deputy tugged his arm hard and nodded to Franklin.

I felt like crowing our success. Instead, I said, "We're showing you the same mercy you showed Darry Declan when you beat him."

Franklin holstered his gun and checked the cuffs. "Sit tight," he told the man. He glanced my way. "The other intruder?"

"Viv's got him at gunpoint."

"I'll bet she does." He withdrew his weapon and hurried to my kitchen.

I followed and peered over his shoulder when he stopped short of the room. He prodded the man with his shoe and got no response. "He's out cold. What'd you nail him with, Holloway?"

"I told you. He walked into my frying pan."

"Remind me never to get between you and your cooking utensils." He studied the man's occupied chest. "Can you get the cat off him?"

"Don't know." I squatted and called Major. "Here, kitty, kitty." The cat didn't budge.

I stood. "Something's off. Maybe he's faking. The cat knows something."

"Point the gun away from Glass, Viv," Franklin said, holstering his weapon.

"I'd rather shoot him," Viv said, "but I'll do as you ask."

"According to our intel, these men are enforcers," Franklin said. "If you kill him, we don't have leverage to identify the guys at the top."

"Logic stinks," Viv said, lowering the weapon.

Franklin holstered his gun, withdrew a knife, and sliced through the zip ties on the man's wrists. "I'll cuff his hands behind his back then he'll be more secure."

But when he bent down to roll the guy over, Glass headbutted Franklin, tried to stand and run, and fell because of the zip-ties on his feet. The cat yowled in the middle of the commotion and leapt off the intruder. The man screamed as cat claws pierced his belly.

Franklin cuffed the man and sat on his heels. "Next time, remind me to pay attention to your cat."

Chapter Forty-Five

After all the nighttime commotion, Pete and I slept late on Friday. No Island Creamery for him, no catering for me. I'd inspected him from head to toe last night, and he'd returned the favor, making sure we were both unharmed. We'd held each other and talked most of the night until the Sandman finally came.

We rolled into the kitchen mid-morning. No sign of Viv or Doug. No coffee started either. I quickly got a pot going and made buttermilk pancakes while I roasted a pound of bacon in the oven.

Wonderful, normal aromas filled the house, and Pete and I were on our second batch of pancakes when the other two joined us. Doug sported two black eyes, like a raccoon.

I whistled at the sight. "Does that hurt?"

"Only when I breathe," he said.

"He's my hero," Viv said, "as are River and Pete. You three fought hard. I sat on the sidelines."

"Doesn't matter who did what," I said. "We caught the guys that beat up your brother. Franklin is working the Alaska shanghaiing angle too. With any luck, that won't happen to anyone else again."

The cat rubbed against my leg again, and I fed him a piece of bacon. "You can have all the bacon you want, Major. You knew Glass was faking it. He tried to outwit us, but he couldn't because Major was on our side."

Maggie Toussaint

"I'm glad you stopped him," Doug said. "Sorry we couldn't hold him in the living room."

"He won't forget my frying pan anytime soon," I said. "Bet he has a monster headache this morning."

"He's likely to have more than that," Pete said. "Franklin probably roasted him on the hotseat all night."

"More power to him," I said. "I'm still zonked after a few hours of sleep. Now I've got to face the disaster in my living room."

"Our living room," Pete said, "and we needed to update the furniture. Now we've got a good reason."

"New furniture is expensive. Let's wait," I said. "You wanted a new place anyway. Furniture we buy for here may not fit another space."

"Been thinking about that too," Pete said. "Why move when this place suits you so well? What about adding onto this space to incorporate a home office for me and a new master suite downstairs?"

My heart sang. "I'd say that's perfect. Did I miss the part where we're rich?"

"I got back 80 percent of my stake from North Merrick. I invested in the ice cream place and now I'm investing in us."

"I love that idea!"

"If you're replacing the living room furniture," Doug said, "I have dibs on the old sofa."

"Yeah," Viv said. "Dibs on the sofa and anything else y'all don't want."

"Okay, okay," I said. "Feels like I've stepped into a hurricane. We're getting new furniture, building a new wing, and you're getting our sofa. Does this mean what I think it means?"

"Yep," Doug said. "Franklin called an hour ago. The sheriff charged Sharpey and Glass with poisoning Curtis. The charges against us were dropped. We're free to go about our lives again."

"What about Darry?" I asked Viv. "What's his outlook?"

"He hailed a cab to drive him here. I hope that's all right."

"It's more than all right. This is wonderful news."

"He also told us where he parked Viv's car. Said he took it to meet Anita only she never showed. Instead Sharpey and Glass found him. We'll pick up the car later today."

"That is very good news."

Major rubbed against my leg, and I rewarded him with another bite of bacon.

"Hey, save some of that for me," Doug said.

"Me too. I'm starved," Viv said.

Round two of breakfast began, and I cooked another batch of pancakes for Darry. He dove into them when he arrived, then he fell asleep on the sofa. With everything under control, Pete left for the Island Creamery. Doug and Viv dashed out to run errands and pick up Darry's prescriptions, so Major and I retired to the back deck.

The air felt springtime fresh and so crisp it hurt to breathe. Thoughts pulsed through my head. Doug and Viv were free. Darry was alive. Pete and I were getting new furniture. I didn't have to move. My cat saved the day. The morning looked golden. I couldn't recall a day that had more promise.

Then, as if a switch flipped on, an eerie sensation raised goosebumps.

The birds stopped singing, a car door slammed in front of the house. Major crouched low under a bench, watching and waiting. I longed for a frying pan, but I still carried a pocketknife. I clung to that thought, though my rational mind told me the bad guys were in custody.

Anita Declan strolled around the house sans children. "There you are. What happened? Your front door is boarded up."

"We had some excitement here last night." I gestured to the other chair, relieved I knew my visitor. "Join me. Can I get you some coffee?"

"No need," she said, shoving a sheaf of papers my way. "These divorce papers are for Darry. I heard he took a cab here."

"He's resting." I paused. "Are you sure about this, Anita? You and Darry have been through so much. Divorce seems so final."

"It is final," she said, moving her hand in a chopping motion. "That's the point. I'm closing this chapter of my life. Darry can see the kids under supervision, but I won't ever trust him again. I thought about what you said. What happened in Alaska wasn't his fault, but he chose to go. Our marriage was in trouble before

Maggie Toussaint

Alaska. Now I'm done with him. I need time to recover from my own trauma."

"I see." And, sadly, I did see. She didn't want Darry. Both of them survived horrific experiences, both needed time to heal.

"If Darry is honest, he wants a divorce too," Anita continued, holding out the papers.

I took them this time. "I'll make sure he sees them."

"Thanks." A frown crossed her face. "Listen, sorry to flit out of here so fast, but the kids are in the car."

"No problem," I said, fingering my necklace chain as she left. I studied the covering of the packet and recognized the preparer's name as that of a local attorney. This was no boilerplate divorce agreement off the internet. Darry would need an attorney to figure it out.

Seemed like overkill to me.

~*~

With the danger behind us, Darry, Doug, and Viv returned to Viv's apartment on Saturday, so that left Pete, the cat, and me at home. My fiancé left for work and I did chores to avoid facing the contract offer from Geneva at Ocean Crest Plaza. But contract thoughts deviled me anyway. Pros: steady work and decent income. Cons: loss of flexibility, cooking standard menus, business promotion not allowed.

Even though I needed to expand the scope of Holloway Catering, this didn't feel right. I didn't want to sign the contract.

I wished Mom were still alive. She'd give her take on the situation. Pete's business savvy centered on earning money, and he'd urged me to "do it." Doug and Viv were busy with each other. That left me and the cat.

"Should I go for it?" I asked Major. "Should I sell out artistry for income?"

Major regarded me steadily, his eyes intent, then he walked away, tail swishing.

Huh.

Chapter Forty-Six

After a good night's rest, I took the cat's advice and walked away from the hotel job and booked a golden anniversary party for early May. The sixty-person gathering could be easily accommodated with minimal help. The couple's children had reserved an outdoor pavilion by the beach and had thought enough ahead to set the event at high tide. Pulled pork and sautéed shrimp topped their menu. It sounded like fun already.

I penciled the event on my calendar, blocking off the day before and half the day after. Looking through the food selections, I created an event ingredient list and got that printed and filed. Electronic files worked fine for most things, but I'd rather have a paper copy I could line out for an actual event.

Once I finished the event preplanning, my thoughts returned to the case. Viv and Doug were cleared. Sharpey and Glass were on ice. Darry had surfaced, but he wasn't whole by any stretch of the imagination.

How nice that Viv and Doug got their life back.

Something worried at me. Took me a few minutes to place the concern. Anita. She'd been wronged by both Darry and Curtis, but she'd come through the ordeals relatively unscathed, while Darry'd been broken by his Alaskan captivity, and Curtis died from poisoning. Except I'd witnessed Anita's hot temper lately. She wouldn't sit idly by if she'd been mistreated.

More than a few times Deputy Franklin mentioned that females used poison to kill. A dark thought flickered in my head.

I'd never once thought of Anita, a young mother, as a murderer, but what if she killed Curtis? She'd been mistreated by both men. Now she was the only one left standing.

Could it be? I got a little breathless. Did Darry choose Alaska to escape her sharp tongue? Maybe Curtis didn't demand favors from Anita as she'd said.

Heavy D and crew said Curtis wanted to be with Viv again. If Anita thought Curtis loved her, but he dumped her for Viv, that temper of hers would've flared.

Oh my gosh.

It fit.

Plus, it made more sense than the Alaska men coming to Georgia to punish Darry for surviving. I still didn't know why they came, but someone orchestrated it. Not only had Anita framed Viv, her rival for Curtis's affections, perhaps she'd maneuvered the Alaskans to take the fall if Viv got exonerated. Even though I didn't know how she reached Sharpey and Glass, it fit.

Diabolical.

Now that I'd viewed the evidence from Anita's perspective, I couldn't stop thinking about Anita being the killer. Could I prove it? I could question her, subtly of course. She'd never suspect I knew about her involvement. Yeah. I liked that plan. And I could invite her over here, on my turf.

I dialed her cell, invited her, and heard her say she'd be right over. True to her word, she was there with little Zoey in ten minutes.

But, my better angels warned, if she's guilty, I could be in danger. I fired off a quick text to Pete. *Anita's here. Think she killed Curtis.*

"Despite everything, you're my friend, River. I'm glad you called," Anita said as I met her on the back deck. "My whole world has been those kids. I don't have a single adult friend outside of Viv and I burned that bridge by divorcing her brother. You and Doug gave me a helping hand. I hope I haven't messed that up."

She had nowhere else to turn, no adult friends. I couldn't imagine feeling so bereft. I gestured toward the house. "Let's talk in the kitchen."

"I heard you guys took down two Alaskans," Anita said, padding behind me with her sleeping child.

"We did, but I'd rather not talk about it. Where's Harry?" I asked as I ushered her inside.

She flexed her fingers as she jittered in place. "With Darry. I didn't know what to do with myself, and then you called."

Anxiety radiated from her body, roiling the kitchen's airwaves. Did she believe Darry would harm his son? This must be a bad case of separation anxiety. "Would you care for iced tea and cookies?"

She nodded at my offer but didn't sit down or relax. She lapped the room before she stopped by the table. "Thanks. Darry signed the papers already. I thought he'd drag the divorce out. I geared up for a dogfight, only now there's no fight and I'm too wired to sit still."

Her news saddened me, but I understood. I poured two glasses of iced tea. "A fresh start is what you both want."

Anita gazed out the window as I placed the tea glasses on the table. "It felt surreal," she said. "He didn't say a word, just shoved the signed papers at me fifteen minutes ago."

I crossed to the cookie jar, withdrew a handful of fresh treats from the jar, plated them, and returned to the table. "I hope you like oatmeal raisin."

"Sure," Anita said, grabbing a glass and staring at the chair as if it were teeming with ticks. "I love your cookies. Do you mind if we move outdoors? It's so peaceful on your deck. I rarely get a chance to enjoy the outdoors without two noisy kids."

"All right." We moved everything and sat outside. I sipped my tea and set it aside.

Anita nattered on about this and that, mostly the kids, but she didn't unwind from that hyper-aware state. When she stopped for a breath, I managed to squeeze in a few words. "Harry is fine with his father," I said, hoping to ease her fears.

"He better be," she said. "What about the case? Is it over?"

"The police think so, but I have a few lingering questions." All of a sudden my stomach felt queasy. A sheen of sweat dotted my brow. I flashed hot and cold. Did I have a fever? I hid my unease so I could continue talking to Anita. "Sharpey and Glass admitted they visited Curtis the day of his death and they admitted shanghaiing and beating Darry. It ties together neatly, but ..."

Anita studied me with catlike intensity. "What?"

"Something about the timing. I think Darry came home earlier than we suspected. And I don't know why or when Sharpey and Glass got here. It doesn't hang together."

"They confessed to being there with Curtis. He didn't do things their way, and they came after him. I'm sure they poisoned Curtis. What more do you want?"

I felt so strange. It took more and more energy to talk. Another wave of dizziness hit. "I get a sense of finality when a case comes together, but I don't have that now. Something's missing."

"Like what?"

"Like the real killer. If those Alaskan's purpose here was to kill Curtis, why didn't they leave after he died? It must be someone else. Darry didn't even know Curtis was dead. He couldn't fake the level of surprise I saw. You hated Curtis. Did you kill him, Anita?"

In the ensuing silence, Anita's foot tapped. I would have glanced at her but I could barely focus on my lap. Moving my head magnified the dizziness. Why didn't she deny killing Curtis?

"I knew you were a problem," Anita said, her voice brutally flat. "You're too smart for your own good."

"Anita, is something wrong?" My voice sounded faraway. I wished Pete were here. Why didn't he answer the text I sent?

"Yeah, something's wrong. You can't stop searching for the truth. In fact, my concern was justified. You're right. I killed Curtis, and I'd do it again if I could."

The world slipped out of phase every few seconds. Nausea welled in my stomach, but I pressed on, the need to know giving me strength. "If you hate Darry and Curtis so much, killing Curtis and making sure Darry ended up broken or dead were the ultimate payback."

"You can't prove anything."

My gotcha moment paled as my headache pulsed with a life of its own. I clutched my temples. This was the worst possible moment to be violently ill, but I couldn't hold it together any longer. "I need to lay down. I'm sick."

"Took you long enough."

Anita's face blurred in and out of focus with a sickening reality. My symptoms did not spring from a sudden illness. "You did this to me?"

"When you prepared the cookie plate, I poisoned your tea. The amount of antifreeze I dumped in your tea is a lethal dose. You'll be dead within the hour. Just like Curtis. I'm sorry about killing you. I always liked you, but you're too clever. I can't let you take your theories to the cops." With that, Anita stood, shouldered the sleeping baby, pocketed my cell phone, grabbed the cookies, and locked the house. She shot me an evil smile. "Enjoy the rest of your short life." She strolled off.

My thoughts fired in no-nonsense bullets.

Anita poisoned me with antifreeze.

Franklin said it was an agonizing death.

No wonder I felt terrible.

How much did I drink?

Not much.

How long did I have?

An hour if I believed her.

911.

I had to call that number.

And I needed to write a note for the EMTs.

I scrambled from the chair and fell to the deck. Ouch. All right. If I couldn't walk, I could crawl. I made it in six grueling hand-steps to the back door. Locked, of course. And the front door nailed shut. I had no keys in my pockets and Anita stole my phone. I sagged against the door.

I must've dozed, because the next thing I knew the cat stood meowing on my legs, the fake rock key enclosure by my right hand.

How'd Major know I needed that?

Didn't matter.

Focus.

I grabbed it on my third try.

The lock seemed impossibly high. I sat on my heels and kept at it until the door opened. I crawled over to where the wall phone hung. I pulled myself up, grabbed the receiver, and dialed the number.

"What's your emergency?" the operator said.

How long until I couldn't talk? Death by antifreeze was an agonizing death. I gathered strength to say what needed to be said. "I've been poisoned with antifreeze," I said, my syllables slurring and running together. "Anita Declan did this to me. Hurry." She asked for my name and address as I slid back down the counter. "Back door is open," I said. "Come around the back."

~*~

Someone shook me. "Ma'am, stay with me. Who lives here with you?"

Words cycled in my brain like socks in the wash but they couldn't reach my mouth. I worked harder to speak, hating the ugly noises I heard. Finally, something coherent came from my lips. "Pete Merrick. Island Creamery."

That effort took a toll. My body ached everywhere. Sharp stabbing pains assailed me, overwhelmed me, as if my insides imploded. I couldn't hold on any longer. Daylight faded to black.

Chapter Forty-Seven

Light glowed beyond my eyelids. Everything ached. I felt warm. Bright light. Warmth. Was I in heaven? There shouldn't be pain. No pain in heaven.

My eyelids flickered and closed.

I heard a noise, felt a steady pressure on my hand.

Alarmed, I opened my eyes wide.

Three concerned faces filled my field of vision.

Pete. Doug. And Viv. My people.

"Am I dead?" I asked.

"Very much alive, though you gave me quite a scare," Pete said. "We have a new rule. You're never getting poisoned again. I can't take it."

Doug punched my fiancé in the shoulder. "Don't give her a hard time, dude. She's lucky to be alive."

"Good to see you," Viv said. "You were unconscious for a day and a half."

Wow. Ignoring my throbbing head, I motioned for the nearby cup of water. Pete held it for me, and I drank heavily, licking my lips as I finished. "Tastes good."

"I'll bet," Viv said, flashing her left hand before my eyes. A diamond ring banded her finger. That was new.

"What'd I miss?" I asked her. "Catch me up."

"The cops arrested Anita for killing Curtis and poisoning you," Pete said, pushing between us. "She was denied bail. Sharpey and Glass will be expedited to Alaska after they stand trial for their

Georgia crimes of felony assault on Darry and us. And, in case you forgot, Doug and Viv are officially cleared."

"How is Darry?" I asked, searching each face.

"He's recovering, but he can't manage the kids," Viv said. "He freaked out about the responsibility and landed in the psych unit again. Doug and I are taking Zoey and Harry."

"As foster parents?"

"For now. Adoption later if Darry can't pull it together. That's not all."

"You're wearing a diamond."

"Yep. Tell her Doug."

"I asked Viv to marry me, and she said yes."

I nodded at the good news. "Congratulations."

"And the news keeps coming." Viv pointed to her belly. "Knocked up. Six weeks by our estimation."

A baby. Oh, how I wished it were me. I hoped my smile wasn't bittersweet because I was happy for her and Doug. "Congratulations again. You guys will be swimming in kids."

Pete cleared his throat. "They asked if we'd consider a double wedding. Since most of our plans are firm, it would be practical and expedient. I'm good with it if you are."

I shrugged. "Sounds good." I tried to move and the monitor beeped. I stilled and unclenched my teeth. My head throbbed but dang if I would mention it. "I want to go home."

"Forget it. You're staying put for a few days," Pete said. "Apparently, there's a delay in symptom appearance from this kind of poisoning. Specifically, your doctor is concerned about your kidneys. Antifreeze can wreck them. Your med team wants another two days of monitoring your body functions, as they track what goes in and comes out."

"But I drank so little of the poison."

"It doesn't take much, and the antifreeze floated on top of your tea. The concentration affected the specific gravity so dosing isn't a straightforward calculation or something like that."

I didn't follow all that, but I caught the gist. "They can't tell how much I drank?"

"They've measured your blood levels but now the concern isn't about the antifreeze as it is about how the body changes antifreeze."

I groaned. "I'm truly stuck here? Isn't there a rule like once I go to the bathroom by myself I can go home?"

The doorway darkened and a woman wearing a white coat spoke from the threshold. "Good to see you awake, Ms. Holloway. I'm Doctor McPhee. Gauging from everyone's happy faces, you sound like yourself and you want to go home."

The dark skinned woman spoke with authority and carried herself like she had martial arts training. She glided into the room and commanded the space. A faint scent of jasmine accompanied her. Her lean body reinforced the command attitude, as did her no-nonsense haircut, navy blue flats, and navy pants. Her expression appeared compassionate but her demeanor radiated I've-got-this. I had no doubt that she could wrangle difficult patients.

"You're good," I said, summoning my reserves for a bright smile. "When can I leave?"

Her eyes narrowed slightly as she recorded numbers on her clipboard. "Shouldn't be too many more days. We have tests to run, but since we got to you right away, we hope you won't have lasting effects."

I tried to sit up again, realized I had a catheter and an IV the same time the monitors shrilled, and I gave up. My headache intensified, and I rubbed my throbbing temples. "What kind of effects?"

"Scary stuff, but most likely not a concern. Your blood titer of the poison and its metabolites is steadily decreasing. We'll run psychological tests for a baseline. How's that headache?"

My hand slipped down onto the covers and cradled my aching belly. If this was feeling better, I was glad to miss the excruciating part. "Lucky guess."

"Educated guess. Known side effect." The doctor frowned at the bed and turned to the male nurse that accompanied her. "Clear the room, please." She fixed my visitors with her steely gaze. "You may return after I examine the patient."

Pete's eyes grew stormy, and he didn't budge.

"It's okay," I said. "The sooner I complete the exam, the sooner I go home."

"I'm not leaving you."

I became increasingly aware of moisture under my bottom. Whatever fluid had leaked out, Pete didn't need to see that I had lost control of a body function. "You are. I don't have much pride left but let me have this exam moment alone with the doctor."

"I can't lose you, River."

"You won't. I'm in the hospital. The doctor is here. They know how to fix me."

"I can take bad news, if that's your concern."

"No secrets. We already agreed to that."

After the male nurse cleared the room, the doctor studied me intently. "Something on your mind?"

"The bed is wet."

Dr. McPhee peered under the covers and called the nurse.

"What is it?" I asked. "Did I dislodge the catheter?"

"The catheter is fine. This is something else. Something I hoped wouldn't occur."

The worst menstrual cramp I'd ever had in my life nearly doubled me over. I cried out. "What's happening? My insides are pulling apart."

"I'm sorry," the doctor said, adjusting the sheets, donning a pair of gloves. "I prayed this wouldn't happen."

I felt the heat of a strong light down there, felt the gush of fluids. "What?"

"I removed the catheter. Feeling the tightness in your belly as well as examining the vaginal flow, I have to ask. How far along are you?"

"Along? Along what?"

"Ms. Holloway, you're having a miscarriage."

~*~

I labored for an hour. Afterward, sleep eluded me and tears seeped from my eyes.

"It's okay to be sad. We lost the child we both wanted," Pete murmured, tucking the warmed blankets tight around me.

"I didn't know," I told him. "After months of not getting pregnant, I thought I needed to see a specialist. I'm weepy and sad, and I wanna curl up in a dark place. I hurt everywhere, especially my heart. I'm sorry I can't pull it together. Oh, Pete, we lost our baby."

Pete caressed my hand. "My heart aches for our baby and for you. I wish I could make it better or have protected you from Anita. I wish I hadn't been away from my phone for the fifteen minutes you needed me."

"Not your fault."

"Feels like it. I nearly lost you and the baby."

"None of us knew how far she'd go."

"She's in police custody. Anita can't hurt you again."

He leaned in and cradled my face. "I'm here with you every step of the way. It's hard for me to be strong because I want to curl up with you and hold you until our tears run dry. You're the most important person in the world to me. Never forget that."

The tears in his eyes and on his face mingled with mine. After a while, a fierce emotion filled the void inside me, and I wiped away our tears. "Anita murdered our baby. You tell Deputy Franklin."

"I will."

Chapter Forty-Eight

It took most of a week to feel whole again. I'd catch myself crying in the pantry, but Dr. McPhee proclaimed that to be normal postpartum behavior. I'd get over it. Kidney and liver function were good. Heart and lungs, going strong. Headaches, a distant memory.

I started cooking again. Cakes, brownies, fudge, cornbread. And I ate carb after carb. My body craved the stuff. Pete brought home ice cream every day. If I kept this up, I'd have a weight problem. Except I kept losing weight.

My fiancé still got a haunted look if I left the room. He'd love nothing more than to keep me locked up in this house so the world had to stay away.

We'd spoken with an architect and Pete showed me the proposed home expansion plans. I approved them with a for-real smile. "Looks great."

"On that, we both agree." He held me close.

Deputy Franklin came to dinner. I made crab cakes, yeast rolls, grilled asparagus, and roasted cauliflower. For dessert I baked peach cobbler to go with Pete's peach ice cream. The deputy and Pete insisted on cleaning up, so I rested on the sofa with Major on my lap. Upon my return from the hospital, Major had darted into the house and claimed my lap. He appeared very concerned about my well-being.

Finally, the men joined me in the living room. "Okay, I've been a good sport and held my case questions until after the meal," I said. "Did Anita confess to murdering Curtis? Because she boasted to me she hadn't left any evidence."

"She blames mental illness for her actions," Franklin said. "Anita said she cracked when her husband left for Alaska. It wouldn't be uncommon for her to have experienced depression and anxiety or worse at being left alone to fend for her family. She lied about her relationship with Curtis. About an hour into her interrogation, she admitted infidelity. Once Darry left, she had a torrid affair with Curtis. She fell in love with him and thought he was her soulmate. But he dumped her to pursue Viv again."

"Wow. Infidelity plus affair plus getting dumped gives Anita a strong motive for framing Viv. Mental illness aside, can we believe anything Anita says?"

"She's a liar and she flunked a polygraph test."

"Hmm. Did you search her place? According to Viv, the only item Curtis valued was the oil painting of Grandma Talley over the hearth. Since it's missing, I wonder if Anita took it to punish Curtis."

"We searched her place when we arrested her. I'll check the inventory, but even if she has the painting, she could claim Curtis gave it to her."

Anita intended to use mental illness as a get-out-of-jail-free card. "How'd she manage all these months with no income? If they couldn't survive on Darry's mill salary, it seems impossible that she paid bills without any income. How'd she pay for gas or keep her heat on during the winter? She isn't the type to suffer in silence."

"On that we agree. Churches and food banks helped her. She lied about her financial situation to everyone, even stealing money from their joint account and hiding it in a personal account to make Darry think they were broke."

I ran through the facts again, my thoughts hitching on her self-diagnosis. "If mental illness is her claim, how'd she pull off two poisonings and who knows what else? How did she consistently parent those kids by herself?"

"She wasn't mom of the year."

"I don't follow you."

"We're still investigating."

Hmm. Maybe I could add something. "Anita confided in me last week that Curtis demanded certain favors for news about Darry in Alaska."

"She mentioned that alleged abuse multiple times in interrogation as well as her torrid affair story. Can't corroborate either version. No ER or doc visits substantiate sexual assault."

"I tried to help her. She must've laughed at me the whole time."

"We put her through a battery of mental exams based on her claims of mental defect. Our doc says she exhibits the traits of a narcissist. She has an inflated sense of self, entitlement issues, a lack of empathy, an overreaction to the slightest criticism, impulsivity in financial decisions, and more."

"A narcissist? I've never known anyone like that, but those traits sound like her. According to Viv, Anita spent freely and loved associating with people of status."

"It fits," Pete said. "Her mother had a similar personality, and narcissism can be inherited."

"I researched this personality disorder," Franklin said. "It's very possible the shame she felt at her husband's abandonment and her relations with Curtis pushed her over the edge."

"Will she get off on the murder charge because of her mental health?" I asked, suddenly fearing her release.

"She's not insane. She's competent to stand trial. Anita wanted Darry dead. Darry came home the weekend after Curtis died, and Anita turned him away. While Darry hid and stole food to survive, Anita confided to her mob-connected neighbor, Beverly, that Darry had returned from Alaska with a tale of imprisonment. That news prompted Beverly's boyfriend Gino Romano to plug the leak. River and Viv got caught in the cleanup sweep."

"That's the part I never understood," I said, jolting at Gino's name. "It made no sense why Alaskans came after me, but Anita set that up. She wanted me gone. That is devious. And premeditated. She tried to kill me twice, with Alaskans and antifreeze."

The bullet hole by my mirror reminded me of my narrow escape. I was still working on forgiveness, but she'd hurt more than me. Her poison took my baby's life. Now the doctor couldn't promise I could even have children again.

"She's behind bars, hon," Pete said. "You're safe."

"Thanks." I exhaled the negativity associated with Anita and focused on the case. "Getting back to what Deputy Franklin said earlier, I assumed Darry was the food burglar, but why did he rob people? Why didn't he go to his sister's place? She would've welcomed him."

"Under questioning, Darry repeatedly said he couldn't go home. He left the island at odds with his wife and sister." The deputy paused before he continued. "From there the story twists. Beverly, the across-the-street neighbor, confirms Anita and Curtis had an affair, whether it was consensual or forced is anyone's guess. The neighbor reported his Mustang there from eight to nine thirty every night."

"Anita spoke to me so impassioned about his abuse," I said. "I believed Curtis preyed on her and from his clockwork presence there, he was a sexual predator. Anita must've felt so trapped and violated."

"Don't get sappy on us," Pete said. "The woman poisoned you."

"She was a victim too," I said. "But if she was the bad guy locally, how does the Alaska piece mesh with the poisoning?"

"Curtis squared his gambling debt to Gino through Darry's conscription," Franklin said. "When Curtis dumped Anita, he said he'd sent Darry to Alaska on purpose so he could seduce her. His duplicity stunned her. Plus, Gino owns the fishing boat where Darry was imprisoned."

The poker guy and Alaskan fishing boat connection linked the last bit together. "Anita killed Curtis and forced Darry out of her life, hoping he'd vanish or die from his injuries?"

"Possibly. We believe Darry recognized Gino's name on the boat from the man's frequent visits to the neighbor's house. With Bev's eagle eye fixed on his Shell Island home, Darry felt unsafe at home and feared Romano coming after him at Viv's place."

Another case fact meshed together in my head. "That explains why he took Viv's car and disappeared. He tried to keep his problem from impacting Viv."

Pete nodded. "With Darry gone, Curtis promised Anita the world but gave her more trouble. Both men were villains in her life."

"How awful. I don't approve of her actions, but she stopped being a victim." I pondered the news. "I don't understand why the Alaskan men came after me."

"According to the neighbor woman, Gino flew Sharpey and Glass here to ensure Darry's silence. He couldn't have Darry blabbing about conscripted labor. But they arrived too late. Darry already told his story to Viv and River. When we questioned Gino about his boat ownership, he said he couldn't lose face with a rival trying to take his spot. By all accounts, Dylan Barresi is giving Gino a run for his money here and in Alaska. For future reference, steer clear of Romano, Barresi, and Danny's Place."

Franklin's point about avoiding dangerous men was duly noted, but the other part didn't mesh. "Wait. Why'd they release Darry if he could blow their operation?"

"They thought he would die. When the Shell Island woman saw him across the street, she told her boyfriend Gino. He called in his fixers."

I did a double take as I connected the dots. "Gino gave the order to have us killed?"

Deputy Franklin nodded.

I shuddered. "My people reading skills must be on the fritz. I knew Gino and Dylan Barresi had shady business dealings but I never figured they were so cutthroat."

"They only showed you one facet of their personality, I'm sure, so don't take it to heart. And there's more bad news. On a daily basis, Anita drugged her kids to make them compliant. You know the rest."

My jaw dropped. "Those poor children. No wonder little Zoey always slept in Anita's arms. I can't fathom any mother doing that, but I've never known any narcissists."

I tried to process the information. Anita was a horrible parent and an unfaithful wife who had bad taste in men. She got even by punishing the men who wronged her. "Wait. I thought the Alaskans confessed to killing Curtis. Did Sheriff Vargas rush to judgment with them?"

"They confessed to arguing with Curtis the day before he died, but they weren't in his house, ever. After Curtis died, both men drove to Jacksonville due to a family matter. Cell phone towers and eyewitnesses corroborate their out-of-state alibi. Their Thursday convenience store argument with Curtis was recorded on video. There's no audio of that conversation and Curtis seemed surprised to see the men. It looked peaceful, so it's unlikely they killed Curtis. But they did assault Darry, so they owe time for that and for the break-in here."

The Alaskans visited Shell Island to tie up loose ends. Since they targeted Darry and me, I believe they would've gone after Curtis if he had lived. Those men used fists and guns. There was no way Anita's lawyer could point to those men as alternate suspects at her trial. "Will Anita's confession hold up in court?"

"Her confession will stand. We did everything by the book."

Anita and Curtis. It boggled the mind. And yet it hadn't lasted. "If she loved Curtis, why not try to get him back? Killing him was final."

"Curtis dumped Anita to woo the love of his life, Viv Declan. Anita said if she couldn't have him, no one could."

"Wow. That's so vindictive. It's a wonder she didn't go after Viv."

"Viv would've been an easy target in her pub crawling days, but about the time Curtis dumped Anita, Viv started dating your brother. Essentially, Anita couldn't get to Viv without going through Doug. They worked together, slept together, played together."

"I'm thankful she didn't poison Doug and Viv. I feel sorry for Anita. Darry and Curtis abused her. Darry left to become the family provider again. Curtis left her for Viv. No wonder Anita didn't want Viv's help. She didn't want Viv to know about Curtis. Seems like Curtis and Darry should serve time for their crimes against Anita."

Franklin's cheek twitched. "Curtis is dead, and Darry will likely struggle with PTSD for the rest of his life so he's serving time if you ask me. From what I've read, Anita's narcissistic tendencies will continue to make her unhappy. She punished her abusers, but the rip current of violence ruined three lives in the process."

"This case had a lot of layers."

"The thanks for solving this one goes to you, River. You kept digging until the truth surfaced. Sheriff Vargas blew a gasket until he realized how to spin the new case resolution to his advantage. You may have seen him on the news talking about his secret investigation to unmask the real killer."

"You kept investigating too, so I can't claim credit, not that I want any. I'm glad Viv and Doug have their lives back." A loose end surfaced in my mind. "What about that painting of Grandma Talley?"

"Anita had it in her garage. It had been slashed repeatedly. Anita admitted to taking it, saying she hated Grandma Talley for looking down her nose at Anita. Apparently the two women knew each other prior to Anita being with Curtis. It must've really upset Anita that Grandma Talley saw her for what she was instead of the image she presented to the world."

"Mercy. Anita didn't turn into a narcissist overnight. She's been one all along and Grandma Talley saw it. Interesting. And what about the Birmingham uncle? Was he really an uncle? It seems weird he didn't take his nephew's ashes or pay for the funeral."

"Ross Talley was an uncle, only not very upstanding. He wanted the family heirlooms to cover his gambling habit. Seems that gambling runs strongly through the male line of the family. The funeral director is suing him for the money owed."

"Sounds like everything is resolved."

Deputy Franklin's phone buzzed. He glanced at it. "I need to return this call. Seems I have a PAC."

"You're leaving?" I asked, thinking he meant he needed to pack a suitcase.

"Not leaving. This Political Action Committee wants me elected sheriff."

"Good. We need a clearheaded man at the top."

Franklin left, and Pete and I watched the sunset.

"You happy?" my fiancé asked.

"Lord knows, I should be happy. I have the guy I want, and he wants me. I have the job I love, and my brother is a responsible adult. But I'm sad about losing the baby, though I hope we have more. And we have Major." I pointed to the purring black lump on my lap. "I love my home, and I love that you want to make it ours. This is the future I've always wanted."

He nodded with a tender smile. "My feelings exactly. Our double wedding is in two weeks. You'll be the one and only Mrs. Pete Merrick."

"I will, but I'm keeping the Holloway, too, for business reasons, just so you know, and I still need a gown."

"We've got time to buy one."

We did. Even though life spiraled out of control at times, the secret to survival meant going with the flow and trusting each other. I had his back, he had mine.

Chapter Forty-Nine

The clip clop of horse hooves pulling the open carriage Viv and I rode in lent a Cinderella glamor to my wedding day. Correction, *our* wedding day, since Viv and my brother were also tying the knot this afternoon. My fiancé arranged for us brides to dress at Village Realty so the carriage ride would roll down the island's main drag to St. Luke's.

Viv waved like mad at passersby. "You look radiant," I said. "No butterflies?"

"Heck no. I'm getting the man of my dreams and a free wedding. I've never had a spotlight moment like this. Remind me to thank Pete later for this special carriage ride."

I beamed. "He knows how much I love horses. One day I hope to have a horse."

"Hands down, you're getting a great guy, but so am I." Viv snuck a glance at me, and I couldn't help noticing that she looked like she'd swallowed a canary.

"What?" I asked.

"I'm sworn to secrecy but as your best friend, I must warn you. You know our small church wedding?"

"Yes."

"It's not so small anymore."

I turned to face her so rapidly, the world took a moment to catch up. I blinked until I saw straight again. "What?"

"Be prepared to see a crowd."

I fought for a breath. "We don't have food for any extra people."

"Relax. We have food out the wazoo. Church ladies made their favs and some of your clients cooked as well."

Okay. That worked. I sipped in some air. "Thanks for the heads-up. I would've hyperventilated for sure once I saw a full parking lot."

"Here's what happened. Father Ben blocked off the date on the church calendar for the Holloway-Merrick wedding and the news went viral on the down-low. When Pete couldn't turn anyone away, Father Ben suggested a potluck reception. Everyone is in on the Big Secret."

"Will people think it's tacky we didn't spring for a reception?"

"Nope. They're excited about surprising and honoring you this way. Word on the street is that if you try to step foot in the kitchen, they'll link arms so you can't enter."

"Gracious. I'm surprised anyone is free on a weekday afternoon."

"No one would miss the event of the year."

We passed from radiant sunshine to a shady patch of oak trees brimming with Spanish moss. "What about a cake?"

Viv laughed out loud. "Taken care of. It'll be awesome. Chef Lorraine from the hotel made it."

"I thought she hated me. Omigosh." I cradled my face in my hands. Talk about backhanded pressure to get me to agree to the hotel catering job I'd already refused.

"Stop that, River. You'll ruin your makeup." Viv swatted my hands. "You do not owe anyone favors because of this. People volunteered. They wanted to do something nice for you. And I know for a fact we have giant tubs of ice cream from Island Creamery. Who cares what anything tastes like when we have ice cream galore?"

"Okay, okay. It's a lot to absorb on the fly. Appreciate the heads-up, very much so."

As we neared the church, there was not a parking place on the street or lot. People in their Sunday best were hurrying to the parish hall with covered dishes. A few turned and waved. My lower lip quivered. All of these people were here for the wedding.

They gave up their afternoon for our double wedding. It was the biggest crowd the church had seen in a long time, and the community support touched my heart.

When the carriage halted in front of the church doors, organ music spilled from the church. Viv rose and Deputy Franklin helped her down from the carriage.

Viv sailed straight into the church, unflappable, and beaming.

I rose on shaky legs, the import of this life milestone hitting me hard. How I would've loved for my mother to be here, but she passed knowing Pete and I would be wed. She'd raised me to be the woman I was today, responsible, compassionate, and generous. I could only hope that one day my kids would think the same about me.

"Regrets?" Franklin asked when I paused.

I took his hand and stepped down. "No regrets."

Moments later, I strolled along the red carpet in a packed church, every face beloved and familiar. Up front, Pete took my hand, his gem green eyes bright with emotion. "You're beautiful."

"Thank you."

As the ceremony flew past, I reflected that though it sometimes felt like Pete and I faced the world alone, we had an entire community wishing us well, and we had each other.

THE END

Grilled Red Snapper with Mango Salsa

Salsa Ingredients
2 tsp chili powder
1 red bell pepper, chopped
1 large mango, chopped
½ tsp cinnamon
1 cucumber, peeled and chopped
¼ cup onion, chopped
3 tbsp lime juice
2 tbsp lime zest
½ cup cilantro
¼ tsp salt

Salsa Directions
In a medium bowl, combine the salsa ingredients. Let sit for at least 10 minutes, tossing before serving.

Fish Ingredients
4 red snapper fillets brushed with 1 tbsp each lime juice and water
Fish rub made with 1 tsp paprika, ¼ tsp allspice, ½ tsp salt, and ¼ tsp black pepper
2 tbsp olive oil

Fish Directions
Heat grill to medium. Place fish on a greased baking sheet. Brush with oil and lightly season with fish rub, getting oil and seasoning on both sides of all fish. Grill for 4 minutes, turn fish over, and grill until fish flakes easily with a fork throughout, about 3 minutes more. Serve salsa on top of fish.

To bake instead of grill, preheat oven to 425F. Bake uncovered in greased pan until fish flakes easily with fork, the duration varies depending on fish thickness. Allow 4-6 mins per ½ inch thickness.

Shrimp Tacos with Sriracha Sauce

Makes 6 tacos.

Shrimp Ingredients
30 medium shrimp peeled and deveined
olive oil
1 tsp paprika
½ tsp garlic salt
¼ tsp black pepper

Slaw Ingredients
2 cups shredded cabbage
¼ cup sliced onion
¼ cup minced cilantro
½ jalapeno pepper, seeded and chopped
1 tbsp olive oil
1 tbsp honey
2 tbsp lime juice
Salt and pepper to taste

Creamy Sriracha Sauce Ingredients
½ cup ranch dressing*
2 tbsp Sriracha (or other pepper sauce) sauce
*Note: You may substitute mayonnaise, cream cheese, sour cream, or Greek yogurt for the ranch dressing.

6 small tortillas, flour or corn

Make the Slaw
Combine and mix the slaw ingredients. Use immediately or cover and refrigerate for a day.

Make the Creamy Sauce
Whisk sriracha and ranch together. Add more sriracha if needed. Refrigerate until needed.

Cook the Shrimp

Combine shrimp and spices in a small plastic bag. Shake to mix. Use or store in the refrigerator for up to 2 days. Warm a large skillet on medium-high heat. Add a generous dollop of olive oil to the pan and then the seasoned shrimp. Cook shrimp until pink, tightly curled, and cooked throughout, about 3 minutes, turning when bottoms pink up. Drain shrimp on paper towels.

Assemble
Top each tortilla with five cooked shrimp and slaw to cover. Drizzle with sriracha sauce. May also serve with lime slices.

River's Peach Supreme*

*To make gluten free and lower in sugar, substitute a 50/50 blend of almond and coconut flour for the all-purpose flour and use an artificial sweeter such as monk fruit for the sugars.

Filling Ingredients
8 thinly sliced fresh peaches
¼ cup white sugar
¼ cup brown sugar
¼ tsp ground cinnamon
¼ tsp ground nutmeg
1 tsp lemon juice
2 tsp cornstarch

Dough Ingredients
1 cup all-purpose flour
¼ cup white sugar
¼ cup brown sugar
1 tsp baking powder
½ tsp salt
6 tbsp unsalted butter, sliced into small chunks
¼ c boiling water

Directions
Preheat oven to 425 F.

In a large bowl, stir together ¼ cup white sugar, ¼ cup brown sugar, ¼ tsp cinnamon, nutmeg, lemon juice, and cornstarch. Add peaches, tossing to ensure even coating. Transfer all into a 2-quart baking dish. Bake 10 minutes.

Next, in a large bowl, combine flour, ¼ cup white sugar, ¼ cup brown sugar, baking powder, and salt. Blend in butter until mixture resembles coarse meal. Stir in hot water until dough holds its shape.

Remove peaches from oven, and spoon topping on top. Sprinkle topping evenly with a mixture of 3 tbsp sugar and 1 tsp ground cinnamon. Bake 30 additional minutes, until topping is golden.

Great alone or served with ice cream.

About the Author

Southern author Maggie Toussaint writes mystery, suspense, and dystopian fiction. Her work won three Silver Falchion Awards, the Readers' Choice Award, and the EPIC Award. She's published twenty novels as well as several short stories and novellas. The final book in her paranormal mystery series, *All Done with It*, released August 2020 and book one in her new culinary cozy series, *Seas the Day*, debuted in April 2020. Maggie served on the national board for Mystery Writers of America, was Chapter President of Southeast Mystery Writers of America, and is Co-VP of Low Country Sisters in Crime. Maggie and her husband live in coastal Georgia where live oaks and heritage cast long shadows. Visit her at https://maggietoussaint.com.

More Books by Maggie Toussaint

Thanks for reading *Spawning Suspicion*. I hope you'll try my other books. A list of my books follows.

Seafood Caper Mystery series, culinary cozies
Seas the Day
Spawning Suspicion
Shrimply Dead, 2021
Dreamwalker Mystery series, paranormal mysteries
Gone and Done It
Bubba Done It
Doggone It
Dadgummit
Confound It
Dreamed It
All Done with It
Lindsey & Ike Romantic Mystery Novella series, cozy mysteries
"Really, Truly Dead"
"Turtle Tribbles"
"Dead Men Tell No Tales"
Cleopatra Jones Mystery series
In for a Penny
On the Nickel
Dime If I Know
"No Quarter" (novella)
Single Title Mysteries
Death, Island Style
Murder in the Buff
Mossy Bog Romantic Suspense series
Muddy Waters
Hot Water
Rough Waters
Single Title Romantic Suspense
House of Lies
No Second Chance

Seeing Red

The Guardian of Earth Futuristic Mystery series

G-1 (writing as Rigel Carson)

G-2 (writing as Rigel Carson)

G-3 (writing as Rigel Carson)

Short Stories

"High Noon at Dollar Central" (a Dreamwalker story)

"Sand Dollar Secrets" (a Cleopatra Jones story)

"The Trouble with Horses" (a Seafood Caper story)

DEATH ISLAND STYLE
Maggie Toussaint

A standalone cozy mystery

Recent widow MaryBeth Cashour moved six hundred miles to escape memories of her late mother's betrayal and her husband's mysterious death. While beachcombing for seashells to use at her artsy Christmas shop, MaryBeth finds a corpse rolling in the surf on Sandy Shores Island.

The horror doesn't end there. When detectives uncover a connection between the murdered man and MaryBeth, she's their prime suspect. It's not her fault the dead guy had one of her hand-painted Christmas sharks in his pocket—she doesn't even know him. Besides, lots of people from the Mid-Atlantic region vacation in coastal Georgia. She insists it's a coincidence he's here. The cops don't believe her.

As her world comes unglued, MaryBeth strips the shellac from her memories, discovering secrets that endanger her life. But time to prove her innocence is running out faster than a rip tide. The killer is crafting up a new murder – MaryBeth's.

Death, Island Style is a cozy mystery flavored with eccentric southerners, Christmas music, and hand-painted holiday decorations. Set in sunny coastal Georgia, the book reveals the struggles of a young woman trying to make her Christmas gift shop profitable while dodging a murder rap. Beach scenes, a hunky pharmacist, and disastrous craft projects add sparkle and humor.

Available at booksellers nationwide and online

Visit www.maggietoussaint.com for details

GONE AND DONE IT

Maggie Toussaint

A Dreamwalker Mystery (#1)

When landscaper Baxley Powell's shovel strikes a human skull, she bargains with the sheriff. If she solves the cold case, she becomes his new crime consultant. She sees the victim's face while dreamwalking, but linking her vision to tangible proof isn't easy.

Meanwhile, Native Americans protest that their burial grounds are being disturbed, prompting a media circus. Then Baxley discovers a murder victim on the same property, landing her in the suspect pool. Worse, her privacy-seeking client fires her.

A telltale white streak develops in Baxley's hair overnight. Between landscaping, pet sitting, and dreamwalking, this single mom can't catch a break.

With a killer dogging her heels and spirits worrying her mind, Baxley dreams of justice for the dead and solace for the living.

Available at booksellers nationwide and online

Visit www.maggietoussaint.com for details

IN FOR A PENNY
Maggie Toussaint

A *Cleopatra Jones Mystery* (#1)

Amateur sleuth Cleopatra Jones of rural Hogan's Glen, Maryland faces an unwanted hazard when she skulls her golf ball across the number six green and it lands in the inseam of a very dead banker. Though the victim is a longtime friend of Cleo's, his ongoing dispute with Cleo's best friend and golfing partner, Jonette, is public knowledge. When the police key in on Jonette as the prime suspect, Cleo sets out to find the real killer.

Amidst the fun of wacky meals, dueling daughters, Mama's heart problem, lovesick Saint Bernards, a sexy golf pro, a repentant ex-husband and a host of murder suspects, Cleo does what she does best. With her trusty spreadsheets and logical accountant's brain, she organizes the information and ferrets out a crazed killer.

Set against the lush splendor of mid-Atlantic springtime, this fun-packed mystery with a dash of romance will keep you turning the pages to see what happens next.

Available at booksellers nationwide and online

Visit www.maggietoussaint.com for details

www.ingramcontent.com/pod-product-compliance
Lightning Source LLC
Chambersburg PA
CBHW060408260626
47160CB00006B/2475